Pedal

Pedal

CHELSEA ROONEY

CAITLIN PRESS

01   02   03   04   05   18   17   16   15   14

Caitlin Press Inc.
8100 Alderwood Road,
Halfmoon Bay, BC V0N 1Y1
www.caitlin-press.com

Text design by Vici Johnstone.
Edited by John Gould.
Cover design by Sheryl McDougald.
Printed in Canada.

Caitlin Press Inc. acknowledges financial support from the Government of
Canada through the Canada Book Fund and the Canada Council for the
Arts, and from the Province of British Columbia through the British Co-
lumbia Arts Council and the Book Publisher's Tax Credit.

Canada Council   Conseil des Arts
for the Arts   du Canada

BRITISH COLUMBIA
ARTS COUNCIL

Library and Archives Canada Cataloguing in Publication

Rooney, Chelsea, 1983-, author
        Pedal / Chelsea Rooney.

ISBN 978-1-927575-56-7 (pbk.)

        I. Title.

PS8635.O642P43 2014   C813'.6   C2014-904120-9

For Laurie

Contents

Part 1

Dirtbag

The night had started out clear in East Vancouver, but from the west a fat finger of tarnished cloud gestured toward us. My best friend Lark and I sat on the wide ledge of her patio, our feet pointed toward each other, our backs pressed against caryatids, bodies reflecting like a mirror. We passed Lark's dirty bong back and forth—an artifact of a past boyfriend who'd crafted it especially for her in his Advanced Glass-Blowing Workshop, its bulbous bottom black with years of smoke. With every hit I took, the silver clouds rolled thicker. Lark sang a song and I watched the orange streetlight grow fuzzy around the edge with dusk. The sky darkened. Her song was about doves.

"The mourning dove." Lark drew a manicured fingertip down her cheek. "With specks on their feathers like tears. The rain dove. The saddest dove." She was feeling maudlin, full of sentiment. "Like those clouds." A delicate hand to the sky. She'd just received a devastating email: the internship at German *Vogue* had gone to someone else. *"Ich habe Deutsch für nichts gelernt!"* she wailed, smoke pouring from her mouth, her nose. I laughed. Tried to summon sympathy. I happened to know she hadn't actually learned much German. She'd missed many classes and then failed the final exam. She'd half-assed her *Vogue* application, too. Facts we ignored. Lark's ankle tattoo flashed as she stomped her bare feet on the ledge. It read, *Havin' a time.*

Lark took a long swig from her glass, her lips and teeth necrotic with red wine. I did the same. We'd been meeting like this for years, near nightly roundtables of cheap booze and medical-grade marijuana, consuming substances to replace our worries, numb our fears. To blur and dim triumphs and add meaning to the sadnesses that passed through us like weather. We sprinted through the daylight hours fulfilling our responsibilities—mine a master's thesis that tore me apart, hers a fashion and culture column in our city's weekly that bored her to tears. She'd stand outside of MEC, frowning. *Fashion in Vancouver? Whatever.* All for that sweet tremble of intoxicant in our bellies, minds vivid and flying, pain and uncertainty transformed into something we figured was better. Wisdom? Enlightenment? At any rate, it was different. That night, the night *Vogue* rejected Lark, was the night before Thierry, my boyfriend of five years, broke up with me. I should have been at home trying to fix it, and I tell myself I would have been had I known it needing fixing. Had I seen the signs.

That morning, Thierry had prepared a traditional Swiss breakfast—homemade *bircher müesli* and soft-boiled eggs in cups—which I took to be a declaration of his homesickness. He ate slowly, and then, out of nowhere, he put his fork down and said, "I should have gone into marine biology." He hadn't finished eating his egg. Marine biology? He'd come from Switzerland six years before to study narrative drawing at Vancouver's Emily Carr University of Art and Design. I knew he liked to draw narwhals sometimes, but marine biology? And there had been that series of sea lions raping their young. He looked at me, said, "I should have been a scientist." He stood up, and walked out of the room.

On the porch, Lark was still singing—*I can hear the mourning doves, right outside my windowpane. Tell me, can you hear my pain*—when the noise happened. A rattling from inside the high hedges surrounding her yard. It sounded like a thousand miniature fireworks exploding in the bushes. Or like the bushes were full of trapped garden gnomes banging metal mugs against their prison bars. "What is that noise!?" we shouted. "What's in the bushes!?" Our voices fell over top of each other. The noise got louder and we were scared. Then, I smelled the wet pavement, warm and itchy in my nose—that acrid taste of powdered concrete rising up—and I realized it was raining. Both of us looked up at the streetlight and saw the fat drops illuminated in the glow.

We laughed. The explosive sound had been a sudden deluge of rain-drops crashing down around us.

Lark squinted through the rain, leaning out toward the street. "Oh! Here comes Smirks!" She pointed west down First Avenue toward Victoria Drive, and I saw a tall, muscular man in a white t-shirt, already drenched, running toward the house. I'd finally get to meet Smirks. He had moved into Lark's apartment last week and she'd told me nothing about him, because, as she said, people were like movies and you had to walk into them without any expectations.

Then why tell me his name? Smirks. Of course I had expectations. He'd be smug and domineering. Probably worked at a bank and said things like, "Nailed it!" When I pictured him, he was faceless and wearing a t-shirt that said I ♥ Las Vegas. But I'd been wrong. This person running toward us had a gravity to his face. Almost an injury. Yes, his arms were sculpted and he clearly spent time at a gym. But it meant something different, I could tell. A training in a strength that wasn't physical. And there was no smirk on his face.

I looked at Lark. She was licking her lips. "You're going to fuck him, aren't you?"

She shrugged. "I haven't decided yet."

Smirks bounded up the stairs. With the orange streetlight cast against the left side of his face, he looked like a Caravaggio model. Round cheeks and full red mouth, half-illuminated like chiaroscuro. His muscles rippled under his wet shirt and he reached his arm out toward me. I grasped it too quickly. His hand was hot, and dwarfed mine. I felt his big knuckles curl into my fingers. His eyes green and hard as sea glass. My chest tightened. "Smirks," he said.

"Julia."

He was older than I'd imagined, mid- to late thirties, but something older there, still. His shaggy, golden-brown hair slicked across his forehead like smeared peanut butter. "Your hair is the colour of peanut butter," I said, disoriented.

He laughed. "Thank you. I love peanut butter." He hopped up on the ledge between Lark and me, facing out toward the street, breaking our mirrored reflection. He looked left, then right, smiling at both of us, and from certain angles I saw small scars on his face. One above his eyebrow, one on his chin. I leaned to the left and glanced at Lark. She was smiling, leaning back, watching Smirks. His body was long and wide and hard, and I imagined it on top of mine, the weight of it, imagined I might mash down like an overripe pear beneath him. I felt bruised and grainy, at twenty-five years old somehow already too old for him. "I may steal that peanut butter simile from you," he said. "For my writing."

And then, Lark's reticence about Smirks made sense. She knew I was suspicious of writers. I didn't understand how they could spend so much time alone with their own thoughts. Any time I'd tried to sit down and work on my thesis, I found myself within minutes skimming the Internet for Lindsay Lohan updates. Or editing my Craigslist post for interview subjects. I kept acquiring new interviewees, while my thesis word count sat at zero. I thought if I wrote something down, an observation or a theory, it would change. Writing, an untrustworthy pursuit. And yet, I surrounded myself with writers: Lark and Thierry. My father, Dirtbag. Though I had no idea if he still wrote, and I liked to say I didn't care.

Dirtbag had written many things, apparently: stories, poems, letters. Most of which were burned in a drunken fit by my mother after he disappeared—after it became obvious he wasn't coming back—in a pyre made from all the furniture he'd built. A shame, really. He was a master woodworker. I'm not sure about his talent as a wordsmith. I'd managed to salvage only one letter he'd written to Mom. I'd found it as a child in Nova Scotia, tucked inside a cookbook between recipes for pies, and I'd stowed it away, shocked always by its realness when I stumbled upon it. Aside from the letter, Dirtbag was intangible. Mythic.

The letter was dated a couple of years before I was born. A verbose apology for a crime he'd committed that went ominously unnamed. When I came of age, I got my Aunt Lucy drunk and prodded her until she gave in and told me. The crime had been a rape. He'd raped a stranger in a hotel just weeks before Dirtbag and Mom's wedding.

In the letter, he called Mom "child-like" three times. A compliment. This trope pervaded my own childhood until he left: he called Mom his good little girl (or bad little girl if that were the case) and I remember waking up many nights to her calling his name in a baby voice. Behaviours I'd thought were normal until I left home.

Aunt Lucy told me it wasn't Dirtbag's apology letter, though, that convinced Mom to take him back. To marry him. Mom married him because the police had shown her a photograph of his victim. Her face, swollen and fluorescent, had paralyzed my mother. She married him days later in a sort of stupor, Lucy said. A stupor that lasted until she woke up one morning to an empty bed. *Child-like.* Three times. I brought the letter with me when I moved to Vancouver. I read it to myself sometimes, when I wanted to feel my pulse. When I wanted to catch my breath in my throat. It made me angry, always, an emotion on which I'd developed a kind of dependency. Smirks called himself a writer, and I felt the familiar uprising of vital signs: my shirt lifting up off my chest by my heartbeat, traitorous animal.

I exhaled, thinking anger could be expelled this way. "A fashion writer, like Lark?"

Smirks chuckled and continued looking out at the rain. I guess he thought I was joking. I thought of Thierry then: short, slender Thierry. He was a cartoonist, but his stories were always relegated to a single panel. Bizarre images inspired by the Clinical Syndrome Axis of my *Diagnostic and Statistical Manual of Mental Disorders.* Trichotillomania: impulse control disorder resulting in the recurrent pulling out of one's own hair. "Pubic hair," Thierry drew. Or: Dissociative Fugue. Symptoms include abrupt travel away from home and partial adoption of a new identity. "Just partial. Like, I'll grow half a moustache." Thierry thought these afflictions were hilarious, and he read the *DSM* over breakfast as though it were the newspaper. He joked that it was research for his own thesis that the human species has survived only in spite of itself. I'd clench my jaw, swallow the urge to bite back.

Smirks turned then and looked at me, finally. "You're a grad student?"

I looked at my hands.

"Lark wouldn't tell me what you study."

Lark chuckled.

"She didn't want to bore you."

He laughed. "I'm rarely bored."

Lark handed me the pot. I took a deep drag. "Counselling Psych." I offered the bong to Smirks. A column of blue smoke twisted up its chamber.

He took it and held it, his big hands curling around its belly. "What's your thesis?"

Good question. I hadn't decided yet. I couldn't stop researching, doing interview after interview with a group of women I'd affectionately nicknamed the Molestas, though that sobriquet was for my ears only. I'd spoken to dozens of women, and maintained relationships with many, but I couldn't bring myself to write about them.

"I'm looking at deconstructing current victim/survivor models of trauma theory."

Lark hummed a little bit of her mourning dove song, which the rain seemed to syncopate in my stoned ears, and I imagined that her voice and the cars driving by and the drizzle were all part of the same rhythm.

"Deconstruct them into what?" Smirks asked. He still hadn't hit the bong. I reached for it again.

"Into less destructive language for people who have experienced abuse."

"For victims."

"I don't like the word 'victim.'"

"Survivor?"

"That word either." I held the bong out toward him again. He shook his head and watched the street. I set it down. Not a pot smoker, I guessed. Had I bored him? "I'm interviewing women who experienced non-physically painful molestation, and who don't consider it 'abuse.'" I used air quotes.

Smirks looked surprised. "There are women who don't consider molestation abuse?"

"A few."

A predictable silence fell between us. This was the moment when people usually asked why I was researching this stuff in the first place. Smirks sighed. "I've never been to a counsellor."

"You probably don't need one."

He looked at me. "And why would you say that?"

"I don't know." I smiled. He smiled back. We stared at each other for too long. He was flirting with me, definitely. I uncrossed my legs so they dangled on either side of the ledge and leaned toward him. "You look pretty together to me."

He jumped down onto the patio, suddenly, jarring me. He hopped from foot to foot, and my brain, which the marijuana had slowed like a cassette on dying batteries, struggled to leap back. "That reminds me," he said. "I gotta tell you guys, today I played the best golf game of my life!"

Lark whooped in celebration and held her hand up for a high five that he enthusiastically returned because he didn't know her well enough to realize she was mocking him. I was too stoned to move. I cursed myself for smoking too much. This new man was coming at me in flashes and blows, and I couldn't form a coherent response to anything he said. He told us of his afternoon on the green, how he'd pulled an "albatross" three times, and one of them was a "barkie." He spoke of being in a "zone." Of being able to see "only the hole." Of everything else besides the hole becoming blurred and inconsequential. He said his focus was like steel. Strong enough to build with. "It was magic. I couldn't fail." His voice built like steel around me. The sound of him saying my name roused me back. My name, Julia, means *down-bearded youth*, a youth who has just begun to shave. Somehow, the way he said it made me sound very young.

"What?" I asked stupidly. Lark laughed.

Smirks put a hand on my shoulder and peered down at me. "I asked if you did your best at anything today."

I looked at his hand. "What a strange question."

"Well?"

I leaned my head against the pillar and thought. What had I done that day? I'd gone bookshop hopping on Commercial Drive, a diverse street in Vancouver's east side, beloved for its multicultural fare and laid-back atmosphere. Outside of Bibliophile stood a man, a road punk, wearing a long green army jacket with band patches sewn into all the pockets. I unlocked my bike and watched him. He was carrying a sign made from a broken-down cardboard box, and the text caught my eye, written in the unseasonable red and green of Christmas. HO HO HO! he'd written. And then, in black: IF I WAS ONE, I WOULDN'T HAVE TO DO THIS. "This," as in walk down the street asking for handouts, I guessed.

I'd balked. If he were a sex-trade worker, he wouldn't have to beg? Sex work was his only other option? And, what made me angriest, the implication that sex workers sold sex simply because they'd failed to rise to the occasion of carrying signs around asking for money. I'd approached him. He looked me up and down and scoffed. I probably wasn't the first feminist to take issue with his sign that day. "So, because you're *not* a prostitute, I'm supposed to give you money?" I asked. He sneered at me. Street punks made me feel silly for wearing clean clothes and having a job.

"It's a joke," he said. "Relax."

I stepped in front of him, wheeling my bike between us as protection. "I wonder if you could be a bit more sensitive to the politics of sex work. It's a pretty complicated issue you're mocking. Some people don't have choices." I bit my lip. I didn't actually know what I was talking about. I didn't know any sex workers personally, but I could still defend them. I thought of the woman with the long brown hair in the tight ponytail who loitered outside my apartment on the corner of Fraser and Kingsway. She carried a cheap blue purse and wore shiny tank tops, the small lip of her belly spilling over the waist of her low-rise jeans. I jogged by her in the evenings, stared at her face as I passed, but she never once looked at me. Her eyes were trained to the street, scrutinizing the dark windshields of oncoming cars, an uneasy smile on her lips, her body tense and ready to run.

The street punk shrugged. "The fewer choices you give yourself, the happier you are." I could tell it was something he liked to say. A slight, mousy woman had slowed her car beside us and held a toonie out. He took it, wordlessly, and turned on his heel, heading north, probably toward the liquor store or the pizza parlour. I watched him go. I wondered, as always, what his childhood had been like, what trauma he'd endured. "Amazing how you can be a homeless loser and still enact the patriarchy!" I yelled after him.

He turned around and started back toward me. I hopped on my bicycle and headed south on the sidewalk, frightening pedestrians who jumped off to the side. "Hey!" he yelled, though I could barely hear him over the pounding of my heart and rush of blood in my ears.

Back on the porch, Smirks' question hung in the air. *Did you do your best at anything today?* "I yelled at a sexist man," I said.

Smirks laughed. "Good for you."

Lark piped up then. "This summer Julia is riding her bicycle across the country." I glared at her. "She leaves in a few weeks. That's pretty outstanding, wouldn't you say?"

Smirks looked at me with a new, indiscernible expression. A very soft smile and curious eyes. "That's incredible," he said, but behind his words were different sentiments. We'll see, his eyes seemed to say. We'll see, young one, if you make it. "Who are you going with?"

"Nobody. I'm going alone."

"Her boyfriend has to work all summer like the rest of us." Lark wanted to make it clear that I wasn't available. "Smirks is taking the summer off too," she told me. "Apparently personal trainers make a lot of money during a Vancouver winter. Which reminds me…" She pressed her hand into Smirks' arm, gripping his biceps. "Maybe you can show me some toning exercises tonight?"

"Maybe." Smirks moved toward the front door, resting his hand on the knob. "And we should all go for a bike ride before you leave." I nodded noncommittally and walked down the porch steps. "Careful," Smirks said. "Slippery."

I looked up at him. His accent had a strange cadence, something unfamiliar. "Where are you from?" I unlocked my bicycle and the lock, wet with rain, slipped from my hands and clattered to the pavement.

"Lots of places."

"Like?"

"All over. Honestly. I've never lived in a city for longer than a year. I was an army brat, and after I left home I just kept moving around."

"Maybe you'll like Vancouver enough to stay."

"We can hope!" said Lark.

"It was really nice to meet you, Julia."

I secured my lock and cruised west toward Fraser Street, wondering what his real name was and if I'd ever ask.

I breathed a sigh of relief when Shelley and I reached Tenth Avenue. Shelley was my bicycle, and Tenth Avenue was the bicycle route, and it was there that we dominated, and it was there that no one asked us strange questions that knocked us off our feet. *Did you do your best at anything today?* The street was inky black with pools of orange streetlight. The rain had kept the fair-weather cyclists indoors, and I swerved through the roundabouts recklessly, not slowing down, not checking for other cyclists headed my way. Thierry said he loved watching me on my bicycle because it was the only time I wasn't afraid of anything. He was right. My bicycle did for me then what drugs hadn't yet. When I mounted Shelley, I felt us slide down and click into this prearranged flight path, as though it wasn't us that moved, but the world that shifted and slid around us. That was the high. The comedown was the virulent disdain I felt for motor vehicles. Their bulk and gross inefficiency. Sometimes I arrived at my destination so pissed off that I wondered if cycling was worth it. Did the health benefits outweigh the stress I was inflicting on my heart and my soul?

That was a question for Smirks. He was, after all, a personal trainer, and surely I would encounter him again when I was less stoned and as capable of extolling my own virtues as he seemed of extolling his. The rain had started again, and I squinted through the mist. A couple of blocks ahead, I spotted a one-tonne truck parked in the middle of the road, its red hazard lights blinking through the darkness like phosphenes.

It irked me when wide loads took up space on Tenth Avenue, but at least this guy had used his four-way flashers.

As I approached the one-tonne, another cyclist entered the bike route ahead of me. He headed toward the truck and, as he moved left to pass, the driver's door swung open and the cyclist swerved, his back tire slipping on wet leaves. I heard him cry out and braced myself for his crash, but he righted himself, somehow, and zoomed past the open door. I heard a "Fuck you" and an "Asshole" thrown out at the same time, not sure who said which, and I felt my blood pump faster. If one thing on Tenth Avenue pisses me off more than absent blinkers, it's absent shoulder checks. How narcissistic could you get? Swinging open doors without looking. Did he think he was the only person moving through the world?

Closer, I glimpsed the shit-eating grin on the motorist's face as he walked around the back of the truck onto the sidewalk. He was short and thick and tanned, spiky frosted hair and a tribal tattoo snaking around his upper arm, bulging with the weight of the boxes. He'd left his door wide open. I looked at the driver and he winked at me. I gave him the finger, and he laughed. Carried the boxes across the lawn. Shelley and I slid to a silent stop beside the truck's open door. I leaned into the cab and grabbed the keys hanging from the ignition. His keychain was a pewter skull with shining red eyes that flashed at me. Making sure the door was locked, I slammed it shut just as he started back down the steps. The sound rang out like a gunshot on the quiet street. "Hey!" he screamed as I raced up the hill toward my house. "Come back here, you stupid bitch!"

I clamped his keys between my palm and my handlebar, their metal teeth grinding into my skin. I pedalled harder, envisioning him running behind me, catching up to me somehow and reaching out to rip at my raincoat. I imagined him pulling me off my bicycle. I'd crash into the street, my shoulders cracking against the pavement. He would whale on me with fat fists, beating my face pulpy. The loose bones of my jaw, cracked nose, broken lips bleeding out. I couldn't shake the image and I raced along Tenth Avenue, wincing and grimacing. His knuckles connecting with my teeth, his weight pinning me down. I cycled faster and faster, my face contorted, my mouth and brow buckling under the imaginary blows. I think I must have groaned, because a nice-looking couple walking their dog turned toward me. They watched me pass, frightened expressions on their faces. Their cocker spaniel peed on the grass, his head tilted up at me, whimpering and flexing his nose.

❁

Thierry was already asleep when I got home. I sat on the corner of the bed, considering whether to wake him to tell him about the truck door. But then, I imagined what would follow: concern about me riding alone this summer. Pleading for me to stay home and wait for a time he could come with me. I placed the trucker's keys on the desk, grabbed my cellphone and cigarettes and went out to the porch to call April. My sister was a nighthawk and I knew she'd be wide awake in Harmony, Nova Scotia, despite the four-hour time difference, probably herself stoned on that awful Nova Scotian weed, painting watercolours. She answered after the first ring.

"Happy birthday," I said. She chuckled.

"Thanks. But it's not midnight in Vancouver, yet. You're calling from the past. I'm speaking from the future."

I told her first about Smirks, our exchange on the porch, the pea-nut-butter hair comment, the *Did you do your best at anything today* question.

"Sounds like a douche."

"But that's the thing. He's not. He's clearly not. He's, like, this really nice, healthy guy who just wants people to feel as good as he does."

"Ugh. He sounds awful." April had no problem insulting people she didn't know. "He sounds like one of those guys who thinks he knows what's best for you."

"That sounds a bit like transference."

She clucked her tongue. Our stepfather, Ralph, thought he knew what was best for our mother. April disagreed. Last week, she'd called Mom's doctor to update him on the dementia's progress. "Ralph wasn't giving them the whole story," she'd told me. She'd also arranged for an Alzheimer's resource worker to come to the house and monitor Mom. This had made Ralph uncharacteristically angry, and he told her to butt out.

"He writes crosswords for a living, Julia!" This wasn't the entire truth. He was a newspaper editor: Ralph at the *Rural Recorder*. But his passion was writing crosswords. This made me smile. April followed up with a whisper. "Do you think he's qualified to make decisions about Mom's care?"

Mom's care. It sounded so strange, taking this benign verb, *to care*, and transforming it into a technical noun specific to a sick, disenfranchised person. Specifically, our mother. It summoned visions of adult diapers and mechanical lifts, wrist restraints for violent spells. Bed sores. Anyway, I thought it was a bit early to be talking about "care." She'd just been diagnosed with early-onset dementia a few months ago. At this point just her language and short-term memory were leaving. She could still take care of herself. But of course things were tense. We all knew that within a few years or less the Mom we had would no longer be the Mom she'd been. This realization came with dozens of caveats and admonishments and regrets, against which we were powerless. All we could do was sit back and watch her change into someone we didn't recognize. A softer woman. A kind of ditzy stranger who didn't fight with us anymore.

As a child and for various reasons, Mom had built up walls around herself, protecting her from invasion. These walls came to be four of her best assets. They allowed her to work in the profession she did—a psychologist at a maximum-security prison, the facility with the bad guys, the murderers and the rapists—to the standard that she did. She was considered a pre-eminent voice in violence psychology, specializing in both domestic violence and sociopathy. While most people in that sort of profession suffer burnout or compassion fatigue, Mom never did. She continued to be lauded and loved by the establishment up until the day she started forgetting her patients' names, patients she'd had for years, recidivists who'd entered the jail at eighteen and revolved through the doors for decades. When Mom had to retire, and had to start taking handfuls of pills every day, and had to have Ralph write down the instructions for how to make coffee, it left this open space where the walls had been. Her defences disappeared.

April had become my liaison between Mom and Ralph. She gave me updates over the telephone, her voice high-pitched and all business as she made dinner. Potatoes, chicken, salad.

Or from her cellphone as she took Rod, her black lab, for a walk through the woods. April was an art therapist, and her client base included patients with dementia, so her perception of Mom had taken a clinical bent that both comforted and unsettled me. All the words she used sounded logical, professional, but her voice sounded manic. On the brink of something, like water about to boil.

I knew we were finished talking about Smirks when I heard the vacuum cleaner start up. "April, it's three in the morning. You're going to wake Mark." I knew this wasn't true. Her husband was a plumber and worked harder than anyone I'd met in my life. He slept the sleep of the dead. But when my sister smoked weed she lost track of time and space. Daytime activities were done late at night, loud chores done over the phone. "How's Mom doing?"

"She absolutely shouldn't be driving anymore, Jules." April shouted over the vacuum. "I'm about to call the DMV."

My sister the multi-tasker, the over-achiever, the obsessive compulsive who repaints her living room every six months and would have a nervous breakdown if she got home and found her Tupperware cupboard disorganized.

"We were on Foster Street yesterday, on our way to Frenchy's, and she got lost. She literally didn't know where to go. She pulled into some random driveway and told me I had to drive. To Frenchy's!" Her concern presented as anger and I remained silent on the other end, uncertain of how to respond. I knew if I were there in Harmony, dealing with it day to day, I could get angry too. Rushing up the South Mountain every morning to straighten Mom's hair because she'd forgotten how to hold the flat iron. Or making all the turkey dinners—

Christmas, Easter and Thanksgiving—because Mom could no longer manage cooking more than one thing at a time.

From my perch in Vancouver, I felt like the prodigal daughter, whiling away my student loans on a graduate degree I didn't care for anyway. Counselling Psychology, who gave a shit? What was I going to be, a therapist? April used to take care of me. She mothered me when Mom couldn't. I would sneak into her bedroom while Mom and Dirtbag fought, brutal fights, screaming and crying and throwing of wine bottles. April would stand with her bedroom door open a crack, peering out, waiting for my arrival. She would usher me in, grab my hand, take me to the bed and hug me until it was over.

"Her cognitive rating is worse than a lot of the patients at the nursing home, you know." April said it like a challenge. I didn't know who she was fighting with. What she was fighting against. Her relationship with Mom had always been more tempestuous than mine. I believed it was because she had it worse with Dirtbag than I had. She wouldn't talk about it, but I knew. He must have forced penetration on her. He must have physically hurt her. Definitely scared her. When I started my master's program, I'd finally had the courage to ask her what he'd done. In the spirit of research, I told myself. She'd started shaking. She said, "I don't want to talk about it," over and over. She'd rocked herself back and forth. I put my hand on her shoulder but she shook it off. And so I sat beside her, not touching, until the tremors passed. I didn't ask her again.

Neither of us ever told Mom about Dirtbag. We'd waited, afraid she wouldn't believe us. A far worse problem than her not knowing at all. In fact, we told ourselves, we didn't have any problems. So why tell Mom at all? But we knew that we did. Have problems. But everyone did. Who's to say where they come from. Maybe it's just being human. But we didn't trust Mom. She read our diaries. And one day, when I was twelve and she was trying to quit smoking, I found her contraband cigarettes in the storage room and she yelled at me, said they were mine. But now that she was sick, and she wasn't that person anymore, it was too late, we'd decided. We'd missed our chance. We'd talked about it twice, and both times had physical reactions. Our breath heaved, and our bodies trembled. Fuck panic. We'd calm ourselves with empathy. Mom was messed up. It wasn't her fault. She, too, was a victim. So if we're all victims, then who can you blame? That's how my conversations with April always ended.

And now, an overwhelming guilt about Mom. I should have been there. "I'll be home soon." Not that she would let me help much.

"Yeah." April shifted the phone. The hard clatter of dry dog food hitting Rod's bowl. "Yeah, you'll be home, soon. If you don't die on your way here." April's voice was tight.

"I'll be fine, sister."

April breathed. "I know. You're right."

I heard the slaps of her sneakers on rubber and the sound of mechanical beeps as she amped up the pace. She was on the treadmill. Speaking wouldn't be comfortable for long.

"How does it feel to be twenty-nine?" I asked her. But I guess she didn't hear me. She said she had to let me go, and I stayed out on the porch smoking cigarettes until, once again, it started to rain.

✿

When April and I were young, we would sit around and fantasize about the ways in which we could get rid of Ralph. These conversations disturbed me, because I'd gleaned from Mom's murmurings about violence and sociopathy that the first step to being a serial killer was to fantasize about killing. But I knew April and I didn't *want* to do the killing. We just wanted to tell a story. A fable to entertain ourselves. And the attention April paid me during those times nourished me. Much nicer than the indifference, or her rage. Not that she ever touched me. There was a strict rule in our house. No hitting.

When we talked about Ralph, April sat on her bed, holding a ski pole as though it were a pointing stick. Though never pointing, for we had no blackboard. I sat on the floor in front of her, trying to emulate her pose. "Remember, Ted Bundy never knew who his real father was." I was expected to remember the serial killers' names and their familial dysfunctions, but I had a hard time keeping track. April's mind sorted information like a computer. "Bundy was born in a Home for Unwed Mothers. His father was either a pilot, a sailor, or his own *grand*father." After she said grandfather, she stared at me. Waited. "And what's that called, again?"

"Incest." The word itself felt gross in my mouth, like a bolus of rotten fruit on my tongue. It was onomatopoeic, its sound, insidious and incessant, inserting itself in my mind at the most inconvenient of times. Masturbating myself to sleep, remembering kissing scenes of Jake and Paulina, my two favourite soap stars. Then the word, *incest*, a sibilant whisper, flashing through the tableau of my scene. Killing the warm, sweet feelings. And I would lie in bed staring at the ceiling, hearing it bounce back and forth between my walls. *Incest*.

"On to Paul Bernardo. He didn't know the identity of his real father either. And what's worse, his stepfather, under the guise of being an upright man taking in a bastard child, was arrested for molestation when Paul was nine."

Those were the people who became murderers.

"Charles Manson, remember him? He never knew his real father either. Do you see the connection?" April angled toward me, eyes squinting, and I nodded, eager to support her.

"So what happens when you don't know your father?" I asked. "Why does it make you a serial killer?" I fidgeted on the floor in front of her, struck with a sudden and fierce need to pee. April tilted her head up to the ceiling. Thoughtful.

"You know how when we move into a new house," she began—we had lived in five houses in our short little lives—"and the floorboards always squeak in a different place? And without realizing it, our bodies and our minds remember where the floorboards squeak. And we start to avoid those floorboards at night?" I nodded. I hadn't noticed that, but she was right. April shrugged. "Adaptation. Conditions *impose* adaptation. Absent fathers *impose* adaptation. They mess with the phenotype." She was fourteen years old and taking her first biology class. I pressed my heel into my crotch. Don't pee. Don't pee.

"The norm of reaction varies wildly in such conditions." I didn't know what the words meant. And neither did she. I looked at the carpet. Pushed my pelvis up toward my belly.

But April didn't want to kill Ralph. Mostly she just didn't trust him. One evening in late summer, at the height of April's plan, she and I sat outside by the pool. Ralph and Mom were inside, cooking dinner. Early September, and the leaves on the cherry tree in our backyard were turning the sharp, painful colour of iodine. I could smell twists of salt in Mom's cooking. I listened to April's whispers. "Being a sociopath doesn't make you a serial killer," she said. "Lots of people are sociopaths. It just means you don't love anything."

I tried to imagine not loving anything. What did I love, at ten years old? I loved my cheerleader pompoms. Choreographing dance routines with my pompoms. Handstands and cartwheels and round-offs, their plastic handles gripped tightly in my fists. The scrape of my knuckles on the hard carpet of our rec-room floor. I charged admission to my shows, twenty-five cents a head, and performed for Mom and Ralph and April. I slept with my pompoms next to me in bed. When the threads got wrinkly and sticky with dried sweat and food, I ran a moist facecloth along each strand.

I loved my mom. In the first few years without Dirtbag, I woke up from nightmares, terrified she was going to die. Visions of finding her prostrate on the kitchen floor, eyes open and fixed on the ceiling. I'd fall to my knees beside her cold body, knowing in that moment I was going to feel lonely forever. On these nights I woke up screaming. Mom would rush into my bedroom and push back my hair with one hand. Lay the other cool hand on my forehead. "By the time I'm old enough to die, they will have invented a medicine that allows people to live forever." Superheroes and mad scientists, they must be. Doctors and witches at work as we spoke. Finding that pill, creating that pill. I prayed to them every night.

I also, secretly, loved Ralph, but I didn't want April to know that. To me, Ralph seemed wonderful. He had barbecued delicious steaks for us all summer. Sweetly charred meat with a perfect horizon of blood setting in the centre. He also wrote crossword puzzles for me. Appalled with the lack of "real history" being taught at my school, he penned clues about the Atlantic slave trade. Residential schools across Canada. Japanese internment camps during World War II. I supplemented my teacher's lessons with Ralph's. Did they know that Francis Drake owned a slave? Did they know about slavery? Are you shocked then that Alberta sanctioned the sterilization of First Nations women up until the 1970s? My teachers loved it and made photocopies for the following year.

I loved Ralph because he made Mom laugh. Once, he made her laugh so hard she farted. They were standing in the kitchen discussing Halloween costumes. Ralph said Mom should be the psychotic nurse from Stephen King's *Misery*, and for some reason this cracked her up. She stumbled back into the oven and, when her bum hit, she let out a big toot. This made them laugh even harder, Mom's face brightening red, her eyes instantly watery. It was the hardest I had ever seen anyone laugh. Her mouth gaping open and silent. She leaned into Ralph's shoulder, and he ran his big fingers through the strands of her hair. Cupping her head as though it were a pompom.

On this particular evening, April imagined pushing Ralph into the pool and drowning him. Ralph's laughter from inside the kitchen. Could he hear us? No. Every night he came outside to skim the pool. He would always announce this mission after dinner. April and I did the dishes, Mom watched CNN, and Ralph would say, "I'm going outside to skim the pool." I loved how the words sounded when they rolled off his tongue. Snowy jump of the *s* and the *k*; the soft lip of *pool*. I would watch him from the window, and he always looked peaceful. A Buddhist monk raking sand. April's plan was to pepper his dinner with sleeping pills. To pour Mom's wine a bit more generously that evening. When Ralph was performing his nightly meditation, a hearty shove from behind would knock him into the water. As he fell, he'd fall asleep and begin to snore. That's what he did. He would drown.

I hated the image. My eyes filled with tears. "I don't want to talk about this." I stared at my goose-pimpled knees.

"Why not?"

"I love him." I flinched. Stole a glance at April. Her face bruised as though I had punched her. "We love him," I said.

She never talked about killing Ralph after that. As adults, we didn't recall those days. Shamed by those adolescent conversations, we grew increasingly protective of Ralph. Until now. Mom's dementia. But I wasn't worried. Our family survived Dirtbag. We could survive anything.

My cigarette smoke thickened in the rain. Forming a kind of putrid soup. The smell clung to my skin and my hair. I knew if I crawled into bed, Thierry would wake up. His nose pricked by the burnt chemical smell. He hated that I smoked, but he hated more how I pushed him away if he tried to kiss me. Even worse if he tried to kiss my hand, where the nicotine stained my skin mustard-yellow. I'd yank it away. Then press it, impulsively into my tongue. Licking the burn. Tasting the poison. "You punish others for your choices," Thierry often said. "But you always punish yourself, too."

Molesta

That night, I dreamt about Smirks. We had planned to meet at a train station, and I wore a red scarf. People rushed past me, and the windows blurred with faces, but none of them was him. In the morning, I woke up feeling misplaced, like a water glass left on a table. I rolled toward Thierry, but he'd already left. In his place was a note with a drawing. He'd rendered a perfect sketch of the trucker's keys. The skull's mouth smiled morbidly at me and he'd even used red pen for the eyes. "To whom do I belong?" he'd written. "Nice Café at 1?" Nice Café was our café. The first place we went for breakfast together. I looked out the window. Rain.

An empty morning apartment. Edges in silver light. Whoosh of car tires and swoosh of rain gear slipping through my fingers onto my skin. My rain gear was an armour. An investment in dryness. On the bike route, other women had gotten caught. Soaked leggings and dripping skirts. Dirty Keds bleeding with rainwater. *Get it together*, I thought pridefully as I rode past.

I had two meetings that morning. One with a potential Molesta. The other with my thesis advisor, Bob. Tenth Avenue was quiet, so I rehearsed my interview questions, but my mind wandered back to Smirks. I imagined intercepting him on his morning jog. The same t-shirt from the night before. Wet again, still clinging to his chest. Peanut-butter hair in his eyes. *Did you do your best at anything today?* When excitement overtook him, his voice cracked like a pubescent boy's. Smirks was the first man I'd felt attracted to since falling for Thierry. The feeling surprised me. I pictured myself with him. Not touching him, just standing near his body. I wanted to be in front of him, so close our toes touched. To feel the buzz and pull.

I pedalled on. The potential Molesta had contacted me through my open call on Craigslist. She lived near campus in Kitsilano, and Bob had lent me his office in the Counselling Psych department. I arrived with just enough time to strip off my sopping gear and settle into the big comfy armchair. Where Bob usually sank and faced me and frowned. I mocked his body language, crossing my arms and shaking my head. He had threatened to abdicate his position as my thesis advisor twice already that year. My research frightened him. He didn't want to be associated with pedophilia. "I have daughters, Julia!" Sweat beaded across his bald brow, his eyes pleading. "Pre-pubescent daughters!"

High heels marched confidently toward my office and a woman, on a call, spoke. I could tell she was a smoker and that she wasn't from Vancouver. "Babe, I *know!*" Emphatic enunciation with a hard edge. She ducked into my office. Mouthed *sorry* and pointed to her cellphone. Rolled her eyes. I liked her. I guessed she came from an interior town. A middling city. Big enough to get lost in but not small enough to disappear. You'd get by with equal parts toughness and sweetness, which this woman had. The scent of her expensive perfume comforted me. I leaned back in my chair. Watched her. Startlingly thin and small-boned, she teetered four inches above the ground on her black stilettos. Pencil-thin skinny jeans. All angles and corners and points. Little shoulders like apples I could pick up and juggle. Sharp, dark face lined with long, black hair. She buzzed like a power bar.

"The girls want strapless pencil-skirt dresses," she spat, "in *rust* orange." Silence. "But you're the bride." Her other hand pinched her waist, red fingernails digging into her stark white dress shirt. "You'll look like a dollop of whipped cream in front of a pumpkin pie." I heard a female voice on the line but couldn't make out the words. "Prohibition era, babe!" the woman cried. "I've been saying it all along." Then her voice softened. "Sheer. Lace. Beads. Buttons. Dropped waists." Silence. A faraway sheen in her eyes. "The birth of feminism. When women started drinking in public! Speakeasies!" Silence. A pragmatic tone.

"Honey. That's when women learned to suck cock." She looked at me and winked. "They took the waistline out of the dresses so that all the emphasis was on the face. The mouth." She nodded. "That's right. That's right. Okay. Bye." She put her phone away and looked at me. "Sorry. Wedding season."

I motioned for her to sit down across from me.

She leaned against the desk instead.

"I'm curious about how sucking cock relates to feminism."

She looked surprised. "That's how we reclaim the penis." She glanced around the office. Walls lined with books. All three of Bob's higher degrees hanging in frames. She leaned in. "Bob Johnson."

"My advisor."

"Well. I don't have one of these. But, if we say the penis dominates us, then it does. I say, instead, we dominate the penis. Or at least love the penis. Love does not have to be an act of submission. Or oppression." She handed me the questionnaire I'd emailed to her, and I skimmed it. Handed it back. "What's wrong?"

"I'm sorry, but you don't qualify for this study."

"I don't understand."

"Well, like my post on Craigslist said, I'm writing about non-painful molestation." The woman cocked her head. "No physical pain. Traumatic abuse is a different matter. I'm not studying it." She remained silent. Squinting. "My clients cannot have experienced any physical pain or force."

"But it wasn't painful. It didn't hurt at all."

"You don't *remember* it hurting."

"That's right."

"I mean that it hurt. But you don't remember."

"That's not true," she said.

I had seen this before, and I'd read about it a lot. It's easy to forget physical pain while retaining the visual memory. She was a tiny six-year-old, probably small for her age. An eighteen-year-old football player raped her. It did hurt. "It must have been painful." I felt it was important that she know this. "It must have hurt."

She breathed in sharply and tilted her head up toward the ceiling. Didn't let the tears fall out. Most of my Molestas detested crying, saw it as weakness. Proof they hadn't moved past or let go of something they should have. "I wouldn't let my mother look at me for weeks. I remember that."

"And your father?"

She snorted. Held a dainty knuckle to her eye, pushed a tear back inside. Straightened up. "He wasn't around."

I nodded. "As soon as any physical force or pain is introduced, or even the threat of pain, it becomes an entirely different issue. It moves from a confusing or pleasurable experience to a traumatic one. And it's not what I'm studying."

"Why not?"

"Because I never experienced it."

"So you can only study what you've experienced?"

"You can only be an expert on what you've experienced."

"Does experience make you an expert?"

"No. But it qualifies you to become one."

"And then how do you become one?"

"Reading. Talking to all kinds of people."

"Are you an expert? On this molestation that isn't physically painful?"

A hesitation. "I think so."

Her eyes narrowed. "So you can speak for other women who've experienced what you experienced."

"I can help women who've experienced what I did."

"But no one experienced what you did. Except you." She sat down. "How did it affect you?"

"I don't think it did. That's the point. The experience wasn't scary or painful. It wasn't traumatic. I didn't even know it was abuse until I started researching it a few years ago."

"Why did you start researching it?"

I'd stumbled into the research five years ago at the height of my drinking problem. Twenty years old and spending half my nights in blackout. I'd just met Thierry, and he liked me. Said things like,

"What's wrong?" And, "Why do you do this to yourself?" One day I typed *binge drinking* into a search engine. Found myself deep into Childhood Sexual Abuse literature, and not relating to any of it.

"I started researching it after rejecting both labels of 'victim' and 'survivor.'"

"And these other women you interview. They feel the same way?"

"Some."

"The ones who know they weren't traumatized are right? And the ones who think they were are wrong?"

"Not wrong. But there is a more beneficial way to interpret their experience. If there was no pain or fear, how could it have been traumatic?"

She shook her head. Glanced down at the questionnaire. "So you've never experienced these things?" She waved the paper through the air. "Depression? Substance abuse? Suicidal ideation?"

"I have. But not because of my molestation."

"How do you know?"

It was so obvious to me. Why wasn't it obvious to everyone else. "In order for something to be a symptom of trauma, it has to have been caused by trauma. My experience was not traumatic."

"But it was shameful."

"No. I don't believe it was."

She chuckled. Placed the questionnaire on the desk. "Tough stuff you're dealing with here."

"At times."

"Sorry for wasting your time."

"Not at all. I'd be happy to refer you to someone in my department who deals with childhood sexual trauma—"

"No, thanks. I'm good." Her Blackberry buzzed at her hip and she checked the display. "I have to take this." She smiled, waved and ducked out of the room. Heels snapping on tile. "Hey, baby," I heard her say. "No, I'm done. I'll tell you about it at home. I love you, too."

I pulled out my own iPhone and texted Thierry. "I love you."

Followed by a series of nonsensical emojis. An hourglass. An elephant. A pile of smiling poo. Thierry usually responded with a narrative tying the images together. I watched for the ellipse. Nothing. This wasn't the first woman to challenge my convictions. A few had left our meetings pissed off. One had told me that by suggesting her experience hadn't been traumatic, I was just as bad as the doctors I was trying to disprove. These women addled me. After they left, I'd return swiftly to the literature. Search for corroboration. Feel peaks of triumph when I saw it written there in permanent ink.

I heard Bob then, shuffling down the hall. Soft moccasins whispering against the tiles. I put my phone away and straightened my hair. Bob's support of my research depended on my being professional. I had to "have my shit together," as they say. He stepped into his office and smiled. He always seemed, at first, happy to see me, and then increasingly unsettled by what I had to say. I offered him his seat, which he sank into and crossed his arms.

"How was today's interview?"

I looked down at my writing pad at the only note I had taken. *Prohibition Era was when women learned to suck cock.* I closed the notebook. "She's not an eligible candidate."

"Why not?"

"Child rape."

He winced and covered his eyes. Peeked through his fingers. "Was he charged?"

I shrugged. "No idea. Why?"

Bob shook his head. "Curious. Your research looks at the mechanisms of victim-blaming. Oppression by diagnosis. You might not be interested in what happens to the men in these cases, but I am."

I focused intensely on not rolling my eyes. "What happens to the men isn't germane to my research."

A wry smile. "So you've said."

"What's funny?"

He made a steeple with his fingers. "Nothing. I think you're ready. You should start writing your thesis."

My jaw clenched. "I'm only at thirty-two eligible participants."

"You need more?"

"I don't know."

"You're never going to feel ready, Julia. You just have to start writing it." He repeated his favourite yogi quote. "To learn, read. To master, teach. To know, write."

"To know, write."

"How was the woman with the soccer coach? She worked out?"

I told him all about the interview with my newest Molesta. Although around Bob I called her my "participant." We'd met over lunch at an Indian buffet. She was a young professional with a trendy hue of lipstick and an active smartphone. The man had been her soccer coach and a family friend from when she was aged five to eight. The man, she called him Coach, stepped in to help her mother after her divorce. Fixing broken washing machines. Giving extra soccer lessons to Molesta in the backyard while her mom was at work. "I don't blame my mother. There's nothing to blame her for." She raised an eyebrow and looked pointedly at my notebook. She wanted me to write that down. When Coach had led her into the shed and told her he wanted to do something nice for her, Molesta was happy. "He lifted me up onto a workbench and pulled down my shorts. I didn't protest. I remember being a little surprised, but I know I wasn't scared. I had no idea what he was doing. I had no idea it was wrong. Why would I be scared?"

"And what was he doing?"

"Oh," she said, as if it were obvious. "He performed cunnilingus on me. He did it for a few minutes, and then he helped me put my shorts back on, and we went back out into the yard and played soccer until Mom got home. It happened several more times over the next three years. He never told me not to tell anyone. He never coerced me to do anything. I never touched his penis. Never even saw it."

"Did you enjoy it?"

She picked up her glass of water and took a long draw. Wiped her lips with a napkin. Looked at me. "Yes," she said. "Mostly, it felt good."

"Why did it stop?"

At this, Molesta shook her head and pulled her shoulders up into a slow shrug. "I've thought about this a lot. One day, I was eight, we were in the shed, and I told him I didn't want to do it anymore. He looked really sad. And he never touched me again."

Years later, Molesta's sister died in a car crash, and she suffered from her first bout of depression at the age of twenty-one. She visited a therapist who, over several sessions, insisted that her depression came from her years of molestation, not her sister's death. "I finally told her to go fuck herself and I left her office and I didn't pay." She laughed and popped a big bite of butter chicken into her mouth.

"So, you hold onto no shame from the experience?" Many of the so-called experts claimed that people who'd experienced molestation as children must be shame-ridden for life. A detrimental narrative to take on.

Molesta held eye contact with me before replying. "The only shame I feel is because I do not feel any shame."

"Can you elaborate?" I asked, pen poised.

"The molestation didn't feel wrong for me. And it never has."

I nodded. "Can I quote you on that?"

"That's why I'm here, isn't it?

"This is exactly the point I'm trying to prove. That it's not as simple as good or bad, right or wrong. But when I make this point to people who haven't had the experience—and some who have—they balk. Which infuriates me."

Molesta put down her fork. "Infuriates you? Why?"

"I get angry when someone tells me how I should feel. What I should do."

"Hmm." Now Molesta turned an analytical eye on me. "I wonder why anger?"

I put my pen down. "It's a violation."

"Sure. But why anger? I feel violated every day and it doesn't make me angry."

Aren't you perfect, I thought. "Everyone responds differently, I guess."

Molesta sighed. "Ain't that the truth." We picked at the pakoras, pushing them into our chutney, chewing, avoiding eye contact. "It *was* wrong, though."

"What was?"

"The molestation. I said it didn't feel wrong. I still know it was wrong."

That dichotomy, thinking versus feeling. It always came up. "If it didn't feel wrong, how do you know it was wrong?"

"Because it has to be. Some things are just wrong."

"I'm trying to stay away from morality."

She laughed. "Then you better stop researching sex."

In Bob's office that day, I told him a version of what Molesta had said. That it didn't feel wrong. I left out the fact she still thought it was wrong.

"There remains, Julia, as always, this tedious issue of consent. Even if the pedophile never threatens them, never coerces them, he is still an authority. He is still in a position of control."

"True. But what is the child consenting to?"

"What do you mean?"

"The child isn't consenting to sex. Or a romantic relationship. The child is only consenting to physical pleasure."

"That comes from unsolicited genital stimulation."

"Not always unsolicited. Some of these Molestas—some of these women—*did* solicit the physical contact. Because it felt good."

Bob stood. His temples flexed as he worked his jaw. "It doesn't matter. It doesn't matter what it felt like. It is wrong."

"That's so simplistic."

"The truth is simple."

"The truth is not simple. Children are not pure, innocent beings. They have sexual impulses. You can't argue with the existence of child sexuality." I reached into my backpack. "I have a video here of a three-year-old having an orgasm." Bob looked horrified. "It's from a Kinsey study in the sixties." Bob shook his head, held his hands out as if to stop me from attacking. The tape showed a little girl mounting a teddy bear, positioning her hips for optimum clitoral alignment, her hip thrusts becoming quicker and more urgent, and her climax lasting seven thrusts in total. I shook the DVD in front of him. "A three-year-old girl! There's nothing wrong about it for her. It's purely a physical gratification. Obviously a child can consent to that."

"Julia." He reached toward me. Took the DVD out of my hand as though it were a gun. Set it gingerly on his desk. "What is a Molesta?"

"Huh?"

"You call them 'Molestas?' The women you're interviewing?"

"It's just a joke."

"A way to minimize."

I crossed my arms. "No. Don't analyze me."

"I don't really have much choice."

"What do you mean?"

"You won't move forward with your work toward graduation. You won't listen to me. What choice do I have but to try and figure out what's wrong?"

"Nothing's wrong."

Bob nodded. "We need some time apart."

"What?"

Bob tried to decide what to say. "I need to think for a while."

I laughed. "Are you breaking up with me?"

He wouldn't look at me. "I need to think about our partnership. Before I continue working with you."

"Why?"

"I don't know." He hesitated. "I don't know if I believe in what you're doing."

His words made it sound as though I'd been planning a crime. The anger spiked. I pushed it down. "And what, exactly, am I doing?"

He shook his head. Threw his hands up in surrender. "You're leaving in a few weeks. Let's reconvene when you get back."

We stared at each other. Bob slumped back in his chair, his thin hair vertical in wispy spikes like a balding troll doll. My vision started to blur. "I'm the expert here. I have the experience, so I have the expertise." Bob nodded. "That's how it works." Bob opened his mouth.

A torrent of heat rushed through me. I threw up my hand. "That's how it has to work." I put the DVD back in my bag and left.

✪

The rain pounded me on my way to meet Thierry at Nice Café. I rode hard and fast, flying down Broadway past steaming, gridlocked cars and forcing my bell on any pedestrian who threatened to step in front of me. I was seeing spots. They floated red past my vision like acidic tumbleweeds. The whole reason Bob had accepted me as a student in the first place was our shared belief that psych discourses had co-opted women's experience to sell therapy and Prozac. Slap the label of Post Traumatic Stress Disorder on any girl who'd had her clitoris touched as a child and you've got a generation of disempowered females looking for saviours. Bob had agreed that the idea of PTSD without pain, or threat of pain, was mythical and profit-driven. But now he was wimping out. I pedalled harder, picturing Thierry waiting for me in our booth in the back right corner. I knew when I told him that Bob had dumped me he'd be happy, and that pissed me off. Thierry didn't like my research either. He thought I should focus on ideas that didn't make me angry. I stayed on Broadway—instead of taking the bike route—just for the cars. The speed and the danger. I tried to breathe out the rage that blistered inside me. Breathe it out, push it out, push it down, get rid of it. I'd promised Thierry I'd work to control it. I couldn't show up in the middle of a tantrum.

I locked Shelley in front of Nice and noted that Thierry's bike wasn't around. I was fifteen minutes late, so I knew he'd have arrived by then, and his missing bike seemed portentous. I swung open the door to our hallowed café and saw him sitting right where he always was. But this time his suitcase sat beside him, its handle pulled up like a long neck with no head. I sat down and gestured toward the bag.

He looked at the bag, then back to me. "Why are you late?"

"Why do you have a suitcase?"

Thierry pressed the handle down, not looking at me. "I got the money. From Switzerland."

I tried to hide my surprise. On a whim, after graduation, he'd applied for a handful of grants from the Switzerland Arts Council. His entire portfolio consisted of pieces from his *DSM* series, making fun of psychiatric disorders. The title page had been his crowning glory: a disparagement of frotteurism, a condition from the *DSM*'s paraphilia index. A bunch of pimply, horny male pledges rushing for the same *frot*. Their groins pressed into each other. Greek letters spelling out something obscene. I clapped my hands together, feigning joy. "Are you serious?"

He laughed. "You didn't think I would."

I said nothing.

"I'm going."

I looked at his suitcase. "Now?"

Thierry frowned and put a set of keys on the table. The dark grey skull looked at up me, red eyes gleaming. "Whose are these?"

The timing was not ideal. "I had an incident."

Thierry waited.

"On the bike route."

He nodded. "You lost your temper?"

Blair—our hippie waiter from Montreal who sang power ballads to us and wrote down his ever-changing postal codes so we could send him "invitations to our wedding"—brought us two coffees. "Everything good?" he asked. We both looked at him. "The usual?" I wasn't sure what he was referring to. "The usual breakfast?" he clarified. We both nodded. He slipped away. When Thierry was upset, a deep trench of a wrinkle appeared just left of centre of his glabella. The flat space between the eyebrows. I had to learn the word for that very small, blank space of the anatomy when I started dating him. I'd had to name it, because it so often buckled with worry for me.

Forgetting the bruise on his face, Thierry moved to rest his cheek in his hand and flinched in pain. The mark I had made there was loud, like one of April's paintings. "Thierry," I said in my best cockney accent. "What do the British call a bruise on the cheekbone?" This was a game we'd invented and played on Sundays when neither of us had to go to work or school. We'd be walking down the sidewalk and it would start to rain and Thierry would call out, "Julia! What do the British call afternoon showers?" And the point was not to think, to just shout the first thing that popped into your head. "Post-meridian drippers!" And we would laugh and laugh.

But that day, at Nice Café, when I called for the British word for cheek bruise, he was silent. Inside me, everything tightened. The soft tissue under the skin of my lips. The muscles in my cheeks, which grew rock hard. And then the light show. Pain always accompanied by anger. Always. A symphony of fireworks, exploding red and orange before my vision and then fading into the middle distance.

To date, I had thrown a telephone, a computer keyboard, and an iPod against a wall. Broken all three. Over five hundred dollars in damages. Now the damage was Thierry's perfect cheek. I used to take pictures of him while he slept. The light next to our bed cast a glow across his nose, frosted like the crest of a wave. And his unearthly cheekbones. Before I ever touched them, I imagined touching them would feel like touching a gaseous planet or a nebula, some celestial body that my fingers would pass right through. Now his left cheekbone was the pale blue of Pluto. The ridge of the bruise a throbbing, Jupiter purple.

It had all happened so quickly, I felt I shouldn't be held responsible. As if it was a thought I'd had that accidentally slipped into reality. Was that my fault? I thought Thierry had deleted everything on my hard drive. I'd turned on the desktop computer, and it was all gone— my research notes, my bookmarked web pages, my pedophile-forum conversations. He'd been talking about how scared he was of being arrested. How irreversible the effects of a child porn charge were. And now suddenly everything was gone. My mind went blank and I turned and hit him across the face with the back of my hand, the way I had seen it done before. I hadn't noticed, in his hands, the brand new laptop he'd streamlined and customized just for me. Tediously and meticulously adding every file and URL and article I'd ever saved. I saw the laptop just a moment too late.

Blair delivered our breakfasts, and I began the process of eating down the pain. The hash browns were the shredded kind, potato ribbons dropped in the deep fryer, gilded and crisp on the outside, slimy on the inside. Blair piled them on top of our plates like mountains of gold. I'd always known Thierry would leave me. I'd told him that from the beginning. Methodically I pushed the potatoes into my mouth. In my head, the refrain: *I told you so. I told you so.* I chewed and swallowed and tasted nothing. Thierry grew up in a small Swiss canton on a lake between the mountains in a perfect home with a mother who never raised her voice above a bird's chirp and a father who communicated his emotions through the painting of whales. Thierry talked about how much he missed them.

He was the only person I'd ever hit. He was the only man I had ever loved. One of my Molestas described the urge to punch someone as a desperate attempt to free a person trapped behind a wall. Who was trapped behind the wall? That didn't matter. Thierry turned his head, and his bruise flashed like a hologram. I felt an urge to throw up.

Blair stood several feet away, leaning against the counter where the ketchup and coffee cups were kept, watching us, his arms crossed. A sad look on his face. I looked everywhere else in the room. My eyes darted up and down, to various customers—did they know what was happening here?—to the kitchen, to the frayed carpet. Back to Blair. He shrugged. He'd caught snippets of our conversation and, of course, could see Thierry's bruise. My potatoes were gone, so I started on the bacon. "Come to Switzerland with me," Thierry said. We had talked about that. He thought it would be good for me, for my temperament. Thought the city was winding me up. "Submit your thesis from Switzerland. Get out of Vancouver. Get away from the Molestas—"

"Don't call them that," I said. I looked down at my plate. It was perfectly clean. I looked at his. He had taken one bite of toast. My lips trembled and breathing became difficult, like a tug-of-war between my lungs and the air. Every anniversary we'd had, Thierry had drawn a portrait of me. "I want to be the first man and the last man to draw your face," he'd said the first time. On the last anniversary, he'd remarked that it had been difficult to complete the drawing. "Because I know you so well now," he'd said.

The thing about breaking up with someone you still love is that it would be much, much easier not to. And so any excuse not to would seem like a miracle. A great, divine relief. That's why Thierry was inviting me to Switzerland. As an out, for himself. I knew, though, what he really wanted. My chest hurt. "I'm going to stay here," I said. And then a sound escaped my throat, and Thierry looked down at his lap and tears fell into it.

Five years before, when he first pressed his hands onto my body, I'd felt something exquisite pass back and forth between us. It felt better than anything I'd ever known. Sadness was a bandage that he had removed. After he left, when I tried to recall that sweet feeling, it would only return to me as pain. Now we stood outside of the Nice in the rain, and he put his hand against my cheek. On my bicycle, I fled from the corner of Main Street. The world was a grey blemish. The world was a windshield covered in rain.

❂

Lark was on a deadline, so when I got home I called April. I needed tears to come out and I knew I wouldn't cry until I told someone what happened. "He left," I said. "He's going to Switzerland for the summer. He broke up with me."

"Why?" shouted April. "You guys are so happy."

I started crying.

"Weren't you?"

"Not always."

"What happened?"

I hadn't told her about the fights. "I hit him."

She didn't say anything. In fact, she was notably silent. No vacuum ran in the background. No programming the coffee pot or rearranging book shelves. I told her about the laptop. The other damaged property.

"Julia. That's terrible."

"I know."

"What are you going to do?"

"What can I do? He's gone."

"I mean, what are you going to do about yourself? About the violence? The drinking."

"It's not as bad as it sounds. It only happened a few times. It won't happen again."

April backed down. We forced some cursory small talk and she let me go. Dinner time on the east coast. *You're not perfect, either,* I thought, but kept my mouth shut. Let her judge me. She couldn't know what was actually going on.

April too had a temper that flew in both directions. At least she had in the past. I remembered the last tantrum of hers I'd ever witnessed. She'd been a junior in high school and I was still a child; it was then that our age difference was most pronounced. One day I was in the kitchen boiling hot dogs, my favourite childhood snack, when she burst through the back door and slammed it so hard the house shook. Her left leg was completely soaked with muddy puddle water. She must have stumbled into a ditch on the way home. I looked at her leg and looked at her face, a startling shade of scarlet. "What happened?" I asked, and she leaned forward, pressing both hands onto a kitchen stool and lifting it up into the air, screaming. She slammed the stool down on the floor, slumped into a chair by the window, pressed her elbows into her thighs, and began slapping herself across the face with so much force I was sure she'd leave bruises. I screamed at her to stop. She didn't, and I watched her mouth, her tight lips, her top teeth like a vise clamping down on her chin. I thought she might bite right through her jaw.

I picked up the phone and dialled the Kid's Help line, the number that played during reruns of *Degrassi Junior High.* This was a definite emergency, I thought, because April could seriously hurt herself. Or hurt me, I realized was my fear, suddenly aware of the handy weapons, the knife I'd used to cut through the vacuum seal on the hot dogs, the glass bottle of ketchup.

April continued to beat herself, and I sat across from her, the phone pressed to my ear. A woman answered, finally, her voice that perfect mixture of comfort and exigency—there must be some specialized training to achieve that timbre—and I shouted into the phone, "My sister is hurting herself and she won't stop!" The woman asked for my sister's name and told me to hand the phone to her, which I did. Magically, April held it to her ear.

"Hello?" Silence. April froze in place, her hand mid-swipe, her cheeks an impossible red. She recited a series of yesses and nos into the receiver, each one seeming to deflate her a bit, until she was leaning back into the chair, her hand resting dumbly on her lap. She said a final okay and handed me the phone. The cicada drone of the dial tone. I placed it gently on the receiver. April watched me, her eyes bewildered. "Thanks," she said. She stood up and left the kitchen.

I heard her tiptoe down the stairs to her bedroom. In a few moments, the wounded crooning of Sarah McLachlan reverberated against the carpeted floor of the upstairs living room. I stood there above her bedroom for a long time, motionless and tense. Like a ballerina in a music box, I felt I was holding something centred, holding something still, though I had no idea what. Soon after that day, April signed up for an art class and discovered a precocious talent for watercolours. Still lifes that didn't stay still; flowers that bled from the walls like wounds. She painted for Ralph, matting and moulding the canvasses in expensive frames, and at first he accepted these gifts warily, wondering at their imagery, until we all began to realize that April was healing and this was what progress looked like. "To say art is 'catharsis' makes the whole process of painting absurd," April would say later. "If you're an artist, you're an artist. Art comes out. It isn't catharsis. It's just being alive."

❁

Thierry never came home. He and his suitcase had evaporated, along with some clothes and a toothbrush and, oddly, the garlic cloves and ginger from the fruit basket in the kitchen. I moved through the rooms and smelled him. I smelled him on his pillow. I smelled him in the armpits of his well-worn t-shirts that he'd left behind. I smelled him in the towel we kept next to the bed, the Love Towel we'd called it, or the Fuck Towel, depending on our mood. I assumed he'd come home after I left for my bike trip. I considered not leaving at all.

I fell out of touch with my loved ones. Lark called and sang silly songs to me over voicemail. *My jewel, my jewel, my Jul-i-a. Come back to me.* I read novels written by women. Their heartbroken female protagonists sounded so cool amidst destruction, as though they could choose which piece of their will to let go of. One woman stopped eating, and made mosaic masterpieces with her dehydrated vegetables as she grew more gaunt and beautiful. Another didn't sleep for four days, and instead wandered the city, taking a photograph of each place she'd ever kissed her lover. I tried to emulate these women, tried to turn my loss into something artistic. My life could be a mumblecore movie, too, I thought. But I couldn't stop eating and I had no energy to revisit places I'd been with Thierry. *Did you do your best at anything today?* My Molestas fell by the wayside. I read pedophile-sympathizer literature. Bob was the only person I wanted to see. When I told him about Thierry, he relented, allowing me to come to his office. "But no thesis stuff," he warned. I went to the psych department almost every day after the breakup in increasing stages of disrepair. I brought him leftover pizza and Indian from delivery I'd ordered the night before. I gave him the European theorists I'd been reading. He looked at the food and the books with equal disdain. Pushed them back at me.

"I don't want these, Julia." He eyed me, not dispassionately. I knew what I looked like. Puffy with sodium and alcohol. Makeupless, frizzy-haired and jogging-panted. He wiped his spectacles on his shirttail, taking his time. "How are your bike-tour preparations coming along?" I hadn't thought about my trip since Thierry left. At least not in a practical sense. Instead I fantasized about asking Smirks to bike with me. When I was with Thierry, I'd wanted a summer alone. Now that I was alone, I wanted a man.

"I may ask a friend to go with me."

"Who?"

"Just a guy I met."

"Just a guy you met, or a guy you just met?"

"Both."

Bob harrumphed. "I think that while you look for your father, you shouldn't have any distractions."

I rolled my eyes. Bob still believed I was actually going to find Dirtbag on my great cross-country quest. That was, after all, the ostensible purpose of my tour: to visit the three cities from which Dirtbag had called since he left. Vacation and cultural journey were secondary, tertiary motivations. I'd pitched them in that order, thinking Bob would only give me time off if he knew my goal was to find Dirtbag. Bob was old-school psychology, imagining that finding my abuser and holding him accountable would help me heal. For Bob, "healing" would mean the end of my pedophilia curiosity. A different path for my thesis. A continuation of the antediluvian victim/perpetrator dialectic.

"Well," I said. "We'll see." I put most of my books back in my bag, but left one on Bob's desk. The treatise of Dutch sexologist Dr. Frits Bernard. The first medical professional to disseminate pedophiliac information. He believed that pedophiles were the scapegoats for westerners' fucked-up relationship with sex. Pedophiles were people too, he claimed, and the modern-day witch-hunt against them precluded any productive research of their condition. How could we learn about pedophilia when it was almost a death sentence to come out as one? But Bob refused to talk about any of that.

He was packing his briefcase, making ready to leave. "What are you going to do today?" he asked.

"Today is April 25," I said. "And I've heard absolutely nothing about Alice Day in Vancouver."

He looked at me blankly. "Why would Alice Day be in Vancouver?"

"Not the actress. The day." Named after Alice Liddell, the wide-eyed, sullen child, Lewis Carroll's muse. Somehow, that photograph of young Liddell dressed as a beggar maid—torn white smock, loose and falling off her shoulder, little body leaning against a rock wall, hand cupped in front of her stomach—had become an iconic image for what many called Pedophilia Pride Day. "Alice Day is meant to be a celebration of child-love. A chance to share information and resources amongst the MAAs."

"The MAAs?" asked Bob.

"Haven't you been reading my emails?"

He smiled. "No." He put on his jacket.

"Minor Attracted Adults," I explained. "I like the acronym because it's straightforward. To the point. No beating around the bush."

Bob frowned. He put a soft hand on my back and guided me to the door. The MAAs were people who admitted preferential attraction to children under the age of consent—who might be infants ages zero to three, prepubescent children, pubescents, or straddling the fine Age of Consent line, children ages fourteen to sixteen. "They don't molest kids. You should look at the website. There's a difference between a pedophile and a child molester."

"I know."

I grabbed Bob's *DSM* from his shelf and flipped it open to the psychiatric disorder index which showed all the paraphilias as mental illnesses. "Homosexuality used to be right here with them."

"Once again, Julia, the two are not comparable."

"In terms of human rights, they are. Non-offending pedophiles live in shame and isolation."

"Yes."

"On Alice Day, supposedly, if you see a man or a woman in a pink shirt, you can approach them and ask for information."

"And where will you go look for this person in the pink shirt?"

I shrugged. "Everywhere. Got nothing else to do."

❂

I found him, hours later, on the seawall. I was drawn there by the anonymity of a vast and boring landmark. The absolute facelessness of Vancouver's face. I hadn't walked around Stanley Park since Thierry and I started dating. We'd gotten caught one day in a downpour without an umbrella. We kissed with wet lips and he wiped mascara from my cheeks.

From a bench on the park's thumbnail where the wall curves into the water, I felt my brain numbed by the chatter of touristic languages—Japanese, French, German—and I stared across the inlet at the glaring yellow sulphur piles on the North Shore. Out of the corner of my eye, I saw a blur of pink. I spotted him. A pudgy white guy in a pink t-shirt. He gripped a handful of flyers, faced away from the water, inland, watching a playground full of children. I stood up, didn't think. Kept my mind resting on the languages I didn't understand. Once near, I reached out. He instinctively leaned away. "May I...?" I asked, looking at the flyers clenched in his meaty fist.

The smile faded from his face and he looked me up and down. "These aren't for—"

"I know what they're for," I said, and I grabbed one, turned on my heel and ran away. I pushed through confused tourists and toppled little children with their stupid sun hats that blocked their views. Someone yelled, "You're going the wrong way!" But I kept running. I ran all the way along the seawall to Sunset Beach, my sneakers crushing into the sand and dragging me down as though in a dream. I realized with a jolt that knocked me to my knees: I'd left Shelley locked to the bench in Stanley Park. I faced the water of English Bay, squinting against the needle-sting of sweat. My palm had soaked the flyer and I carefully unfolded it. The world around me dimmed. I had done it. I'd found it. It was happening. The MAAs had a meeting scheduled in Vancouver the following Monday.

I walked back to Shelley who leaned against the bench with an abandoned look in her frame. *You took off so fast,* she seemed to say. *You didn't even look back.* I mounted the bicycle and aimed toward the Lions Gate Bridge, direction North Vancouver. I'd worked there as a Personal Care Attendant for my boss Elaine for the past five years. An academic herself, Elaine accommodated my school conflicts as much as she could. That evening, while helping her with dinner, I asked if she could find someone else for the Monday shift.

"Doing something fun?" she asked.

"Not really. Just school stuff."

"Umm hmm. More pedophiles, I think." She was perspicacious. Said she had to pay closer attention to people due to her condition. "This is shaping up to be a sex-offender-themed day." A Calgarian serial rapist, recently released from federal prison, had decided to settle down in North Vancouver. Elaine hadn't ascertained his address, but we knew his face, had printed it off the CBC website and posted it on her refrigerator for all of her workers to study. *If you see this man, kick his balls.* Media called him the Baby-faced Rapist because he was young, twenty-two years old, when he went on his rampage raping three women, holding them at knifepoint, threatening to kill them if they screamed. I had watched for him as I rode my bicycle up Lonsdale that evening on my way to Elaine's. I wanted to spot him, the way you want to strain your neck to view a car crash. My father was a rapist. Not of children. Of women, my mother included. Under the Criminal Code of Canada, a man cannot be simultaneously a husband and a rapist. He cannot be tried as a husband who raped his wife. He can only be tried as a rapist.

I'd met Elaine in a Women's Studies class, Women and Body, in my first year of university. She was a teacher's assistant, and taught the memoir on the syllabus. A story of a woman who had been raped and beaten, almost to death, while on a walk through the woods. At first, due to an overwhelming sense of shame, she'd told her friends she had only been beaten. She didn't reveal the rape. They were flabbergasted, bewildered that someone would commit such violence "for no reason." It wasn't until she told them she had also been raped that they understood. The rape gave the reason. "Beating a woman makes more sense to us when it is accompanied by rape," Elaine had said. Her being in a wheelchair compounded the gravity of her words. "Anyone care to speak to how fucked up that is?" It was the first time I'd heard a university instructor say "fuck."

It was time to help Elaine get ready for bed. I removed her petite clothing and gazed, unabashedly, at her smooth, pale body. She had the figure of a twelve-year-old—limb-girdle muscular dystrophy had stunted her growth. Bones shorter and thinner, muscles soft and wasting. She'd been diagnosed during puberty and her physique had stayed there, mid-pubescent. Tonight she was sore and wanted to stay in the shower for a long time. I bathed her slowly, her body white as thinly stretched dough, and I knew that had the galactic alignment of her chromosomes been different, her physique would have been that of a dancer's, narrow-hipped and pointy-shouldered.

After our Women's Studies class had ended, Elaine asked me if I would be interested in working for her. In my job interview we quickly moved beyond typical questions into some serious sex talk. She lamented the fact that men her age, then twenty-five, looked at her and saw a disability, not a sexual being. They saw a wheelchair and no vagina. "I just want to get laid. But don't tell my mother that." Though Elaine lived alone, her mother, Beth, remained heavily involved in the hiring of her attendants. Beth drove me home, appraising me, after my interview.

"There're sickos out there," she said. "Sickos who would only want to work with her so they could touch her. I know the type. Perverts. Fetishists."

I'd tried to help Elaine. We went to a woman-friendly sex shop on Commercial Drive and bought a small vibrator that I would place by her crotch at nighttime before leaving her alone. I would turn on the toy, which looked like a fat, white index finger, and Elaine would roll her body on top of it. We called it Craig after Elaine's mentor in the Law department with whom she had fallen in love. After she orgasmed, Elaine would roll off of Craig, and his soft buzz as the rechargeable batteries dwindled would lull her to sleep.

The system worked great, until one night Beth came over just after I had left. She was used to a high level of access to her daughter's life and entered Elaine's bedroom and turned on the light just in time to watch her daughter bucking and moaning in the throes of orgasm. Of course, Beth knew immediately that I had been the one to help position Craig. From that day on, she was cold to me. Sometimes, I guess if she were feeling particularly prudish, she'd come to Elaine's apartment and take over the work during the last stages of the night shift. She didn't trust me.

This evening, sure enough, when I turned off the shower water and helped Elaine out of her sling and back into her commode, we heard Beth in the kitchen, putting away dishes washed. I opened the bathroom door and found her staring at the photo of the Baby-faced Rapist. She turned to us. "My baby!" She embraced Elaine, kissing both cheeks and pinching her nose. Looked at me. "I see you know about the rapist."

"I printed that photo, Mom. And I wrote the caption."

"Well. I'm sure it won't be long until he's in jail again."

Elaine shuddered. "That would require he rape again, so let's hope not."

Beth took hold of the chair's push bars. "You're cold. Let's get you into your PJs."

Outside I lit a cigarette. The avenue was quiet and smelled of cherry blossoms. I smoked slowly. It would take Beth exactly twelve minutes to help Elaine into her bed, fuss some more in the kitchen, turn out the light and lock the door. I slid my hand into my pocket and felt Craig, five years old and going strong. I stepped away from the flowered tree, its pink buzz lingering in my nose, and crept up the alleyway to Lonsdale, ready for any sign of the Baby-faced Rapist. Any rustling in the bushes, any suspicious figure standing in the shadows of a street lamp. I clicked on the vibrator, imagining its drone alerting the rapist, pulling him toward me like a dog to a whistle. But he never came. Just the sound of Beth leaving Elaine's building, slamming the door of her old hatchback and driving away. I stamped out my cigarette and, Craig in hand, headed back inside.

Smirks

The day of the MAA meeting came hard, impregnating Vancouver with spring in a fury and flurry of cherry blossoms. Trees overhead suddenly pink, and air that soaked my lungs like an elixir. Nostrum made up of early daffodils and massive ferns whose leaves were umbrellas against the soft rain. I needed spring like I needed water, or food, or the sex I was no longer getting. I loved how thick it came in Vancouver, how smelly and virile. I cycled past gardens and breathed in all the fucking of the flowers as the bees buzzed from genital to floral genital.

I'd decided I would pose as a homosexual hebephile—Greek for juvenile-lover—attracted to girls just starting to grow hips and breasts, just starting to bleed in time with the moon. I'd slept fitfully through the night, had woken feeling part of me had stayed unconscious. Sloppily dressed and hairbrush forsaken, I left the house without applying toner or makeup. I tried to look like I had no hope. With fine lines showing and my appearance unkempt, perhaps I looked older. But I couldn't be too paranoid about my authenticity being questioned, even if I was the only woman there. Regardless of the demographics, all participants would be paranoid, all would be carrying a deep shame and sense of hiding which would make them at once suspicious of me but also desperately willing to believe I was one of them. Or so I hoped.

The all-day MAA meeting was to take place in a warehouse space in industrial East Vancouver where all the secondary businesses lived—catering equipment rentals and commercial cabinet installations. The warehouse was a few blocks south of the water where streets were wide and empty of design. Corrugated aluminum facades in pale blues and yellows. Huge, darkened windows. A sliding chain link fence barricaded the parking lot next to the meeting place, and wooden pallets were stacked outside like Jenga pieces. The awning said *Express Paper Converters* and made a promise to perform the "best die-cutting service in the Lower Mainland." Whatever that meant. The parking lot was empty of people, and the doors were closed. The address on the flyer matched the one above the door, so I stepped inside.

A tall, slim man with shiny skin and spectacles greeted me at the doorway. "Are you here for the MAA meeting?" His cheekbones were high and rounded, overtaking his eyes from below. A bird-like gaze, eyes darting down his pointed nose. In my head, I called him Bird. He bent at his waist and shuffled through the documents I'd require for participation. I looked beyond him into the room. About thirty men, in their late twenties to early seventies, milled awkwardly. Some stood near the coffee urns, some sat on orange plastic chairs that had been arranged in a circle. My eyes leapt from man to man and finally to three women, all within a few feet of each other, none of them conversing. "Welcome, Joy!" Bird chirped. I'd chosen an obvious pseudonym. I wondered if anyone else had made similar jokes.

I sat near the refreshments. Two large beverage machines, one for coffee, one for tea. Milk and sugar. Muffins from Safeway on Styrofoam trays with the plastic wrap peeled back. I imagined the pedophile who had prepared the snacks. It must have been Bird, arriving early, turning on the lights, arranging the food on the table, poking his thumb into the stretchy Saran wrap and tearing it open like skin.

The women ranged in age from late thirties to late forties. One of them was beautiful. She had golden-blonde hair that, even in the garish warehouse lighting, shone luminously, swept up into a loose bun on top of her head. Her eyes, the blue of map water, darted up and then fell, darted then fell, like jays that couldn't keep flight. A deep horizontal line cleaved her forehead, revealing years of arduous thoughts with physical impact. Her eyes lit on mine and lingered, a recognition in them. *I see you*, she seemed to say. *Do you see me?* I wondered what little boys, or girls, if any, she had touched. I wondered if they had liked it.

A few of the men talked to one another. About sports and weather. An elementary school teacher, a lawyer, a construction worker, an accountant. Where did their bosses think they were? The woman chose a chair a couple of seats down from me. We nodded to each other. I was afraid she would speak to me, and I leafed through the various pamphlets splayed on each of our seats. One, *Minor Attracted Adults: Dispelling Myths*. Another, *The History of Pedophilia*. The prosaic titles bored me, and I began making up my own. *Nepiophilia (attraction to infants): You've Come a Long Way, Baby!* Or, *Ephebophilia: Barely Legal*.

"Joy?"

I looked up without thinking. Smirks. Before I'd looked up, I knew it was him. Even before my brain sent signals to my neck to tilt my jaw back. His face was round and white. Violet under-eye circles and chewed lips swollen with blood. I read his name tag.

"Jacob." We frowned at each other. I had the urge to stand and hug him, but I resisted. Touched my face to stop myself from touching him. Jacob. Smirks wasn't pseudonym enough? Maintaining eye contact, he sat in the chair beside me. I was next to him, again. Again, moved by the size of him. The energy racing through his muscles. I looked away. It would be odd if we appeared to know each other. The other pedophiles might worry. His eyes stayed on me. *Did you do your best at anything today?*

"Joy?" he said again, this time questioning my choice of name.

I whispered, hardly moving my mouth. "Julia means 'pubescent youth.'"

He sniffed. People around us pretended not to notice. Finally, he asked, "What are you doing here?"

I stuck to my plan. "I'm attracted to pubescent girls." The lie crashed between us. A sudden hard rain.

Smirks smiled. "Right."

I asked, "What are you doing here?"

He leaned back against the chair, stretched out his long legs and linked them at the ankles. His biceps strained against his t-shirt as he crossed his arms, the pamphlets in his hand crinkled pink, yellow and green.

I couldn't reconcile his soft face with his hard body. He looked me up and down.

"You look like shit."

I laughed, and then he laughed, and everyone sitting around us flinched. The blonde woman's eyes grew wide. *Why are they laughing?* she must have thought. *What are they doing here, if they are light-hearted enough to laugh?*

I closed my mouth. I looked at Smirks. I wanted to tell him the truth. I wanted him to tell me the truth. He chewed softly on his lower lip and watched me. He put his hand on my leg. "You really do look awful. Are you okay?"

"My boyfriend left me."

Smirks nodded once, squeezed my thigh and pulled his hand away. "Wasn't into little girls?"

"Why are you here?" I asked again. Smirks broke eye contact and re-crossed his arms. He shook his head. Bird flitted in and out of my peripheral vision. "You can tell me." He looked at me and scoffed. I nodded, shrugged. Obviously he could tell me. I was studying pedophilia. I was the best person to tell. He pushed his baseball cap down on his forehead.

"Welcome to the inaugural conference of the Vancouver MAAs," Bird announced. "Could everyone find a seat." The chairs filled up and the meeting began.

I wanted to absorb every word. I'd been too paranoid to bring in a voice recorder, and couldn't take notes, so I had to listen as Bird spoke. His voice shook at first, and then grew smooth. He found his pace. His body loosened and he animated. "I've been trying to organize an MAA in Vancouver for four years now. It is very difficult to establish a community, which will be one of the topics we discuss today. We'd like this meeting to be a step toward creating a permanent MAA community in Vancouver. Today will be an introduction to our history, the MAA, and your history. Where we come from. Before we can even begin to tackle the practical, legal and strategic issues of the MAA agenda, we must get to know each other. *In here* is an open place where you can feel free to express all the things you can't express *out there*.

"My first sexual experience was with a neighbour friend when I was six and she was five. I know this was not the start of my pedophilia. Most people have their first sexual experience at this age. Though they may not know, at the time, that it is sexual. They just know it feels good, and that they should keep it private. We played 'doctor' together, as the cliché goes. She rubbed my genitals to climax, and I rubbed her genitals to climax. At least, I believe I did. I don't think five-year-olds have learned to fake orgasms yet." Bird held for laughter. Silence, and then a lame chuckle from someone. Wrong joke for the wrong crowd. Smirks was as still as a painting.

"Our physical relationship continued until her parents moved away three years later. I'm telling you this experience only because it was my first sexual encounter. Not because I believe it had any impact on my being a pedophile. I do believe, and research supports, that pedophilia is like any other sexual orientation. You are born with it or not, and while early experiences may coincide with or influence what attracts you later on in life, they do not determine your sexual orientation. Only being born can do that.

"I remember knowing I was 'different' at the age of twelve, when I found myself yearning for and masturbating to my little sister's friends. I was never attracted to my own little sister. Incest and pedophilia are two different things. By the age of seventeen, when my peers were chasing after girls our age like hungry dogs, my worst fears solidified. I have a journal entry from that time which I'll read." With this, he removed a piece of paper from his pocket. "Lisa was the child of my mother's friend," he said. "She was eight years old." And then he began to read. His words sounded like words I'd written as an adolescent. Dismayed by my own hormones and actions. So much shame directed at the self, at the body. At physical impulses we did not understand.

"I did it again last night. I had Lisa sit on my lap, under the blanket, and as she bounced around and danced to the cartoon, I held her pelvis in place, not firmly, but gently, and I masturbated against her bum through my jeans. She had no idea. She laughed and laughed. I came really fast. I set her down and went to the bathroom. I looked in the mirror at a monster. I looked at Dad's porn. Tried so hard to get hard. Big tits and wide hips and pubic hair. It made me want to puke. And then I did puke. I want to kill myself. I'm a monster. I want to kill myself. I want to die. I'm fucking disgusting. I deserve to die."

Bird folded up the paper and replaced it in his pocket with shaking hands. "Shortly after this journal entry, I graduated from high school and moved away to college. I started drinking and became a half-hearted alcoholic, going to school during the weekdays, drowning myself in my studies, and then drinking to blackouts on the weekends. If I closed my eyes long enough, I thought, I would wake up from the nightmare. It truly felt like a nightmare. I was completely alone in my hell." As he spoke, from the corner of my eye, I thought I saw Smirks nod his head.

We could all relate to the terror of sex beyond our control. In the first few years after Dirtbag left, I took what he had taught me and continued masturbating on my own. I started engaging my friend Cheryl in sex play. One day we were sitting on the living-room floor while her mom watched a soap opera. Two characters onscreen were embracing and kissing passionately. I remember the woman's breasts pushing out of her low-cut blouse and against the man's chest. That round flesh lit up something inside us. Cheryl and I squealed in a performance of disgust and dashed to her bedroom. Without words, we tumbled into each other. Sloppy kisses, wet and thick-tongued, our thighs pressed tightly between legs. Her mother must have seen through our pretence, discerned our nascent horniness, because she burst through the door seconds later. "You are not to touch each other in that way!" she screamed. "It is disgusting and wrong!"

It. Kept saying "it." *What was it, though*, I thought wildly. *How did she know? What had we discovered?* Finally, she uttered its name. "*Masturbation.* We were masturbating," she said, and "it was bad." I had to look the word up in the dictionary when I got home. Cheryl stopped inviting me over after that day. This taught me that masturbation was shameful, and for it I would be punished. But I couldn't stop doing it.

I needed it to fall asleep. In my diary, I wrote in tiny script, speaking in code. "I did it again last night. I am disgusting. I am never going to do it again. Please give me the strength to not do it again." I don't know whose help I was invoking. Some uninformed concept of God. I locked and hid those diaries, anxious my mother would find out my secret. I imagined her monitoring me at nighttime to make sure I didn't do it. Standing in the corner of my bedroom, watching.

The silence that followed Bird's confession brought me back into the room with the pedophiles. Smirks pulsed beside me. I watched his feet, the toe of his right tennis shoe rubbing against his left. I looked at our speaker. Bird was more confident, more real. "Before we ask for your stories," he said, "I would like to read the important ethical criteria outlined by IPCE."

I'd read about the IPCE. They'd dissolved the root words of their acronym due to their political implications, but it used to stand for International Pedophile and Child Emancipation. *Pedophile* had become synonymous with *evil*, and *child* had become synonymous with *innocence*. "As you probably know," continued Bird, "the IPCE's mission is to understand and emancipate mutual, consensual and free relationships between children and adults through scholarly discussion of child love." Problem was, the IPCE couldn't get any real discussion going. Most scholars wouldn't touch the issue. "There are strict behavioural guidelines one must follow to meet IPCE's standard of ethics. I'll read them now."

I knew the guidelines by heart. They had comforted and saddened me when I began my pedophile research, in the way I imagined sitting with a sick friend would both comfort and sadden. "Criterion number one: the minor should experience the relationship as positive; should be able to withdraw from the relationship at any moment; should desire sexual contact and not provide it as a favour to the adult. Criterion number two: the child should undergo no physical harm. This includes no unwanted pregnancy. Three: any and all erotic contact should be initiated by the child. Normally there will be no penetration, as this would, in most children, inflict physical harm. Four: the adult should be honest with the minor in terms of the nature and extent of the adult's feelings, in order to avoid disappointment on behalf of the minor. The minor's personal, social, and relational freedom should not be in any way limited by the adult. Five: parents of the minor should be fully informed about the relationship. If the crossing of cultural and legal boundaries will negatively affect the child's self-perception, no such boundaries should be crossed. Six: the adult should not spoil the minor. Frequency of erotic contact should be moderate to avoid so-called sex addiction. Seven: the adult should make the minor aware of real sexual abuse, and warn them about non-consensual sex. Eight: the minor should not have to keep secrets about the relationship from any adults with whom they share a close emotional bond. Nine: the disbandment of any erotic relationship should continue platonically for as long as the child needs to not feel abandoned or used."

And then, at the end of this surreal and elegiac list, Bird delivered the final caveat: "Most consensual relationships will end up being reinterpreted later as abuse. This misinterpretation, however false, will have damaging psychological effects for the former child. For this reason, it is not a good idea, morally, for an adult to engage in a consensual relationship with a minor."

That list flies in the face of what most people think of pedophiles. It was generous and protective. I'd shown it to Bob when the whole Jerry Sandusky trial blew up. Sandusky had been charged with dozens of accounts of sexual abuse of boys he mentored. Boys he was supposed to take care of. The story incited a fresh round of public vitriol for pedophiles, and Bob had suggested—pleaded—that I sideline my pedophile research and focus on victims. I printed off the IPCE guidelines and tacked them on his office bulletin board. In red ink, I'd written, "*Pedophile* is not synonymous with *rapist*. Most pedophiles never molest." Bob had told me I was living in a fantasy world. Said it was impossible to know that without any research. My point exactly.

I glanced at Smirks. Had he heard the IPCE's guidelines before? His body, guarded by muscle, gave nothing away.

Bird opened up the floor to the pedophiles, and several told their stories. Each person's account sounded like a variation of Bird's. I'd hoped for some insight into the effects of molestation. Hadn't some old pedo had an erotic relationship with a young girl who then went on to become his best friend later in life? Looking for the unicorn. A bad researcher. I didn't want to hear the clichés. Molested girl becomes prostitute. Molested girl becomes stripper. But no one in the meeting that day admitted to actually molesting anyone, and Smirks didn't volunteer to speak, so my mind wandered outside of the meeting, out of the warehouse, out of Vancouver and back to Harmony. Where my old friend Drew still lived, now with her baby boy.

I tried not to think about Drew very much. But sometimes, out of nowhere, I'd remember her grey eyes blinking behind her small, upturned nose. In middle school, she had waited on the sidelines of popularity, giving away her homemade chocolate chip cookies at recess. Laughing at everyone's jokes. Never making her own. I must have sensed she'd be compliant. We began spending recesses and lunch hours together at school, and then one day she invited me to her house for a sleepover. When her mother turned out the lights, and we lay breathily whispering under her quilted bedspread, I rolled toward her and stuck my hand between her legs. She pushed me away. "Don't you ever do this?" She didn't say anything. I wrapped my leg around her.

Drew had wanted friends, and I had somehow wheedled my way into the popular crowd, and she knew, instinctively, as I knew, instinctively, that if she didn't submit to me that night, I would banish her from the circle for good. And so she yielded. Spread her legs a little bit and let me rub her. She looked the other way, her face turned to the wall, when I mounted her thigh and pressed my crotch against her skin, humping her leg until I came.

That same scenario played out half a dozen times. In the mornings, she never said anything. She was always quiet and sad, it seemed, and I always felt nauseated. We would wait silently at the end of her gravel drive for my mother to pick me up and I would imagine puking my blueberry pancakes onto the road. Then, one night, she made me stop. I reached for her and she rolled away. In a voice I had never heard her use, she said, "I don't want to do that." The *don't* still echoes in my head all these years later. It was so hard and final. I was shocked still, and lay awake for hours waiting for the sun to come up so I could leave.

But then I made it worse. That Monday at school I spread a rumour that Drew's mom beat her with a wooden spoon every night. Everyone stopped talking to her. She switched schools after grade eight and ten years later sent me a friend request on Facebook. I browsed her photos. Those stormy eyes of hers hadn't changed. An unsmiling baby hung from her neck. Strange posts on her wall. "Where are you?" Friends asked. And: "What happened to you last night? Answer your phone!" I denied her friend request, and blocked her from my profile. We'd have nothing to say to each other, I told myself. What could I possibly say?

Children should be watched as well, for abuse. Little pre-conscience assholes. I'd had no idea what impact my actions would have on Drew. And what impact did they have? Was I responsible for her dark eyes? Her fatherless child? As her abuser I had to admit that, to an extent, I was. I'd known as a child in her bed in the darkness that she didn't want to do the things I made her do. But how to atone for my younger self? Would calling her to apologize help her? Would it help me? Dust better left unstirred. Everyone had something in their past they needed to let go of. I hoped she'd let go of me.

❂

When the MAA meeting ended, Bird encouraged us all to sign up for the email list. "It's secure, we promise."

Smirks didn't sign up. I did. I had my university degree to fall back on as proof that I was researching. He watched me write down my real email address. "I'll forward you their messages."

He frowned and shook his head. "Let's go." We left the others standing about awkwardly. The blue-eyed woman watched me leave. *Take me with you*, her eyes seemed to say, as though I could save her. Smirks and I did not speak as we walked toward his truck. He opened the passenger door for me and offered his hand. It was warm. I felt a jolt through my fingers and up my arm. He was strong. Usually, big muscles repelled me. I'd told Thierry that big muscles signified vanity and also a low IQ, but maybe the reason was Dirtbag. He was a big burly Irishman with intimidating upper body strength. Thierry's thin arms, smaller than mine. How safe I'd felt in them.

Smirks settled in beside me, his face turned west and washed with sun. Seven o'clock and we were approaching the golden hour. Spring evenings beginning to stretch out their long, warm arms to summer. Smirks circled through his iPod and settled on something soft and rhythmic and rich. The music massaged my ears and I found myself comfortable amongst his things. I looked around his truck: a smattering of sports equipment littered the back seat—soccer cleats, a basketball and an array of pinnies. "Pinnies," I said. A memory on my tongue. "I haven't seen a pinnie since grade nine gym class." Outside, Shelley was locked to a street sign. Her front wheel cocked toward me, she seemed to say, *Where are you going?*

"We're going to the beach," Smirks said. We drove west.

I loved Wreck Beach, when the tide was out, vast bars of sand spilling into the Georgia Strait. Brown sun worshippers, prostrate starfish, soaking up every photon possible. The shore of Wreck Beach was the only place in Vancouver where you couldn't see any sign of modern civilization. Save for the speedboats that occasionally docked there, full of young people drunk with too much money, and the container ships shifting imperceptibly in the distance, a few more every year. But no buildings, no roads. Everything tucked just around the corner, to the north. Out of sight. We chose a log close to the water and laid a blanket down. Smirks looked at me. "You can't wear clothes on Wreck Beach," he said, unbuttoning his jeans. "It's obscene." I followed suit. I gazed at his penis. It was formidable, larger than Thierry's, and I wondered if it had ever entered the tiny vagina of a little girl.

We sat down against a log and stared toward the water. A few yards away, a beautiful, naked woman played Frisbee with her beautiful, naked daughter. They both had deeply brown bodies and long, black hair, the woman a few years older than me, the girl maybe nine.

I watched the woman's body, athletic and lean, softer between her hip-bones, a little belly. She was trying to teach her daughter how to throw the disc, but her various instructions went unheeded. "Loosen your wrist," I heard her say, her voice sweet and sharp, like a knife playing on the rim of a glass. "Tighten your fingers! Follow through." But the little girl continued to chuck the disc either straight down into the sand or off toward the water. Smirks chuckled and stood up.

"Duty calls," he said, and walked over to the pair. I stayed by the log, my eyes glued to Smirks' swinging dick. Penises fascinated me, how they moved and hung, how soft they were, like satin sacks of moist cotton balls. So vulnerable, there. He introduced himself to the girl, and from where I sat about fifteen metres away, I could tell that the mother was already enamoured with him. They chatted for a minute, the woman nodding vigorously, and I thought: a nudist on Wreck Beach, of course, would never question a visit from a fellow nudist. That's the whole reason she was there. To shed her inhibitions and celebrate her freedom, et cetera.

Smirks squatted beside the little girl, whose body was a sharp contrast to her mother's. Flat narrow chest and straight hips, twig legs. Did the child arouse Smirks? Not her supplely-breasted mother? He reached around the child's neck and placed the Frisbee in her hand. His fingers held her wrist as though she were a sculpture. His other fingers pressed lightly into her waist, informing her stance. I leaned in, squinting through the backdrop of the setting sun. His dick never hardened. Together, they threw the disc. It sailed in a perfect arc and curve, and the mother whooped, giving Smirks a high-five and lifting her daughter up into the air. Smirks came back to our log and sat down.

"Smirks—"

"I am not ready to talk about this with you."

I'd learned in Counselling Psych that asking questions, in the beginning, didn't work. He curled up in the sand like a child and, strangely, fell asleep. The mother with the long hair kept looking at me. *Lucky you,* her eyes said. Shivering, I got dressed and spread a blanket over Smirks' goose-pimpled body. I watched him, his hand cupping his cheek, until, after some time, he woke up. We climbed the four hundred and fifty stairs back to the real world. In his truck, Smirks sat petrified and staring ahead. I put my hand on his shoulder. It was rock hard. I squeezed and tried to dig my fingers into some softness. He collapsed against his steering wheel, his forehead rolling from side to side, and cried.

❁

After Dirtbag left, everything improved, particularly Sunday mornings. I always woke first. Tiptoed past Mom's bedroom door. Turned the television on low and ate my Cinnamon Toast Crunch while watching Billy Graham at the pulpit. He'd brandish his right hand, balance the bible in his left, mellifluous voice like a powerful poet. I was a godless civilian, a child without church, but I loved his voice. How he yelled, roared, without sounding angry. I was moved often after his sermon to go outside and smell the grass. To listen to the birds. Later, I'd fry one egg—three if Ralph had slept over—over easy, and like an altar server I'd carry it to my mother's bedroom. Push the door open and breathe in her stale smells, the hot unventilated air. Half-empty wine glass stagnant on her nightstand. I'd wave the breakfast plate by her head, and she would stir. Squint at me. Quiet moments passing in the dark before recognition, then a smile and her arms stretching toward me. Blinds up: light in.

We'd leave April sleeping and point the truck at the next town east down the Old Highway through the Annapolis Valley. I loved the stretches where I couldn't see any houses, or churches, or stores. In those spaces, I'd will my mother to slow down, to prolong the moment we spent outside of the world of other people, inside a pocket of trees and road and hill and sky, where only we existed.

At the second-hand bookstore I would sneak off to the Harlequin section, find the most promising-looking paperback, and flip to the trusty penultimate chapter—the last chapter primarily reserved for tidy resolutions to outrageous storylines. But the penultimate chapter invariably held the good stuff. I'd scan the pages for the salacious words, trying to trap them in my head. *Ass. Tease. Flesh. Lips. Thighs.* These words caused the bottom of my stomach to drop out and made me dizzy. I wished for a photographic memory so I could remember every detail. Meanwhile, Mom browsed the true-crime section for books about serial killers and rapists. She'd call my name from the cash register and I'd sneak around to the teen section emerging with an old Christopher Pike. We loved our horror stories, all of us.

In the truck on the way home she'd hand me her selection while she drove. She knew I liked to look at the photographs that split up white and glossy through their middles. I'd try to still the tremors between my legs as I ran my fingers along her books' shiny titles, embossed and bumpy as gooseflesh. She assumed, I suppose, that I was interested in the gory crime-scene photos, but what I really studied were the faces of the men before they got caught. The murderers and the rapists posing as husbands and fathers. "Rapers," Mom would say. "Rapist sounds too much like 'artist.'"

The gory crime-scene photos, in fact, made me feel sick. As if I were on a roller coaster with the world rushing up above me. I had my own selection of true-crime photographs hidden at home, but Mom didn't know that. There were three of them, and I kept them in a shoebox marked "Christmas Stuff" at the back of my closet. They were Polaroids, and along the bottom white strip a social worker had written "December 19, 1993, 02:00." One photograph showed my mother's body from the front, one of her profile, and one of her back. She was naked and her mouth was open. They had made her smile to show her missing teeth.

She had always told me her teeth had fallen out when she was a child because her parents couldn't afford floss. She turned this fable into a rhyming admonishment: "You don't have to floss all your teeth! Just the ones you want to keep!" She'd sing this and point to her own mouth, bobbing her head to the beat. The staff at the women's shelter had photographed her and urged her to go to the police. It was, after all, the third time in a year she had fled, drunk and bleeding, from Dirtbag, a wife-beater so useless he just let her go, waving from the front door, his anger washed out of him, his body limp and wrung like a rag.

I'd found the photographs of Mom the same day I met Lark. The two events became inextricably linked in my mind as key moments that changed my life's trajectory. Lark arrived at Harmony High School on the day we were to start sex education, and we were paired together in our first PDR class—personal development and relationships. She shook my hand as though we were adults and then burst into laughter, hoisting her long black hair like a thick rope over her shoulder. She walked around the perimeter of the classroom, gold palazzo pants shimmering, pausing at the diagrams of penises and ovaries on the walls. On her tiptoes she studied the images then, over her shoulder, asked our teacher to please lower the reproductive anatomy posters "because art should hang at eye level." Finally, the lights in the classroom dimmed and in a frenzied state of agitation we watched slides of cross-sectioned genitalia, holding our breath, each imagining our own bodies sliced open, our own halved organs on display. A boy beside us whispered, bragging about finding his father's pornographic magazines. Lark pouted. "I want a pornographic magazine." She turned to me. "Do you have a dad?"

"I have a stepdad."

She smiled. "Even better." I followed her home from school that day to my house, to my storage room in the basement, where she was convinced we'd find them. "The X-rags," she said with studied aplomb. We poked through boxes and looked behind old paintings that leaned against the walls. We found nothing.

"Ralph isn't like other dads," I said, and Lark nodded. Her dad had died when she was little. She didn't really know what other dads were like, and neither did I. I'd seen my girlfriends with their fathers. Tiny hands disappearing into big, strong fists. Riding on their shoulders, laughing, looking proud and special, like a princess on a float. Serene fathers smiling. Who were these upstanding men? At sleepovers, movie nights with their family, my friend in a thin nightgown, cross-legged with panties showing, cuddled up on her father's lap. As if there was nothing in the world that could go wrong with that.

I didn't have that type of physical connection with Ralph—not with anyone, really. As a child, hugging made me nervous, an anxiety I would later outgrow for boyfriends, but never for anyone else. Unless I was drunk. The limbs of other people seemed ominous to me, like frayed electrical wire. When invited over for dinner, I watched the legs of the fathers underneath tables. If they leaned toward me to pass the butter, I pulled away. That night in the storage room, Lark, reaching up to a top shelf, knocked a shoebox to the floor, and the cluster of Polaroids of my mother's bleeding face scattered at our feet. Neither of us moved. Later Lark said, "Your mom's a survivor." This, after the horror had receded and left behind a rough awe. "She's badass," she said, and I knew it was true.

My mother was badass. Working in a maximum-security prison and being married to a violent alcoholic had placed her in the hands of danger many times. Her life before Ralph was full of stories that could have opened any of her true-crime books. Like the story of an infamous inmate, Jimmy Lachrymose, so nicknamed for his perpetual closeness to tears. Jimmy had always been sweet with Mom, sweet on Mom, and one day she let her guard down, closed her office door so he could let loose on a particularly loud crying jag. Within seconds, he had her against the wall, a knife to her throat. "All I could think," Mom would say when telling this story to a captive audience, "was where the *hell* did he get the knife?"

Jimmy told her if she didn't call the doctor and order him a prescription of Valium, he'd kill her. She picked up the phone and dialled security. "Hello, doctor," she said, and made the request. The security guard laughed. Told her she'd dialled the wrong extension again, and almost hung up. "I *realize* that, doctor. But I assure you, it's urgent." Before Mom hung up the telephone, the guards stormed her office, guns drawn, deep, baritone voices shocking Jimmy Lachrymose into submission and then, of course, into tears. Mom had saved herself.

She would tell that story over bottles of wine to her engrossed friends who had boring jobs like selling makeup and cleaning teeth. April and I were allowed to stay in the kitchen until the story was finished, and every time, at the end, we would cheer and dance around her, pulling at her shirttail, willing her to look down at us and smile.

As I got older, Mom rented movies where women plotted against abusive husbands, movies where women kicked men in the balls. "*Good* girl," Mom would say emphatically to the screen. She'd tell us stories about sex offenders arriving at her jail. The medical staff would try to keep the details of their crimes away from the guards and other inmates, but somehow the secret always leaked. "That guy raped a nine-year-old girl. That guy fucked a dog." And then the goons would descend, viciously beating the deviant, often within an inch of his life, while the guards of the prison stood by and watched. Laughed. Sometimes found excuses to pummel the new intakes themselves.

Once at the dinner table after such an incident Mom had sliced angrily into her steak. "They're all a bunch of football players, if you know what I mean." Ralph had nodded, as if he did know what she meant, but he didn't. Ralph was as peaceful as a comma curled between two nice words, and the only games he ever participated in were played out on a board or a piece of paper. "They just look for fights," Mom said. Her knife screeched against her porcelain plate. "Rape's a great excuse to beat the shit out of somebody."

Shortly after this conversation, she enrolled me in a self-defence class taught at the jail that housed and employed the very men my parents hoped to arm me against. Lark joined with me. We were the only teenagers in a class full of middle-aged women with floppy arms and neon tank tops, nervous smiles. A retired police officer named Frank showed us how to find the weak spot in a set of hands that might grab at us at night in a darkened alley. Find the weak spot and twist, yank, pull at such angles so our bodies and limbs became propellers, twirling, lifting us up and away from the perps. At fourteen, almost everything I learned simply felt like a new dance step, a fun new way to move my body, and I couldn't seem to summon the anger to perform the escapes. And then, during the last class, Frank took me by surprise, snuck up behind me and put his hands around my neck, and I felt a blitz of madness blow through me. I threw my arms up in the air and hurled my heel back and then Frank was down on the ground holding his groin and wheezing.

"Good girl." He groaned. In pain, but satisfied. "There's the anger. There it is."

And there it stayed.

❂

The night after the MAA meeting, I couldn't sleep. I tossed and turned in bed for hours. The darkness wrapped around my neck like a gag. I crawled out of bed at dawn, and under trees raining cherry blossoms I biked to Lark's house as the sky lightened. I let myself in with the key she'd made. Bypassing her room, I pushed open Smirks' door. He was awake, and he opened his arms to me, and I sank into bed and pressed my head into his chest. "Will you bike with me this summer?" I asked. I knew something about him no one else did, I thought. It was a kind of control over him. It was a kind of control I liked. The window brightened with morning, and through the glass we watched cherry blossoms dip and swirl.

The idea that a fresh season brings renewal is apocryphal. There is a steady tilt and travel of the planet, ancient anaphora disguised as death and birth, disguised as change. A narrative we impose. But nothing changes. Until a new thing is said, we are anaphoras: the same words repeated, over and over, signalling change, and bringing none.

Shelley

That year, spring heated up fast in Vancouver. The clothes came off and hipsters came out in great numbers. Everything seemed amplified and rushed. Lark and I, single together for the first time in half a decade, fell into a languid, heady pseudo-pattern, acyclic and unhealthy, varying wildly save for the mornings when I would wake up on her couch. Dressed in only my underwear. Bare legs sticking out from under a throw and mascara crumbling into my eyes like ash. Smirks would creep past me in his running shoes, carrying a banana, on his way to coach basketball or work a shift at the YMCA. Trying not to wake me.

One morning the front door clicked behind him and I woke to a particularly vicious hangover. The kind where even the thought of standing caused my stomach to roll over. My mouth tasted like an ashtray soaked in cat piss and I lay on the couch recalling, reluctantly, a broken memory from the night before. After the bar, I'd knocked on Smirks' door. Why? What had I said to him? I remembered only the look on his face. Embarrassment, for me. His head shook back and forth, a little smile on his lips. He closed his door. Leaving me in the hallway alone.

Lark's bedroom door opened, and her voice, raspy with last night's cigarettes, croaked my name. "Julia, come. It's time for you to learn." I pulled myself off the couch and my stomach swung like a pendulum, heavy with stale liquor. We squinted at each other through bleary eyes. She held up the outfit I had worn the night before. "This is not," she said with gravity, "a long t-shirt." I shrugged. "I heard you call it a long t-shirt." I shrugged again. "It's a shift." I stared at the garment in

73

her hands as she clutched its shoulders and held it up to her body. Its straight cut was a narrow triangle hiding the curves of her hips.

"Shift," I said. I needed coffee.

"That's right." Lark eyed the piece at arm's length. "Words that are nouns and verbs. Smirks has turned me onto them. I keep finding them everywhere."

I nodded. "So," I said, settling on her bed, "were *you* wearing a long t-shirt last night?"

She frowned. "Nobody was wearing a long t-shirt last night." She walked over to her closet and pulled out her piece, royal-blue and shimmering, and placed it against her body. "This is a tunic."

"Tunic," I repeated.

"Yes." She gestured to the design. "Note the collar, and the sleeves, the vaguely Grecian tone." I nodded. Lark opened her walk-in closet wider. It overflowed with colours and fabric and, one by one, she gave name to sleeves and necks and textiles that had previously been anonymous. Peter Pan collars and smocking shirts and Juliette sleeves. Chambray and chenille and charmeuse. Skirt length modifiers: mini, tea, ballerina, maxi. "Learn your pantones, especially the ones in verbs: spice, buff, smoke, tangle. How you put *on* your clothing is important as well. Have you ever thought of that?" I hadn't. A "placket" is the slit in the skirt's waist that allows you to shimmy in. Your pocket is a flap, a patch, or—adorably—a smile. The warp is the lengthwise thread, and the weft is the thread that crosses it to make cloth. "The warp and weft of life," Lark said with a sweeping gesture. "The fabric we live in." She ran her hand along a blouse made from organdy. Organdy, a heavy word, a heavy fabric, its name summoning images of organs and orchids, kidneys or livers blooming like flowers in one of April's paintings. "When a fabric *feels* nice, you say, 'it has a nice hand to it.'"

"It has a nice hand to it."

"Smirks wears nice clothes," Lark said.

"Smirks is a pedophile."

"Well, not nice clothes. But cool clothes." She continued to touch the organdy blouse.

"Lark. Smirks is a pedophile."

Her hand fell and she looked at me. Shook her head. "No."

"Yes. He was at the MAA meeting."

Her mouth dropped open. "What?" Her gaze turned inward, to her memories, to all her interactions with Smirks from the day she'd met him. She ran through each encounter, reconsidered every word, rehashed every touch they'd exchanged. "No," she said again. She continued to shake her head. I continued to nod. She brushed past me toward his bedroom. Pushed open the door and peered inside. His bed was crisply made. Novels lined the bookshelves alphabetically. A bulletin board displayed quadrants of concert tickets, photographs, business cards and birthday greetings. Everything had a place. He'd even folded the plastic wrap in his garbage can. Lark stood there for a long time.

She didn't believe me for a while. She couldn't talk to Smirks about it because I'd made her swear an oath of silence. She was a great actor, though, and her behaviour around him didn't change one bit. She flirted with him, touching his muscles. Making lewd jokes. And then she'd barrage me with questions once he left. "Has he ever touched a child?"

"I don't know."

"Is it little girls or little boys?"

"I don't know."

"But he's so smart! So handsome!"

"I know."

"Was he molested?

"I don't know."

Eventually, she stopped.

Then one morning Smirks left as usual out the front door with his basketball and, as soon as the lock of the deadbolt clicked, Lark's bedroom door burst open and I heard her scampering down the hall. She jumped in front of me, wearing a bike helmet and bike gloves, with her right pant leg rolled up to her knee in bike-commuter fashion. "He's a pedophile!" she shouted, and I nodded, standing up, wondering if she'd fallen out of bed in her sleep and smacked her head on the floor. "And now," she said, jumping up and down, "you'll make him a PEDAL-PHILE!" With this, she buckled over at the waist, laughing maniacally, and I joined her, overcome with a relief so powerful it felt like the breaking of bones. We collapsed into each other, unable to breathe, we laughed so hard, like children, our lungs clawing for oxygen, our teeth bared in defiance against the world.

❂

The next morning Smirks knelt beside the couch and woke me. I could smell the toothpaste on his breath and a drop of water from his wet hair fell on my hand. "I need a bike, Julia," he said, nodding, and I knew for sure he was coming with me. I took him to The Bike Doctor. He wanted the same one as me, a Devinci Stockholm, black and sleek, modern. Aluminum frame, twenty-four speed Shimano Alivio gearing, the Trans-Canada Highway ours for $700 plus utilities.

Our mechanic, a small, blonde-haired man with a thick eastern-European accent, envied our plan. "I came to Canada because I could not believe there is a country so big." He attached a sturdy back rack to Smirks' rig. "To bike across it must be so…enigma." He wrenched his Allen key, and Smirks and I glanced at each other, smiling. The mechanic raised the seat and lowered the handlebars, attached the brackets for the front panniers. He gazed at us happily. "You are on a train now," he said. "Enjoy the slow view."

Smirks and I left the shop and rode down a quiet street. "What are you going to name your bike?" I asked.

"I dunno. Hadn't thought about it." We continued riding. "Why is your bicycle's name Shelley?"

"After my hairdresser." Shelley still lived in Harmony, where she had cut my hair from the first time to the last time before I left Nova Scotia for Vancouver—the big city—and she gave me bangs because, as she claimed, they were more urban.

"They'll call it 'fringe,' though," she had said in her thick, fourth-generation valley accent. "They" being the hairdressers of the west.

City hairdressers, who'd have a different vernacular than those from our rural town. "They'll call themselves 'stylists.' Hair dye is 'colour.' And when your colour starts to grow out, they'll call your roots 're-growth,' and then, later, they'll call it 'ombre.'" She was a tiny, amused woman. I'd always loved the colour of her hair: cooked carrots. I'd asked her several times throughout high school to please dye my hair that hue. She refused. "This colour doesn't come in a box, honey." She'd grin at me in the mirror.

I named my bicycle Shelley because I'd always felt as if Shelley knew me in a way no one else did. Not that we'd discuss anything intensely private. Just typical salon fare: boyfriends, girlfriends, test scores, teachers. The true gossip carried more in tone of voice than words. She didn't know anything about my childhood or my father, only that he was a drunk and then he was gone. But she had watched me, for fifteen years, watch myself in the mirror, and I imagined this gave her some privileged perspective. She could see my insecurities and my hopes, saw the times I liked myself and the times I hated. When I initially hopped on my bicycle, an image of Shelley popped into my head, standing behind me, looking right at me, through a mirrored reflection. I whispered her name and it stuck.

Smirks and I started going on long bike rides around the Lower Mainland. We took Adanac Street out of East Van and through Burnaby, the short, severe hill at Boundary bearing portents of the Rocky Mountains, which we imagined—wrongly—would be the most difficult part of our journey. We chose the hardest routes we could find. We didn't research elevation, the grades or the slopes. I think part of us worried the maps and charts would overwhelm us and lock us in Vancouver forever. It was best to go blind and wondrous, to not know what was coming. A hill off Dollarton Highway heading west toward Lonsdale infuriated us both: it rose what seemed like straight up, for several blocks, and we felt as though our bodies were the perpendicular run to the hill's rise, our knees pumping choppily over a series of barrels. We did it five days in a row, and by the fifth day it felt easier. At the top, Smirks leaned over and slapped my thigh, hard as rock.

We were getting to know each other. Smirks suffered from a series of poetic afflictions. For one, he scarred easily. His face had at least four scars on it, small and curiously placed, and he doled out their causes to me over the weeks before we left. The one on his ear, which I had mistaken for a new pimple, was actually the mark of a claw of his ex-girlfriend's cat.

"You had a girlfriend?" I asked. I tried to sound casual, but my mind spiked at the possibility of more information. We were lying on the beach in the rain. We had cycled from Deep Cove to UBC, starting in the late afternoon, taking our time, and arriving at the bottom of the stairs of Wreck Beach just in time for sunset. I loved sunset at Wreck Beach. The nudists cheered as though they were watching the most magnificent fireworks. That night, though, the clouds were thick and the rain poured down, but we didn't care. We were hot and satisfied, or at least I was. I had fallen for him, in that sad and peculiar way one wants something that one can never actually have. Like to have been born with carrot-red hair. When we reached the bottom of the stairs, Smirks had lain flat on his back, his hair pressed into the soaking wet sand, and I collapsed beside him, put my head on his chest.

"You had a girlfriend?" I asked again. He still didn't respond. And as I lay there with my head against his ribcage, listening to his heart, I heard his second poetic affliction: heart arrhythmia. His pulse a train steadily chug-chugging along a series of ancient tracks and then—suddenly—a skip of a beat. A moment of silence where the heart should have been. A hollow louder for the space it left behind.

And then later, at Walmart at the end of the SkyTrain line, against his will, shopping for the cheapest of the cheap flip-flops to wear on the lakeshores of southern British Columbia, summer dresses weighing nothing that I could stuff in the side pocket of my pannier and unfurl on a Saturday night in the middle of rural Canada, after we'd been biking for days and man, oh man, did I ever need a beer and some bona fide male attention—in Walmart, I held up two dresses toward Smirks, same style but different shades of blue, asking for his opinion, but he couldn't see the difference. He was colour blind.

We ditched our bikes for the evening and wandered to Trout Lake, my second favourite place in Vancouver, a little oasis in the concrete, a lung of water—however murky and contaminated—surrounded by verdant water lilies and ferns, sprawling green lawn, huge oak and maple trees, and the North Shore mountains sparkling out beyond it all. We took the alley along the baseball fields so I could watch the Little League game. Small boys and girls in their blue and white uniforms, East Side Bombers, their tiny, shiny helmets reminding me of Lego men as they ran around the diamond that had been halved to accommodate their small bodies.

We passed by garages, their open doors displaying greenhouses, woodworking shops, drum kits, intricate homebrew setups. Smirks avoided the baseball game and instead surveyed the backyards. From ahead we heard a searing noise, sharp and tinny, and saw a small light, hot and purple. Somebody was welding. An old man wearing an industrial, rectangular mask, a narrow black slit for eyes. Smirks reached toward my face and gently turned my chin away. "Don't look at the light." As a boy he'd looked for too long at a welding light, and still had a permanent burn on his retina. A black glow where the world should be. A blind spot.

We settled in on the sand that curls along the south end of Trout Lake. I could still hear the baseball coach yelling at the children. "You run like a girl, Toby! Smarten up!" I looked at Smirks. Do men really still speak like this to children?

He nodded. "The world of sports can be pretty awful." He sounded sad. "That's one of the reasons I got into coaching." He took off his sneakers and dug his toes into the cool, wet sand. "The things we say to children are so important." He stared toward the baseball diamond. I waited. "Everything you say to a child is an instruction. Almost everything they hear is new. You have to be so careful." I looked around us. A young boy stood at the water's edge, watching a row of ducklings chase their mother through the lily pads. The boy was smiling, his tiny hands at his sides shaking with excitement. I didn't notice children very often, didn't think of them as Smirks did: like students of life awaiting instruction. They were still mysterious to me. Opaque. Books, though, I knew. I opened my bag and pulled out my copy of *Pedophilia: The Radical Case*. Handed it to Smirks.

He took it, and I watched the child. Little yellow rubber boots. His mother stood off to the side, keeping an eye, but also letting him be. In *The Radical Case,* O'Carroll suggests lowering the age of consent. Decriminalizing incest. He claims that the dysfunctional families are the ones who do not encourage sexual contact between their children and loving pedophiles.

Smirks flipped through the pages too quickly, not pausing on one long enough to let any information sink in. He kept frowning and sighing and finally he closed the book and looked at me. "There have been two girls." My stomach softened and I held his gaze. The child in the yellow boots by the water laughed, a sharp sound like glass breaking. "The first was ten, and I was twenty-seven. She was the daughter of a woman I was dating."

"Your ex?"

"Yes."

"Did you date her to get closer to the daughter?"

"Yes."

But just to be close to her. He was not going to touch her, he had told himself. She had hair the colour of new pennies. He called her Penny, and taught her how to spit cherry seeds farther than all of her friends. They made up intricate handshakes, which Penny could never get through without dissolving into laughter. Penny fell in love with Smirks. In the mornings, she came into her mother's bedroom and crawled up on top of him, as soft and light as a kitten. He was never going to touch her. She had eyes the colour of wet pavement.

They had a relationship. And he did what he said he would. He never touched her there. She never touched him there. But, I was thinking, prepubescent children are sexual—at an early stage of their sexuality, but still sexual. A body is sex, personified. Sex, alive. Even before puberty. How did we draw these distinctions? Smirks never touched her there. "When I left—I had to leave—she cried.

It hurt to leave, but I had to. And that is the story of Penny."

"And the other girl?"

"Is another story." He handed *The Radical Case* back to me. "And none of those stories are in these books."

"But the literature—"

"Isn't for me." He put his sneakers back on. "Not everyone finds their answers there, Julia." I put my shoes back on too. "Come on," he said, offering his hand and pulling me up. "Let's race." He turned and started running, and I scrambled to catch up, trailing him past the families barbecuing hot dogs and the children playing baseball. I watched his firm calves pump faster and faster as he got away from me. Like that, I chased him all the way home.

❁

Two weeks before Smirks and I were supposed to leave for our bicycle trip, Lark was hired as a staff writer by *Flare Canada*—"Interning is so last year," she said—and within two days she was packed and on an airplane east for Toronto Fashion Week where she would sit among other fashion forecasters and watch her favourite designers strut their new collections down the runways. Except now it was called "World Mastercard Fashionweek," which Lark did not think could be any less cool. "Corporate sponsors with their eponymous colonization," she said. "What are we, living in the Year of the Depend Adult Undergarment?" I moved into her bedroom, and the apartment became a base camp for training. I texted Thierry my updates every few days, letting him know I'd permanently left the apartment, wondering when we should put it up for rent. I never heard from him.

Lark emailed me from Toronto. Brainstorming article ideas. Photographs from fashion shows. What would be on trend the coming season. Cutouts, apparently, would reign supreme as a pattern. Digital images of thin, hard models, like children, their bodies painted in structured fabrics with geometric patches missing. The white of their skin like an ambulance, or brown like varnished alder. And material made of iridescence, painting the model's body like an abalone shell. No one smiled, and all wore sharp heels. Loose trouser pants. Skinny jeans won't be around forever, said Lark. The colour orange. Straight up orange. Crush orange would be everyone's accent piece next season, just wait.

And two-tone. Outfits divided like fractions. Two-thirds black, one red. Half-white, a quarter of yellow, and a quarter of green. Do you call it chartreuse or lime-green? Lark tried to show me the colour over Skype, holding up her latest *Vogue* to the screen. "It's on all the runways, and it varies. A bit. What should I call it? *Flare* is very parsimonious with word count. *Parsimonious*. This isn't quite lime-green. But it's not chartreuse. Let's go with chartreuse. Sounds like the name of the pretty girl in a John Hughes movie." And then, days later, a photo-text from her, that, when I first opened to view, shocked me dumb. I jostled my head and looked away, looked back, certain I could not be looking at what I thought I was looking at.

Her text came seconds later. "I'm so fashionable, even my poop is two-toned!"

What would I have done without her?

❂

We needed to learn how to repair our bicycles. Neither of us had ever so much as replaced a bike tube. We eschewed the communal public workshops at the East Van co-ops whose mechanics favoured fixed-gear bicycles. One day, biking south on Main Street, a series of black-denim-clad bike couriers overtook us, smelling of Pabst and Belmonts, two of them muttering "gear fag" as they rode by. Why would they say that? It scared me away. We decided to venture out of Vancouver proper for our bicycle education.

We found our private mechanic online. A grandpa-type who'd made the cross-country trip three times, twice alone, and once as a guide for a group of cyclists raising money for leukemia research. The three-hour lesson took place in his backyard garage in Burnaby. Ceiling-mounted bike stands. Dozens of tires and chain lengths on hooks. Old leather saddles hanging like tribal masks from the walls.

Grandpa shuffled slowly, pushing tools around, fiddling with the radio dial until "Sonata Pathéthique" warbled, a sweet ache, through the speakers of his ancient boombox.

"Those slackers had a support van the whole time. Those cancer riders." He scratched his moustache as though it itched. Esoteric tools peeling from the walls, their shapes outlined against the plywood with black Sharpie. I would learn the tools' names: socket wrench, headset wrench, pedal wrench. "But I carried my own damn gear with those leukemia kids." He bent down to point out boxes of spokes, stood to show us chain pins and link connectors. "Just like you kids are doing, I did that. I refused to throw even one ball of socks onto that stupid support bus." *Support* as though it were a dirty word. "Kinda defeats the purpose of riding across the country." He held up a brake clamp in one hand and a pair of brake pliers in another, looked at us. "Don't you think?"

Smirks and I both shrugged. We didn't know. Neither of us yet knew our purpose. Grandpa told us. "The purpose is to feel the whole country underneath you. To feel the weight of your load in your legs. You get an idea, real quick, of just how much stuff you need when it's your own ass hauling it seven thousand kilometres across Canada. I guarantee you—I'll bet money—no matter how lightly you kids pack, you'll post at least ten pounds of stuff home within the first two weeks. Guaranteed. You think you need something. *I need this. I need that.* But then you're out there, on the road, on a mountain, in the trees..." He trailed off. The grace notes of the sonata's first movement spiked the air, stirring up my chest. I smelled oil and chain lube. Rusted metal and pine. He looked at us. "Wish I could do it again."

He started with the basics, the bike parts, and for this, he flipped his own bicycle upside down so its seat sat on the floor and its tires spun in the air. "The first thing you must learn," he said, "is how to handle your bicycle. Flip your vehicle over as I just did: with complete control and balance." He showed us how. Stand on the left side of the frame. Bend over the top. Grasp the right-side fork and seat stay. Stand up, keeping the bike well balanced in front of you. Flip it over and rest the saddle and handlebar on the ground, taking care not to damage the handlebar accessories: mirror, computer, bell. Perhaps a bar-bag with a clear top pocket to display our maps. "We can't move forward," he said, "until you can both complete this process with complete control and balance."

Smirks and I flipped over our bicycles, perfectly, the first time. We looked at the underbellies of our machines. Pieces that I had summarized into one term called "Shelley" revealed to me their sophistication: rear derailleur, cogset, chain-stay, pinch bolt, stem, head tube. This, a poetry I understood. I recited the words, wanting fluency in something as flawless as a bicycle. Something so pure in purpose and function. Something that did no damage, only good. To learn a bicycle, to master its tenets, would surely lead to my apotheosis. Light-headed on clarity. Always knowing what to do next, always knowing the right step to take. I craved it.

Start with the chain. Clean it, and oil it. Some say oiling a chain will cause it to gum up and wear down. But the fact of the matter is, you need oil to run smoothly. "I'll trade a little wear for a smoother ride, won't you?" asked Grandpa. He passed us cloths damp with lubricant and told us to cup our chains inside them, rotate our pedals, and let the metal slip through our hands like sand. As we did this, he stood behind me and hung a bright yellow whistle around my neck. Identical to the one Mom had given me when I moved out to Vancouver.

"Rape whistle," I said.

Grandpa laughed, handing one to Smirks. "I call them 'alert whistles,' but yes, it's the same idea." He told us there would be a time on the road when Smirks and I would get so far apart we wouldn't be able to hear each other yell. A time when a sharp, piercing blow would be more effective than our voice. A time when one of us would need to stop and the other, oblivious, would keep on going.

"Or, a time when one of us is being raped," I said. Grandpa and Smirks frowned. "Jokes."

"Let's hope so." Grandpa handed us pencils and diagrams of bicycles with blanks where the parts' names should be. "Fill these out." I stared at the simple line drawing, and imagined the crude names

Thierry would put in the blanks. Grandpa finally sat down on a stool. "So, what's your cause?"

I looked at him.

"Most foot-pedallers these days gotta have some cause to move their asses for. What's yours? Cancer? Diabetes? The global warming?"

The crisp, white sheet of paper with a bicycle on it, drawn in *ligne-claire* style, a bicycle that Tintin would ride. Thierry had read and reread his Hergé comics his whole life. When I'd shared with him the lie I told Bob—that I wanted to take the summer off school to find Dirtbag—his glabella had buckled. "I don't think that's a lie," he'd said. I assured him it was. Bob wouldn't let me take time off unless it was related to school. If I involved Dirtbag, it became research. But Thierry didn't want me to find him by myself. He wanted to be there.

"I'm not going to find him," I'd told him.

But now I wanted to. Like a bicycle, there was a logical next step. The tightening of the gear cable. The pumping of a tire. The finding of the father.

"I'm looking for my father." At this, Grandpa nodded. Smirks stopped filling in his bicycle diagram and looked up at me. I continued. "When I was a kid, he molested me. Well, actually, he taught me how to masturbate. And now I want to find him and ask him some questions about it." Grandpa's hand froze in mid-reach toward his moustache. Nobody said anything, so I kept talking. "I'm studying counselling psychology and working with women who, as children, experienced sexual relations with adults. But I guess I feel as if a piece of my research is missing. In order for me, as someone who was molested, to be as objective as possible, I'll need his version of the story as well. Maybe ask him his intention. Or. Not his intention, but what he was thinking. Did he think about the impact he might have on me? Had he planned the molestation, or did it just happen, beyond his control?" Still, nobody talked. "Actually, I don't really like the word 'molestation,' which has two definitions, the first being 'to force unwanted sexual attention onto somebody, especially a child,' and the second, 'to pester, bother, or annoy.' In many cases, mine included, nothing was ever forced on me. Nor was I ever pestered, bothered, or annoyed by the touching that went on between my father and me. That's why I think certain instances of sexual relations between adults and children need a name other than molestation."

I looked at Smirks, gripping his pencil so tight his hand shook. "Julia."

"Smirks?"

"You never told me that."

"I know."

Smirks put his pencil down and leaned toward me. "How did it affect you?"

Grandpa's stool squeaked under his weight.

"The molestation?"

Smirks nodded.

"It didn't."

Smirks had told me that all his characters in the stories he wrote started with a goal. They were defined by their goal. Every action they took sprang from that goal. I yearned for such definition. Such a clear line drawn around me.

"The feminists don't like that idea. They don't like my research. But, as I always say, the belief that pedophilia is solely the result of a patriarchal society is specious. It's not always *just* a male exerting his will over a female. Other factors play a role. There are results other than victimization and oppression."

Grandpa straightened his back and turned toward me. He examined the handlebars of my bicycle and then looked at me. "Well, honey. The first thing you're gonna need to get yourself is a rear-view mirror."

"Oh, yeah?" I said. "Why's that?"

"In my experience," he said, "a deadbeat father is always behind you. Never ahead."

❂

After our workshop, Smirks and I rode the ten kilometres home on our freshly tuned bikes, trued and lubed and pumped and adjusted by our own hands. How wonderful it felt, falling down the hill at Boundary, shooting west, blossoms of cherry leaves kicking up at our wheels, sending sprays of cotton candy pink into the air, Lark's voice in my head: *Gross! The ground is barfing unicorn blood.*

"I really wish you'd told me that," Smirks said. "About your father."

"You never asked why I was biking."

"I didn't think to."

"Would it have made a difference?" I asked.

He was quiet for a while. Then, "What exactly did he do to you?" We were on Adanac Street, the bike path, side by side, riding slow and aimless, having fulfilled our only duty of the day.

"Nothing, really."

From here you could see the entire downtown core, silver and grey, an island of commerce in Burrard Inlet. The sprawl of West Vancouver creeping slowly up the North Shore mountains like a beautiful disease. Like rosacea.

"Nothing like he did to April, my sister. I think he did worse things to her. She won't tell me, but I think he abused her. Forced her. She's much more traumatized than me. There was definitely fear involved with her, maybe pain."

I waited for Smirks to speak. He didn't.

"All he did was touch me. Rubbed my clit until I came. It was a nightly thing, sitting on the rocking chair in the living room under the guise of 'reading lessons.' My mother liked to say I knew how to read when I was ten months old. But only because Dirtbag would point at the words and say them into my ear a million times until I was finally trained to match the sound of his voice to the symbol on the page and repeat it."

"That's reading," said Smirks.

"I suppose."

"And that's molestation."

"No, it isn't."

We rolled past a construction sign entreating cyclists to please dismount. We didn't dismount, never listened. Rode by an animal control van with its back doors spread wide, a cage awaiting some transgressive creature. We watched the open front door of the contiguous house, listened to the scuffling noises inside. We wanted to see the captive. A racoon? Skunk? Cougar? Our tires carried us farther, and the moment passed.

I'd heard from Dirtbag exactly three times since he left Nova Scotia when I was seven years old. Once from Banff, Alberta. Once from Redvers, Saskatchewan. And once from Kingston, Ontario. "We're going to visit each of those towns," I told Smirks.

He grunted. "Are you serious?"

"Yes." I was, I realized. I was going to look for Dirtbag. "You don't have to come."

"I just don't understand why you want to find him."

"To unite the adult with the child. To acknowledge the agency of both parties." I was thinking aloud. "It could form a new conversation. One in which there is no victim. No oppressor." I took my hands off the bars, stretched my arms out beside me. Looked at Smirks. "Don't you see how beneficial that could be?" The road was otherwise empty. The cherry blossoms whirred at our feet.

Smirks kept his grip firmly on his handlebars. "I'm the wrong person to ask," he said.

Part 2

Slipstream

My cellphone played the marimba next to my ear. Harsh midi tones like fingers jabbing my eyes, my head. My body, sweating and inert. My limbs, heavy bricks. I twisted my neck across the pillow to see the screen. Thierry. My hangover pounded through every vein in my body like the heartbeat of a giant. Thierry. He knew I was leaving on my bike trip today. He wanted me to stay. I answered. "Thierry."

"Julia."

"Hi."

"Hi." Silence. Did he want me to speak first? "I got your message?" Upspeak. As if it was a question. My message. Shit. I plunged into my memory of the night before. I'd vowed to stay in. Pack. Mentally prepare for the journey ahead. Write in my diary or something. Be civilized. But then, I'd poured a glass of wine. Smirks went to bed. I had another, another. On my desk, I had laid out all of my Dirtbag Documentation. Thomas's *Collected Poems*. The confessional letter/rape apology. Another glass of wine. Purple lips, dry tongue. The telephone numbers from the three cities he had called me from. Banff. Redvers. Kingston. Telephone numbers I'd written down as a child and carried in my wallet, in a keepsakes box, tucked inside a book. Three of the few telephone numbers I knew by heart. "I could call these numbers right now," I'd thought. Save myself the trip. Instead I texted Emma, a party-time drinking buddy since Lark left.

"Doing anything fun?"

A trill of relief rang through my belly when I saw the ellipse of her imminent response. "The Narrow. Double highballs." Slammed the last glass of wine. Escaped the sleeping apartment and rode Shelley to Main Street. After my first double, whiskey soda, fuzzy recollections. Crowded bodies in the galley like a rush-hour SkyTrain. Sundresses and cutoffs. The fizz of boozy breath. I was leaning over the bar, reaching for a bottle. Emma's flammable laughter as she stole a sandal off my foot. Spinning around the parking meter as if it were a stripping pole. A tall British man with yellow hair yelling up at the heavens "You're ugly! You're an ugly god!" His thin face looking down at me, telling me I pronounced *patronizing* wrong. And then nothing. The blackness of an empty sky.

"Julia?" Thierry sounded impatient.

"My message?"

"You don't remember." A statement, not a question.

I sighed, just happy to hear his voice, even if it was sad. And worse than sad: annoyed. "I don't remember."

"Jesus."

"What did I say?"

"It doesn't matter. You're leaving today?"

"Unless."

"Unless what?"

"Unless you want to talk?"

He laughed. "How's...what's his name, Smirks?"

"Smirks is. Fine."

"You meet him before or after we broke up?"

"I met him the night before you dumped me."

"And it's love already, you think?"

I mashed my tongue between my teeth. Fuck. Dug the nail of my index finger into my thigh. "Did I say that?"

"Oh, yes. You said many things. About the size of his dick. The scars on his face."

I buried my face in my pillow, defeated. I considered telling Thierry that Smirks was a pedophile, but that would just make me sound even more crazy. I'd lost. That was clear.

"I've sublet the apartment for the summer, so you don't have to worry about rent. You don't have to worry about anything." Thierry's voice had tightened and shrunk. Wavered. He was hurt. I had hurt him.

"Thierry—"

"Have a nice life, Julia."

He hung up.

Later, Smirks came home from the gym and found me despondent on the couch. "Did you go out last night?"

I nodded.

He made power smoothies out of kale and honey and plain yogurt and crushed aspirin, forcing me to drink two full glasses of water before handing me the green elixir. I sat by the window, expecting friends to show up. A cohort of congratulators to see us off. Maybe our bike-happy mayor, the one who'd changed all the traffic lights and installed the roundabouts, maybe he'd come to see us off. But nobody notices when you leave unless you tell them to. It was a sunny day, but that didn't matter. I felt gutted and pressed like charcuterie. Smirks skirted around me for a while. The silence pulsed and the living room brightened as the day got hotter. He dragged my panniers out of the bedroom, splayed them on the floor in front of me.

"Pack."

"In a minute."

"What happened?"

"I don't even know."

Finally, the jangle and buzz of Skype's ringtone. Lark wanted the webcam to face the living room as we packed up our panniers so she could monitor and adjudicate our choices. From her hotel room in Toronto she watched, her head at an anxious angle, lips pursed into a frown. "Is that the only dress you're bringing?"

"Yes, Lark. This is the only dress I am bringing on my bicycle trip across Canada."

"In my closet I left some—"

"Bike tools and cookware have taken up most of my pannier space."

"I just think you should have options." Lark had options for everything: outfits, breakfast, fuck buddies, ways to die. She believed that maintaining an arsenal of options was the only way left for the middle class to assert agency.

"There will be Walmarts along the way," Smirks said, bending down toward the webcam, his round face filling the screen. Our weeks of training had left him even more fit and lean. Not tan—his pale skin seemed impervious to the sun—but cheeks bright and rosy. Lark lit up at the sight of him, her smile fading when he scurried off to roll more microfibre clothes into bundles the size of socks.

"No Walmarts. When you get to Banff I'll have plenty of pieces to lend you. We'll rock the Rockies."

If we stayed on schedule, Lark would be in Banff the weekend we passed through. *Flare* had her writing about an Eco-Fashion show, an offshoot of Calgary Fashion Week.

I flipped through the book I'd found hidden in Lark's closet.

"And what, do you know, is illegal in Banff?"

"Acting drunk. You are not allowed to *act* drunk in any National Park in Canada."

"You can *be* drunk though, right?"

"Mos def," said Lark. She'd left us the book as a surprise going-away gift. A little tongue-in-cheek joke for the pedal-philes. *You Can't Do That in Canada* was full of bizarre, outdated bylaws in towns across the country. In York, Ontario, no bathing on the side of the road. In Halifax, Nova Scotia, no riding a sheep down a sidewalk. Lark twisted a strand of hair in her fingers. "Break at least one law in each town you pass through. Okay, Smirks?"

"I'll see what I can do."

For the final farewell, Smirks and I crowded the camera, our faces gleaming white from the sun that shone through the window, our mouths almost invisible in the glare. "Bye, Lark!" we chorused. The only person to whom we said goodbye, and the first person we would see again.

We locked her door, tucked the key into a fake yellow rose in her trellis. Slipped into a smile-pocket of the world, like two toothpicks, invisible and forgotten. Removed from play, an isolated travelling society.

A circus. No one paid attention when we swerved the roundabouts on Adanac. My hangover tapered to a dull point at my glabella. A rope pulling me forward. Around every corner we expected to see someone to say goodbye to, but no one showed. The better I felt, physically, the more emotion settled in. I was leaving Thierry. Thierry had left me. I'd lost the only person who ever loved me. Headwind drew thin, wet lines from the corner of my eyes. We headed east in silence. New weight of our panniers pulling us down tight to the earth, a foreign gravity. Too soon, it couldn't really be happening, we swung onto Barnet Highway. Cruised past the Burrard Inlet where it broke into Indian Arm. Sulphur mills gleaming like giant pollen heads in the sun.

"The last view of the ocean marks the point of no return," I said. An old aviation term: the point of no return. The moment when a jet no longer has enough fuel to turn back. I felt like a pioneer. The only direction was forward. No map, just forward. One hour, two hours, three hours. Quaint suburbs escalating into stretches of massive, big-box, brick-and-mortar commerce. A Best Buy larger than a city block. An Applebees serving hundreds. And then, this mania wilting to the pastoral, the bucolic. Colours of nature. Brown cows, green fields, purple mountains. Here was Canada. Not so far away. We made our first discovery as pioneers: the slipstream. It happened on the way down a long hill out of Chilliwack. Riding behind Smirks, I immediately overtook him and, once in front, he immediately overtook me. We continued this way down the hill until we got to the bottom and rode side by side along the Fraser Valley floor. We'd heard of it, but had never been riding fast enough to feel it. Not until you feel something can you understand it. Drafting: when one cyclist cruises behind or beside the other cyclist, carried in the vortex of her slipstream.

"It's not a vortex," Smirks said. "It's a wake."

"You're awake."

The event of our discovery was momentous enough to name, so we named it The Slipstream Movement, which reminded me of Thierry, a Vonnegut fanatic and general connoisseur of slipstream fiction, the genre that dissolves the borders between the strange and the literary.

Riding the slipstream was like being pulled along by an invisible, weightless rope tied around my waist. Beside a river, I closed my eyes and trusted the slipstream to suck me forward. Across flat land, I'd watch Smirks work so hard to break through the wind, and I'd be right there beside him, in a ghostly sidecar, cruising. We fell into a pattern of timed intervals: five minutes in the slipstream, five minutes at the prow. The prow, we called it, as if we were captains of a ship.

That first night, I dreamt in slipstream movements. In my coffin tent, its canvas tickled by light, whispery rain, I drifted in and out, at times feeling intense motion and power in my legs, my core. Other times feeling as though I were asleep in a hand, carried. Energy organizing itself into slipstream movements.

"I carry you halfway across the country, and then, you carry me," wrote Smirks in a poem that he read to me at the foot of a steep incline just outside of Manning Park. Three days into our trip and we'd formed a leisurely pattern of rewarding ourselves before the hard work. The road had started to tilt upwards and patches of snow had appeared, signalling a sharp spike in altitude. So, before beginning the climb, Smirks and I took our leave from the road and settled amongst some fallen tree trunks and sun-warmed boulders. I lay on the ground and stretched my body as long as I could, pushing my sore muscles into pebbles and divots.

"More," I said. "More poetry." I wanted a poem about love. About one of his girls.

He set aside his notebook and retrieved another from his bag. The flipping of pages. I stared at the sky. Pine branches waved in slow motion, moving like belly dancers. The chuckles of chickadees and the hiccups of the mountain finches swelling then fading with the wind. I breathed deep, trying to relax. Trying not to try. Smirks started to read.

"No person shall wantonly unhinge, take away or hide any front gate to anyone's house." He was reading from the book Lark gave us, the obsolete laws of our land. "No person shall deliberately frighten a mouse." He turned a page. "Draw the blinds if you're naked inside your own house." Another page. "During federal elections, do not be a souse." He closed the book.

I nudged him with my foot. "Nice rhymes." No response. He was looking toward the hill we would soon have to climb. I closed my eyes and brought my rape whistle up to my lips, blowing softly the first few bars of "In the Hall of the Mountain King."

Smirks stood. "Hello!" he called, and I stood too, just in time to see the yellow-clad cyclist barrelling toward us. We jumped out of his way and he skidded to a stop, gravel spraying, brakes screaming. He was an odd-looking, middle-aged man with a shapeless upper body and skinny white legs. His face was smooth and, despite his features, featureless. He reminded me of a peeled potato.

He whipped out a kerchief and wiped his brow. "How long have the bears sat there?" His voice was high-pitched and squeaky.

Smirks and I looked at each other, shook our heads.

"Have you not seen them?" He had a Scandinavian accent. Wire-rimmed bifocals sliding down his amorphous nose. "Did you not see me pass by ten minutes ago?" He looked astounded.

"No," I said.

"When I saw the bears, I thought you have also turned around."
"Bears?"

He chuckled at our stupidity. Dismounted his bike and set up his kickstand. Everything about this man was wee: slender bike, miniature panniers, little body. He told us that up the hill, around that bend, a mama bear and her two cubs sat on the side of the road eating garbage. "The bears are quite comfortable. But I am not. I am not Canadian," he said by way of explanation. "I don't know how to act around a bear." I had never seen a bear before either. "I like Canada, though," he assured us. "Especially this part of the country, outside of the city. The people are more...wholesome."

I knew what he meant. The people are more white. "Where are you from?" I asked.

"Norway."

That morning I'd read a link on my Twitterfeed about the trial of a Norwegian terrorist who murdered seventy-seven people because they were Muslim. The tweet asked if the killer should be tried as an insane person. Does promoting indiscriminate violence against all Muslims make you crazy? Did reports of him being a "challenging and aggressive" four-year-old, and a pre-teen "lacking joy and spontaneity," prove he'd been crazy his whole life? The twitterbugs thought the talk of his sanity was due to his whiteness. Had he been brown, no one would question his ability to murder. To be a terrorist. But because he was white, he must be crazy.

"What do you think will happen in the Norway Terrorist Attacks trial?" I asked.

"The Norway Attacks," he corrected. "He'll get twenty-one years. That's all they ever get."

"That's crazy," I said.

Smirks shrugged. "That's restorative justice."

"He has a three-room cell in jail," I said. "And a television."

"Yeah, and he can sunbathe on the roof of his prison. And it makes him less likely to murder again."

"This is just one way our countries are different," said the Norwegian. "Prison is not for breaking people. It is for healing." He had his hands pressed into the small of his back and was arching away, stretching. "It is a problem, though," he said, shrugging and remounting his bike.

"Preventive detention?" Smirks asked.

"No. The Muslims." He took a long draw from his water bottle and then looked at me. "You couldn't be here, you know." He gestured to my body. "In those clothes." A tank top. Spandex shorts. He pointed at Smirks. "With this man. If you were Muslim."

I laughed. I hated him, instantly. "That's a weird thing to say. You wouldn't be here if you were a duck." Resisted the impulse to swear. Hoped he couldn't see the heat in my face, my thumping heart. My skin tingling at my hairline.

The Norwegian shook his head and mounted his bike. Done with us. "Will you head north at Keremeos?"

"Our plan is to stay south until Christina Lake," Smirks said.

The Norwegian giggled. A wheezing squeal that reminded me of a pig. "You're in for quite the climb. Quite the climb indeed!" He headed back up the hill, chuckling.

My breath returned. I looked at Smirks. "Quite the climb?"

He shrugged. "It's Canada." We watched the Norwegian turn the bend and waited for him to come back. He didn't. "Bears must be gone."

"You think twenty-one years is enough?"

Smirks shrugged. "Enough for what? Punishment is weird. It doesn't work." A breeze came on. He held up Lark's law book and slipped it into his pannier. "You and I are both criminals in some country, right?"

His Twitter account was full of statements like this. Me, I had no idea. And thus, I didn't tweet. Or was it that I didn't tweet, and so I didn't know? When I moved to compose a tweet, my heart raced. I had difficulty breathing. Couldn't think clearly. The battle between thinking and feeling. Cerebral and physical. I strove to find a balance.

"How are you a criminal?" I asked. "What have you done? Besides washed your body in a river by the road." An infraction in Mission, BC. Smirks just smiled. We climbed the hill, riding past a pile of torn garbage bags. Food waste scattered across the highway like a finish line. Save for the rosy finch calling, no other signs of wildlife. I swallowed my disappointment. I had wanted to see the bears.

Two days later we hit that Norwegian's hill. Biking east out of Osoyoos, a wine town on the border of Washington State, we climbed three thousand feet up Anarchist Mountain. We were hungover, the local cabernet sauvignon flowing freely the night before. Our stomachs empty of food and full of Powerade, and we could smell sugar seep from our glands. Switchback after switchback after switchback for thirty-two kilometres. Twelve hundred metres, no plateau, thirty-degree heat.

Metres before we reached the top, before we saw it, we could hear it: the song of the summit sign squeaking. Old, rusted chains swinging in the wind. And once at the apex: euphoria. Washington State spread south, Canada north. Our bodies holding everything, that mountain inside us, in our blood. No drug-induced high could compare to what I felt at the Anarchist Summit. Smirks filmed everything on his camera and in the footage I look possessed. "There is no greater sight," I screamed, "than the summit sign waving!" We could have ended it right there, he and I. Could have turned around and biked home. It was the only time I saw him dance like a ballerina, but he acted as if it happened all the time. Swinging from the summit sign, his arm curved high and graceful, *port de bras, pas de chat. Plié, plié, plié.*

Later, in the valley of that mountain, the happiness lingered. Wouldn't fade. My problems seemed far away and beautiful, like stars. What was happening? Smirks and I ate hot dogs from a roadside diner and I felt the juices wind through the tributaries of my taste buds. That relaxation I'd tried so hard to find in Manning had found me. I knew it wouldn't last but I wanted to know what it was. Ralph would know. Ralph would appreciate this altered state. I called Harmony. The ringtone purred in my ear. I needed Ralph, crossword-puzzle creator, trivia-expert-extraordinaire, to give this sensation some context. To take it out of the abstract and fit it into a small and tidy set of squares.

Ralph's voice was warm. He sipped chamomile tea. "They don't know exactly what it is, Julia. Endorphins play a role, obviously. But there's still some mystery to the level of euphoria you're experiencing." He paused, let this idea sink in. Mystery. "Isn't that nice?" It was. He'd plotted our bike route and researched landmarks more than we had. "Do you know why they call it the Anarchist Summit?"

"No."

"Richard G. Sidley, the Justice of the Peace in that area in the late 1800s. He was an anarchist. He was fired for his extreme political views."

"What were they?"

"I couldn't find out, exactly. He may have had something to do with the Haymarket Affair."

I could feel my heartbeat begin to slow. The first licks of fatigue finally dampened the edge of my thoughts. I was relieved for this normalcy.

"I've got another question for you," Ralph said. "What's the most ubiquitous roadside litter along your Route Three, southern Canada?"

"The banana peel."

"Yes. Do you know why?"

"Because of the floppy surface area of the peel. It creates drag. A thrown peel lands close to the road. A thrown apple core sails further."

"Farther," said Ralph. "Yes."

❁

Next came Christina Lake, a lush valley town boasting the warmest waters in Canada. Baseball diamonds settling with dust and clapboard houses faded with weather. Safe Haven Campground hugged the water's north rim. The owner, Janice, and her two children, Si and Sally, all three blonde and sun-kissed, greeted us at the entrance. Smirks kneeled in front of the kids. "Your name, Si, could also be a noun and a verb." Si scrunched up his face and hid behind his mother's knee. To illustrate, Smirks exhaled an exaggerated sigh. "Si." He turned to Sally and solemnly held out his hand. "Your name, Sally, is also a noun and a verb."

"I know," Sally replied. "It means going on a trip."

"Sort of," Smirks said.

"Like, let's sally forth to the boat." She pointed to a canoe that rested on the water's edge and grabbed Smirks' hand. He didn't flinch.

Janice laughed. "Sally, relax. They haven't even chosen a site yet." She looked at us and rolled her eyes. Her daughter wandered over to our bicycles. She stared at our panniers and our tents tied to our back racks. Nothing surprised her, I could tell, from the various visitors she must meet every summer. I sensed she was like a cat who'd been fed once by strangers and now kept coming back for more. I guessed she was ten years old. She pointed at our gear.

"Two tents."

Her mother stepped to retrieve her. "Sally."

Sally looked at me. "You don't sleep together?"

I laughed. "No."

Janice grabbed Sally's hand. "Sorry," she said to us.

"No worries," said Smirks. "Everyone assumes we're a couple."

I looked around. Safe Haven would have been paradise for a child. Living by a lake, in a forest, surrounded by travellers, vacationers, people happy to be anywhere but where they were from. The families would leave their toys, from Barbie dolls to inflatable boats, which Si and Sally would adopt as their own, a cornucopia of curios, made special and rare by their sudden appearance, by the disappearance of their previous owner, like a baby left on a doorstep in the night.

"Choose any site you want," said Janice, to Smirks in particular it seemed, and ushered the children away.

We avoided the family for the rest of the day. The pine trees towered over us and, after three days in the desert, we didn't want to leave the shade. We bought laundry soap from the vending machine and washed our bike clothes that had grown stiff with days of sweat. I took a long, hot shower, dirt curling, moulting off my body. We started a campfire in the afternoon, urged by Janice to use all the wood we wanted. "There was a terrible storm here last month. A bunch of trees came down. We need to get rid of them." She threw another log on our fire. "A boy died," she said. "Burn as much as you can." Later, Smirks and I sat in the hot tub until our lungs and our heads felt as hot and heavy as soaked sponges.

When the sun went down, we huddled by the fire, our laptops glowing blue, illuminating our faces with a harsh, artificial light we'd only left five days ago but which already felt so foreign. A case of bottled beer sat between us on the picnic table. We had the wireless network name, and the multi-digit network key, but our fingers hovered above our keyboards like indecisive fruit flies. Did we want to access that world? The sleek, shiny one, with windows and tabs you could open and swipe through and close? Smirks looked from his screen to the slip of paper containing the wireless information that Janice had given us. "I should Skype with my mother," he said. It was only the second time he'd ever mentioned her. I knew she had been a stay-at-home mom, and that he now fell in and out of contact, sometimes going months without returning her calls.

"Have you been in touch with her since we left?"

"No."

"You could email her."

Smirks opened another bottle of beer. Breathed a bit harder.

"Let her know you're okay."

He closed his laptop and set it aside, his face disappearing into the dark.

"Why do you ignore her sometimes?" I asked.

Silence.

"Your parents must worry about you when you dodge them like that."

"I don't think so."

"Really?"

"I know them pretty well."

"Obviously. But—"

"They have their own problems. They don't worry about me. I'm an adult."

"Why do you think—"

"I don't want to talk about it."

I closed my computer too. Twisted a cap off a bottle and threw it into the fire. We watched the sparks. The beer went down like water. "I hate talking to my parents too sometimes," I said. The firelight pumped like a red heart in the night. "Everything has to be just right for me to be able to call them." Smirks nodded. "Something good has to have happened. Or something really, really bad." Somewhere in another campsite, laughter. The volume of the radio turned up. Whitney Houston sang out. I wanna dance with somebody. "Are you attracted to Sally?"

Smirks sighed. "Julia—"

"What?" I asked, suddenly defensive. I was tired of tiptoeing around Smirks' feelings. I was tired of skirting the obvious. It was exhausting.

"I really don't want to talk about this."

"Okay." I pushed my stick into the fire, sending up a spray of bright ashes. "I'm just getting a little pissed off. I've told you so much about me, about my work, and you know I'm on your side and here to help—"

"I don't need your help," Smirks said loudly. It was the first time I'd heard him raise his voice. He stared at me. "You need help." Firelight churned shadows across his face. "You're the one who needs help."

The anger inside me stilled, hovered for a moment, retreated. "I need help?"

Smirks nodded. "You sit there, with your books written by pedophiles, and your tolerance and your understanding, and you look like a big fucking idiot. Do you know that? You might as well write a book about what it's like to be black. There is no part of you that can understand who I am. No part. I'm not your father."

"I know that."

"No, you don't know that. You believe that deep down your father and I are the same. That's why I'm here. Isn't it?"

I didn't think that was true. "No," I said. He was there because I was in love with him. But I didn't want to tell him that. The fire was dying down, and neither Smirks nor I made a move to reignite it.

"I'm here so you can teach me. Or learn from me. Either way, it's all about you."

I didn't respond. Aware of our loud voices. The music from the other campsite had shut off. I was calm. No red spots. Just a tenderness radiating from my solar plexus. We drank from our bottles. "Why do you think I need help?"

Smirks thought for a moment. "You can't just be with a person, Julia. Without trying to change them. Yourself included."

"I want people to be better. What's wrong with that?"

Smirks exhaled. Shook his head.

I said, "Let's bring Sally to the beach tomorrow."

He didn't respond, didn't move, didn't look at me. I could imagine them together. In the canoe. In the middle of the lake. Where no one could see. Where no one was watching. I could picture her sitting in his lap and Smirks reaching in between her legs. I could see it all. I could see it happening. It could happen, and then what? And then nothing. And then nothing. Nothing would happen to Sally. She would not be afraid. She would not be hurt.

"Julia," Smirks said. "If she were your niece—"

My niece, Lila. Not really my niece. My cousin Sandra's daughter. Little Lila with her big brown cartoon eyes that she got from her mother Sandra and her silken, almost silver hair from her father Joe. Seven years old and a hellion, obstreperous, unstoppable. Teachers said she had "discipline problems" but I saw something better. A tenacity and a questioning of authority that could only be good for her, in the future, surely. She wasn't unhappy and she wasn't disrespectful. She was her own person, a small person, a little adult. "What about Lila?" I asked.

"If Lila were here, would you offer her to me? Would you give us time alone? Would you let me touch her?" He threw a log on the fire, and the world lit up in an instant of orange, then faded as quickly to dark.

I'd spent the summer with Lila the year before. Her parents, my cousin Sandra and her husband, Joe, ran a restaurant up north in Fort Nelson. A truck stop, natural-gas pit on the edge of the Greater Sierra oil field. Fort Nelson was a town in the middle of the bush. That's what they call it up there, "the bush," because you couldn't really call it a forest. They barely looked like trees, those spindly pines and firs, skinny from the frigid temperatures and dry air. My favourite formation was the *krummholz* black spruce, German for "bent wood." Trunks and limbs, exposed to decades of freezing wind, twisted and deformed like arthritic knuckles clawing north. I'd gone to help with Lila, who'd become a handful. Sandra and Joe offered me free room and board for the summer to nanny while they ran their restaurant, Port Mantoe, a French-Canadian diner on the west bank of the Prophet River, serving bicultural fare such as cheeseburgers on baguettes, or coq au vin with a Montreal style bagel.

The population of the town was 4,500, and most of these people were truckers and diggers, natural gas executives from India, mechanics,

A&W employees. It was a strange place on the border of the Yukon, four hundred kilometres from any town on every side, frontier land with no greater purpose than pumping fuel down to the cities and suburbs sprawling half a country away. Sandra and Joe had a beautiful log cabin on the edge of town, isolated from the trailer parks and motels that lined the Alaska Highway. In the summertime the sun didn't set. Sandra and I would stand on her back patio at two in the morning smoking cigarettes and watching the soft, orange orb sink to the horizon and hesitate there before swinging, slowly, back up toward day.

Lila was enthralled with me: a new, young, energetic adult, paid to pay her attention, which I did. I poured my attention into her, grateful for the break from my research and from the fights with Thierry. This was before the Molestas, when I'd been hiding inside my books for too long. Lila breathed life into my research. It was the first time I'd spent any significant amount of time with a child since I'd been one myself.

Sandra and Joe would wake up early every morning, gone by six, and Lila would rouse around nine. I'd make her breakfast and she would sit on the floor and watch cartoons. After eating we'd head out to the field where we would, each with our shovels, gather the horse poop of three horses and pile it in the middle of the pasture until the mound was higher than Lila herself. The mares, Passion, X and Synth, would roam, suspicious, around our perimeter, eyeballing us with chary expressions, looking away if I caught their gaze. I always felt they were holding something back, some vital part of their personality that they only exposed once we'd gone inside.

On days when I was distracted, Lila would manage to throw herself into the heap of shit while I wasn't looking, as though it were a pile of leaves we'd raked, and I'd spend the rest of the morning with her in the bathtub, scrubbing manure out from all her nooks and crannies. At these times, I would be acutely aware of the realness of her body. It made me uncomfortable. Her flat, sexless chest. Everything narrow and nascent and smooth, like a sunflower seed.

I always wondered: didn't Sandra worry about me? She knew about my father. She knew about the storied "cycle of abuse." Didn't she fear perversion on my part, taking care of Lila every day, bathing her, dressing her? I asked her once, after a few beers, terrified at her response.

"No, Julia," she said, looking me in the eye. "You would never do that to someone. You've been through it. You would never do it to someone else. The buck stops with you, remember." She stamped her cigarette out for emphasis. We cracked open two more cans. I had felt we'd both missed the point.

One day Lila and I took a nap together on the couch. Her little body was warm and supple, snug into my chest, cozy between my legs. I woke up before she did, and tried to imagine becoming aroused by her. We were spooning, essentially, and her bum was against my crotch, and I stared down at our bodies for a while. I lifted the waist of her pink jogging pants and peered past her belly to her underwear. Tiny, like a doll's. She was about as sexy as a sleeping cat. There was no physical or psychological reaction from me. There was nothing arousing about it. I remember gratitude in that moment, and I actually said out loud, "Thank God," though I realized later it was a perfunctory performance of relief, because I'd still known I wasn't safe. What if Lila were twelve? What if she were developing breasts? What if she weren't my niece? Might I be aroused then? I held these questions at arm's length.

Months later, long after I had left Fort Nelson and returned to Vancouver, I received a voicemail from Sandra. "I've had your diary here since the summer, you know. Just sitting on my bedside table. I kept waiting for you to ask me to send it to you. But you never did. So I read it last night." A pause as she took a drag from her smoke. "Dude, you're hilarious. A pedophile? You? Ha. Come on, bud. You're not a sick fuck. You're a little fucking crazy, I think maybe a bit. But you're not sick. Call me. I need you to tell me what 'perfunctory' means."

Smirks asked me again. "What if it were Lila?"

"That's not a fair question."

"What's fair?" he asked.

"I don't know about Lila."

"Do unto others."

"That's an essentialist argument."

"How so?"

"What's right for me isn't right for everyone."

"Isn't it? Think."

He was right. I had to think. According to the literature, many of the long-term effects of childhood sexual abuse don't activate until a certain stage of emotional development. The research suggested that if the perpetrator of the abuse is a parent or relative, the symptoms of depression worsen because of the perception of the betrayal of trust. But this perception was what I questioned. Did I—did others—actually feel betrayed, or were we told we should feel betrayed? There was no way to know.

There was one way to know.

I was in a dark place, and I was beer-drunk. Heavy. Angry. "I have to go to bed."

In my tent, I bit my lips until they bled. Pained groans tight in my throat. I hated that Smirks thought I needed help. What could he see? Which one of my defects had slid into view? The loon on the lake called out. A song so familiar that you imagine you could emulate it by opening up your throat, your chest. You imagine your own sadness and wisdom could make the same sounds as a loon. But of course, if you tried, you'd just sound like a human, crying.

✪

The next morning, I dipped my toes into Christina Lake and recoiled. Could this really be the warmest lake in Canada? I spread my blanket out on the sand and sat cross-legged facing the water. Sally's mother kept the canoe docked at the corner of the small beach, and Sally had brought her lifejacket, even though Smirks had insisted he was not going to take her out on the water.

"I don't have the skill," he'd lied to Janice. Of course Smirks knew how to row a boat.

"Oh, it's *fine*, Smirks," Janice had said. "She just wants to float around out there, anyway. She's just going to jump off and swim, the little fish. Trust me." Sally held her mother's hand, looking at the ground, digging a toe into the dirt. The quality of her summer days depended on the willingness of the campers. Would they play with her or wouldn't they? Si and Sally had probably escorted dozens of campers on the lake, in the woods, over the course of their short lives.

Janice was tall and regal-looking, like a formidable tree. Late thirties, probably a couple of years older than Smirks, the same blonde hair as her daughter's and a brown face that, rather than wrinkled, had been smoothed with age, like a stone. Ice blue eyes just a shade too far apart. A beautiful lake creature. She touched Smirks' shoulder, and I froze the image in my mind. Smirks and Janice, happy couple. "If it's really too much of a hassle—"

"No, it's fine."

He would take her. I saw a flash of relief in Janice's eyes. She liked Smirks. She inherently trusted him. What an idiot. A surge of rage tingled from my thighs, through my core, into my throat. My innards liquefied. I felt the anger and did nothing. Rode the sensation right out of my body. The situation unfolded and I stood there, jaw fused. I knew I should say something. Obviously I should say something. I should stop it. Should. I wondered if I were a sociopath. Smirks reached out and took Sally's fingers in one hand and her lifejacket in the other. Together, they walked toward the water.

Once at the water's edge, Sally jumped up and down. "Let's go for a float, Smirks!" He laughed and gave her a high-five. Some momentum had taken hold of him, and it slowed all movement for me. I felt caught by opposing forces, the potential energy of his body and mind causing him to move so fast, light years ahead of me, while I was getting smaller, sitting on my beach blanket, watching them, voice lost, withering.

"You gotta put your life jacket on, sweetie." He held out the little orange vest. Her arms slipped in, thin as broom handles. Smirks kneeled in front of her and fastened her jacket, taking care not to catch her long blonde hair in the teeth of the zipper. I didn't breathe. He reached his hands, as big as her head, around both sides of her neck, and for a moment it looked as though he was going to kiss her, but instead he tucked his fingers under her hair and drew it out from her life jacket. It spread across her back, golden in the sun. "You ready?"

"Yeah!" she exclaimed, and threw her arms around him in a sloppy embrace. I thought of the scene in Kubrick's *Lolita*, when Dolores and Humbert Humbert are driving in the car and she clambers up from the back seat, embracing him, kissing him. The word "coltish" kept coming to mind. *But children are not animals*, I thought.

Smirks looked at me. "You sure you don't want to come?" Was that a threat in his voice? A hint of *I'm calling your bluff?* I felt as though he were challenging me. I'll do it, he seemed to be saying. I'll do it and it will be your fault.

I shook my head. "No." My voice choked. I held up my book, Faulkner's *The Sound and the Fury*. I had never read Faulkner and had thought, stupidly, that a vacation would be a good time to start. Sally ran toward me and put her hands on my shoulders and looked into my eyes. A remarkably adult gesture. I looked at the ground. I wanted to reach up and grab her waist and hold her there. Hold her there until the tsunami that was washing over us stopped flowing. Receded. Disappeared. Sally followed my eyes until they finally landed on hers. Young, trusting girl. Little girl with a slender neck. How did children— so fragile, so easy to break—make it out? How did they survive?

Satisfied with my eye contact, she spoke. "Don't worry. I'll take care of him."

"You'll take care of him?"

She laughed, and trotted back to Smirks. He grasped her under her armpits and lifted her up into the canoe. She was so excited, bouncing her knees, lifting her bum up and down on the yoke. Smirks pushed the canoe into the water, lake lapping up to his knees.

"Woo!" he shouted, "Chilly!"

"Chilly!" mimicked Sally, bursting into a giggle. *All children sound the same when laughing.* That was a line from a book I read once. What book was it? Right before the woman kills herself. She hears children laughing. I pressed my hands into my knees, felt the hard ridge of my kneecaps, dug my fingertips in, probing for cracks. Smirks hopped in the boat and inexpertly guided it toward the middle of the lake. I watched how he slopped the oars into the water and made shallow and ineffective attempts to steer, and I realized he wasn't faking his ineptitude. He actually couldn't row. How could a man who grew up learning every other sport and living near different bodies of water not have learned how to row? He and Sally were out in the water like two children.

Sally traipsed all over the boat, perching on first the bow seat, then the stern. She grabbed Smirks' biceps for balance. Muscle can be a noun and a verb. Intransitive and transitive. *I muscled my way into the situation.* Or, *all that cycling has muscled her legs.* I had a compulsion to tell Smirks he was a loser. I made a mental note to do it when he got back. Any self-respecting athlete should be able to paddle without looking like a fucking moron. I remembered that conversation on the patio. One hundred years ago. His smugness disguised as inquiry. *Did you do your best at anything today?*

Smirks reached an arm around Sally's waist. He gripped her there, guided her to sit down in front of him. They drifted farther away until they were shining shadows of themselves, the sun reflecting off the water and their bodies. I could make out movement but not specifics. Their bodies were close together, then apart, like drops of black oil bonding and breaking. I squinted against the sun, tried to discern details. There could be kisses, maybe. There could be touching, but I couldn't see. Smirks' hands disappeared between her legs. Or was he still paddling? They were in the same spot for a while, it seemed. I shielded my eyes with my hand. Sally reached her arms up high above her head. Why wasn't she wearing her life jacket? I thought I saw Smirks press his lips to her hairless armpit.

I ran into the water. I still had my shoes on, and I swam. The water pummelled me, coated me in icy armour and all I could think to do was breathe and swim, my mind an anaphora. Right arm, left arm, right arm, left arm, chaotic breaststroke that felt more like drowning. My feet were tied together. I caught glimpses of the blue sky.

The tree line. The water's edge. A blurry metal boat in front of me with people playing inside. I swallowed green water that tasted like freezer burn and stone. I swam for so long, twice as long as the distance should have allowed, before I finally slapped my hands up over the edge of the canoe and peered inside the hull.

Smirks was sitting on the bow seat and Sally on the stern. She held one foot tight to her body, close to her chest. The way she sat, with her leg bent up, I could see the crotch of her bathing suit. Had it been pushed to the side? She was sobbing. I couldn't breathe. My lungs dragged. I sputtered, shimmied toward her with my hands on the gunwale. Smirks was talking, but there was a rush in my ears, water leaving them, Sally's sobs entering them, I couldn't hear him, didn't look at him, just moved toward her. Sally. "What happened, Sally?" I asked finally, my lungs finding some air. Sally couldn't speak, she was bawling too hard.

Smirks' voice. "She hurt her toe, Julia. She stubbed her toe and slipped." I looked at him. He was shaking his head. "She hurt herself." I looked at Sally. With Smirks' retelling of her trauma she started wailing even louder. Reliving the sharp pain in her mind made it worse. I looked at her foot and saw a trickle of bright red blood twisting up around her ankle like henna. "She was about to jump into the water, and she stubbed her toe. She hurt herself."

Sally nodded desperately. Smirks pulled me up into the boat with the adeptness of a lifeguard. Before I knew it, he was rowing us skilfully back to the shore, expert swipes and digs with the oars, the hull cutting a fast line through the water. I held Sally in my lap and watched him, dumbfounded. We made it to the beach. Janice was already standing there, arms akimbo.

"She does this," she said. She grabbed her daughter's wrist. "She cries, for no reason. Just cries and cries." She jerked Sally's arm, harder than necessary.

I pointed to Sally's foot. "She cut her toe."

Janice looked, softened a bit at the blood. "Oh. Sweetie." She kneeled down, kissed her fingers, pressing them to her daughter's skin.

She looked up at us. "It could have been a lot worse. Right?"

Smirks touched Sally's forehead, wiped a strand of hair from her eyes. "I'm sorry, Sally."

Sally had her thumb in her mouth.

Janice pulled it out. "Don't worry about it. She's really too old to be crying like this." She hushed Sally, pulling her toward the campground. Sally looked over her shoulder. She looked at us as though we were strangers.

Smirks and I watched them go. I could sense him scowling. "People are so fucked up," he said, and he moved to tie up the boat. He was talking about Janice. He was talking about me. Me, I felt incredible. Like a star had exploded in my heart chakra and shot photons to every cell in my body. He hadn't touched her, and it thrilled me. I'd escaped prison. I'd escaped war. We left Christina Lake that afternoon, and for the first few kilometres, until the town was out of sight and off our minds, we stayed far away from each other's slipstream. I knew Smirks was furious, with me and with Janice and with himself. But I felt liberated. Every time he turned around to look at me, I turned the corners of my mouth down. But the smile would creep back, and the work felt important and the world looked beautiful. I bit my lip to keep from hollering my joy.

Dylan

Two quiet nights after leaving Safe Haven we landed in Sirdar, a tiny lake town in the middle of the Kootenay Mountains. Population: 300 and falling. A fifth of those people were at the Sirdar Pub that night watching a show by local musician Kootenay Buck. He sang and played his own country songs like a happier Johnny Cash. The tension between Smirks and me had wrung itself out with strained conversations and sweet offerings to prepare each other's meals. "I'll make the coffee." "Okay, I'll boil the oats." "Do you want half of this can of tuna?" By Sirdar, we were back to joking and making fun of each other. Ready to drink. To bury Christina Lake under a swimming pool full of beer.

The people in Sirdar Pub looked like my kind of people. Rural folk who filled the local social house in Harmony. Lumberyard workers, rig pigs, biker chicks. Raw wood floors cracked and sagged, beer soaked. Faded posters from last year's concerts on the walls. Blue light on the stage making Kootenay Buck's teeth gleam. Our aging waitress had teased hair like a tiara. We started drinking, and after the third old man put his hand around my waist, Smirks pretended to be my boyfriend, cupping his hand on the back of my neck and even paying for booze. By the fourth round of drinks I was ready to dance, and I pulled him up to the floor and he spun me around expertly before pulling me tight into his body. He led with strength and ease. I shouted above the raucous guitar. "You can dance!"

He smiled. "I can dance." I wanted him so badly. I moved my face toward his and he dipped me down so low my hair swept the floor.

I laughed and told him to do it again and again. Rye and flat ginger. In the bathroom I bought a condom from the vending machine. A chorus of hoots and hollers from the ladies. High-fives. Kootenay Buck fell off his stool and Smirks leapt up on stage to help. Free drinks. "All the way to Nova Scotia?" "Holy shit!" "Here's to you!" Beer pong in the back room, a wet kiss to the victor with one eye open for Smirks' reaction. Jealous? No. We closed the bar down, finally kicked out by the owner, who gave us two bottles of beer for the road.

"'Cause yer ridin' them bicycles," she said. "Crazy kids. Road pops!" Her cackling followed us out the door. The hot midnight air teeming with mosquitoes. We crossed the empty road and weedy train tracks to our tents hiding behind the bush. I was so drunk the world was tilting.

"Can I sleep with you tonight, Smirks?" My voice soft like a child's. Smirks stopped unzipping his tent and turned to look at me. He opened his mouth, and then let out a long, loud fart that blasted through the air like a horn.

I shrieked. "Gross!" I stomped over to my tent. As I bent down to unzip it, I let out a fart of my own. A softer, squeakier version of his.

"The seal has been broken! We're fart buddies now."

"Is that like fuck buddies?"

"Goodnight, Julia."

I could hear him laughing softly through the nylon. Was it so funny to imagine sleeping with me? I waited until his breathing became steady and even. Then I touched myself, thinking of him, of his body, of what he would feel like inside me, until I fell asleep.

That night I had an awful dream of my mother. We were trapped in a huge Nova Scotian farmhouse. Drooling old people in faded denim. They rolled their eyes and smacked their lips, toothless mouths. I could see the ocean outside the window, but the doors were locked and the glass wouldn't break. One by one, the old people floated up to the vaulted ceiling, suspended by some invisible force. A demon. I started panicking. Mom was drinking red wine and she offered me her glass. Her words slurred. "You need to shear your head."

"You mean *clear* my head."

She laughed. "Whatever."

I woke up with her laughter echoing through my hangover. Hot, stuffy tent and mosquito bites on my face. I fumbled for the zipper and ran to the train tracks, emptying my stomach onto the steel rails. Crumbling wood. Nails the size of my arm. I heaved until the yellow bile came. My poor stomach. We needed to get out of Sirdar.

You need to shear your head.

Lots of noise breaking camp until Smirks finally woke up. He was hungover and sullen, still not used to a headache and nausea. I worried, for a moment, about how I was corrupting him with these nights of excess. Pushed the thought from my head. He was his own adult.

We rode past the pub. It seemed much smaller than it had the night before.

❂

Radium, British Columbia, marked our first 1,000 kilometres. Gateway to the Rocky Mountains, the town teemed with tourists and I wanted to hug all of them. Touch their shiny, expensive haircuts and ride in their luxury rentals. Breathe in their tasteful fragrances, lavender and honey. Basil and mint. City folk out for a breath of the Canadian wild. The antiseptic to our dirty week. Wholesome and wealthy and normal. Smirks seemed happy too, smiling at passersby as he struck yoga poses on the front lawn of the grocery store. Beside him, a wooden grizzly bear stood on its hind legs. Inside, I stole a box of ice cream bars because I didn't feel that I should have to wait in line. I held my breath as I walked back out the front doors. Imagined someone grabbing my shoulder. What I would say. "I biked here, mother fuckers!" We ate them, shameless, on the grass, sprawling our bodies along the manicured lawn, our bike gear scattered around us. "Lark told us to do something illegal in each town," I justified, but really I believed that the bike trip was work and that somebody should be paying us to do it. Smirks shrugged, licked the vanilla cream. I watched his tongue slide between the crusts.

We rented a campsite at the Hot Springs, a pine-filled, sprawling, rustic resort with ominous *Beware of Bears and Cougars* signs tacked to every other tree. I felt certain that with this many campers, no bear or cougar would venture near, but we heard stories from other travellers of fabled maulings and slayings by the claws and teeth of wildlife. A Danish man had stopped us on our way to our site, asked us about our bicycles. "You don't want to disturb the natural order of things," he said, pouring cups of natural ice tea. His family, blonde and pristine, sat at the picnic table, eating cheese and bread and yogurt. "We should not even be here." He motioned to his RV, our bicycles, the garbage cans, the man-made paths through the forest. His children ate with their mouths open and stared at us vacantly. His wife looked from him to us, back and forth, shaking her head and shrugging. She didn't speak English. "We should all, in fact, be ashamed of ourselves. Trying to take something that is not naturally ours."

The Radium Hot Springs were named for the trace presence of radon found in the mineral wells. Smirks wanted to research radon, the decay product of radium, on his laptop before entering the pool. I slipped into my bikini and stretched out on the picnic table at our campsite. I shivered in the shade. Smirks spouted radon facts to me, and I closed my eyes, enjoying the sound of his voice. We were a couple on holiday, I pretended. About to go for a swim. Out of nowhere, a pang through my entire body: *Thierry.* Where was he? He would rub my arms to smooth the goosebumps. He would carry me on his back through the woods and I would bury my face in his neck. Smell his skin. Pencil shavings and Old Spice. Smirks read on. "Radioactive gas decays into something called 'radon daughters.'"

"Sexist."

"Exposure to radon daughters has been linked to lung cancer."

I took a drag from my cigarette and blew the smoke straight up. "Too late." Smoke caught in the breeze, carried west.

"Radon daughters are solids and they stick to solids such as dust particles in the air. If inhaled—"

"What about radon sons. Are they harmful at all?" Smirks didn't answer. I thought I was being very clever. "Radon fathers? Now, there's something to watch out for." I blew a stream of smoke his way.

He coughed. "If you inhale radon daughters, your chance of developing lung cancer increases by—"

"If you had a daughter, do you think you would be physically attracted to her?"

Smirks slammed his laptop shut. "Let's go to the pool."

"Finally."

The pathway to the springs dipped deep into the forest along a shelf of a sheer cliff lined with evergreens. A cougar could spring out of the darkness between the trees. Bears didn't frighten me; they seemed lumbering and clumsy. I imagined, stupidly, that if I had to I could outrun one.

Cougars, however, were a source of nightmares. I had encountered one as a child, at three years old, though I have no recollection of it. My mother had recounted the story many times over the years, to me and to strangers, while I sat listening, feeling as though what happened must have happened to someone else. To some other little girl sitting in a kiddie pool outside a mountain resort. Our parents had taken April and me there when we were very young. Most likely in an attempt to either fix a failing marriage or to appear to be trying to fix a failing marriage. No one ever talked about anything else from the trip. The only narrative that survived was the one of the cougar.

"Dirtbag was off somewhere with April," Mom would say. Where were they? I always wondered. April would have been six years old at the time, prime age for Dirtbag. I'd asked her once if she remembered where they were during the cougar incident, but she didn't want to talk about the time in the mountains. "And I was washing dishes in the kitchen," Mom continued, always with her mug of wine in one hand and her cigarette in the other. "It was a beautiful day. I'd put Julia in the kiddie pool with about two inches of water." At this point in the story she would turn to me and say, "I know you can drown in two inches of water, but I was watching you like a hawk out the kitchen window, you were never in peril of drowning, okay?"

Then, back to her audience, "When out from the trees came a cougar. An actual mountain lion. Do you know how beautiful those things are? Slinking down the hill like an oil slick. Its mouth hanging open. I just remember thinking: how black it is inside there. I couldn't see its teeth. It was just this black abyss. And I must have been in shock. I thought: he doesn't have any teeth. Thank god, my baby is safe, he doesn't have any teeth." At this point, she would pause for effect, and take a long drag from her cigarette. Everyone in the room would be watching me, looking for a scar, maybe. Or a reaction.

"And I froze," Mom would say, her hands braced in the air. "My hands froze in the dishwater. I still remember that feeling on my skin, the soap and the grease, and I watched the cougar, and then I looked at Julia. She must have sensed him, or heard him, and she looked up, and immediately thought: 'Kitty!' I could see her eyes think it! Kitty! And she raised her hands up in the air and went to stand. And I thought: she's going to fall. She's going to try to stand up, and then she's going to fall, and the cougar is going to pounce, and I am going to watch my baby be eaten by a mountain lion." A gasp from the audience, a squeal. Mom would pat a hand on my shoulder, or touch my hair.

"But she stood up smoothly, with perfect balance, the best I'd ever seen her stand at that point, all by the power of her legs—you had those powerful legs even back then, got those from your father—and she just stayed there, arms high up in the air, straight as an arrow, eyebrows raised, mouth open, and all of a sudden, the cougar ran away. Shot like a dart back into the woods. And Julia tilted her head to the side, and her face did that thing where it crumpled, in silence, and then she started to bawl. I rushed outside, grabbed her, brought her inside and slammed the glass sliding door so hard it rattled the whole cabin, and Dirtbag came running into the room screaming 'What the fuck was that?' and I told him. 'OUR BABY ALMOST GOT EATEN BY A COUGAR!'"

At this point, the audience would look to me, and I would shake my head in wonder. "I remember nothing." I'd shrug. Apologize. And the listeners would murmur and sigh. Tell their own stories of close encounters. While I'd remain shaken, a trembling deep in the bone. Cold shade from pine boughs. Icy water between my knees.

I remembered something. Somewhere within my body. The woods of the Pacific Northwest always triggered a reaction. A shudder within. The nuclei of the amygdala stirring in their caves. An anonymous crackle of twigs or a shaking in the bushes would freeze me and I'd forget—as though I'd never known—if I should stare a cougar in the eyes, or if I should look away. Should I stare a cougar in the eyes, or should I look away? What was the story my mother always told? What had I done that had saved me? In the moment, I could never remember.

But there were no cougars in the Radium woods. We made it out of the forest and into the Hot Springs. They were crowded and touristic, which I found comforting. I headed to the showers, grateful for human presence and the steam of hot, soapy water. Little girls in soggy bathing suits and mothers in shower caps. Laughter and flip-flops. Lockers hung open in trust. I scrubbed myself red before entering the pool, wanting to give Smirks time to find a spot of his own. On the deck, I scanned the crowd for him and spied him lounging against the back wall. He waved to me, and through my sunglasses I pretended not to see him. I wanted some time alone. At the opposite end, I slid into the warm water. Even though I knew it was impossible, even though I knew the radon presence was hardly detectable, I imagined it glowed blue with radiation, and that I was sinking into radioactive decay, unstable gases and elements working on my body, daughter nuclides swimming at me, into my skin. Me, a contaminated hot spot. Flesh tattooed with trefoils and scintillating in the dark.

We were cycling out of Radium when I felt my cellphone buzz in my pocket. I pulled over, letting Smirks ride along without blowing my rape whistle. My sister spoke, and I watched him cycle slowly. He didn't want to hurry into the Rockies. He didn't know what to expect. His back was a blue GPS dot moving away from me, pulsing with every pedal. April's voice was high today.

"And I told him, I don't want any stupid iPhone apps! What could I possibly use one for? I've lived this long without them, right?" April's voice was trying to be funny but came out sounding afraid. For some reason, I thought: the people I love the most are the people I want to change the most. Not alter them completely, just perform a sort of lobotomy, wherein I would remove a part of their brain that I thought hindered them. April was loving, and wounded, so when the weather changed, or her car wouldn't start, she took it personally. As if she was being punished. "Do you think I need apps?" Her small voice. She'd held out till the last minute, but finally had no choice. No other option. The world operated on smartphones.

I told her to download the SkyView app. To hold her camera up to the sky, look through her viewfinder, and see the solar system. See the planets, their orbits, and the constellation she was born under. Aries. Where were her stars now? Had her Saturn return begun? How did she feel? In the day, she could see the moon. "Out at the lake, when you're on the dock in the dark, hold it up to the sky. It will circle every star and name it. Stars you've never heard of. Alsuhail. Zubeneshhamali. Phact."

"I believe you."

"No. P–h–a–c–t. It's the name of a star. And if you lie down on the floor at nighttime, and hold your iPhone against your chest, you can see the sun resting there. And it looks like it's on top of your heart, but really it's underneath the world. With Australia."

April sighed. Smirks had finally stopped and turned around. Saw I was on the phone. Reached into his bag and pulled out his notebook, started writing. I could tell April wanted to change the subject.

"What's up?"

"Mom's not doing too well."

"What's wrong?"

"What's the difference between 'danger' and 'risky'?"

"Noun, adjective."

"So would one be the five-letter synonym for the other in a crossword?"

"No. That would be peril."

"Exactly. Peril." I heard April run water into a sink or a tub. She was about to wash either dishes or Rod. "She couldn't even spell it correctly. She said she'd never heard the word before." The clacking scratch of claws on tile. A splash as Rod jumped into the bath. Grunts from April as she scrubbed him clean.

Mom used to complete four crossword puzzles a day: the local, the provincial, the national and the international—The *New York Times* crossword, which, even on Sundays, never took her more than forty-five minutes. And forty-five minutes was a slow day. Her skill was supernormal, and it was this skill that led her to Ralph in the first place. The famed story of their first meeting. I'd heard it so many times, it had become a memory of my own.

One day, two years after Dirtbag leaves, Mom completes the local paper's crossword. She takes particular umbrage at one of Ralph's clues. Feeling for whatever reason emboldened, she drives to the *Rural Recorder*. She knocks on his office door and he beckons her inside. He is handsome, but because she is beautiful herself, she is not so easily stricken, and says, "Are you Ralph Goodman?" He, on the other hand, is stricken by her beauty. For a moment, he just stares. He has a full, neat beard and wears a blue plaid shirt tucked into his jeans. Thick-framed glasses, warm brown eyes. A pencil tucked artfully behind his ear, the way Mom carries her cigarettes. Mom cannot resist a man in glasses.

He raises his eyebrows at her, a half-smile on his lips, and taps his pen on the placard in front of him. It reads: RALPH GOODMAN. This is a cool move. "That's me." He slips the pen behind his ear, knocking away the pencil that's already there. It hits the floor with an impotent clatter. "Oops," he says. An uncool move. Mom, reassured by his awkwardness, holds up that day's crossword.

"I suppose you've received many complaints about this already?" She doesn't suppose, but also doesn't want to (publicly) presume to be the first.

"Actually, you're the first person to speak to me all day. Most people lodge their complaints behind my back." Mom is pleased. She takes a seat in front of him. "Have a seat." He is chuckling with his eyes.

Mom says, "I wanted to correct you on one of your clues in this morning's crossword."

A groundswell of butterflies rises up from Ralph's ankles into his chest. "Thirty-six down?" he asks.

Here Mom falters, because he is right. The clue asked the opposite of castration anxiety. "Yes, in fact, it is thirty-six down." A bit of the air deflates from Mom, from her pumped-up conviction. "There is no opposite to castration anxiety because there is no opposite to a man." She pauses. Ralph nods. "There is no opposite to a woman. Or a human, for that matter. Males and females are not antonymous. They are autonomous. Saying a woman is the opposite of a man is like saying the sun is the opposite of the moon." Mom bites her lip. She does not want to sound so hippy-dippy, so yin and yang, so Mars and Venus. "Or a black person is the opposite of a white person."

Ralph smiles, nods. "But I didn't mean that a woman is the opposite of a man. I meant that castration anxiety is the opposite of penis envy. The fear of losing one's penis is the opposite of wishing one had one."

"I disagree. Since only women can suffer from so-called penis envy—"

"Is that true?" Ralph asks.

And Mom laughs. She notices that Ralph wears no ring on his finger, and that his beard looks soft, not scratchy. She tells him she has to get home to her daughters.

"Are they crossword puzzlers themselves?" Ralph asks. "Maybe I will meet them someday."

And he did, meet us someday. Mom must have wondered how to broach it, how to introduce him, when would be the right time. But that all happened behind the scenes. All I was privy to was a phone call home from work one day. "I have a friend coming over after work."

"Okay."

"It's a man."

"A man."

I was ten, and I knew what she meant. A man was someone to kiss. A man was someone with whom to share a bed. But there hadn't been one in the house since Dirtbag. After Mom's phone call, I lingered near the window for the rest of the afternoon. Who was this man? What would he look like? I watched our neighbour across the street climb up and down a ladder, repairing his roof. He wore white coveralls splattered in paint, and every time he swung his leg over the side of his house to step down, I leaned forward, fingertips on the glass. But he never fell. Then, Mom's car. The passenger-side door. The man: thin, short. A button-up shirt and glasses. He looked like my teacher at school. He took grocery bags from my mother's arms. I watched their fingers touch. He smiled at her. I couldn't stop staring. They walked up the front stairs, and Mom waved at me. "Hi," she mouthed, but I averted my eyes, looked toward the neighbour who was making another journey onto his roof. Mom deadheaded a few wilted pansies from the pots on the steps. The man watched our neighbour on the roof. Mom opened the front door. "Julia, this is Ralph." She took the groceries and shuffled off to the kitchen.

I still didn't move, didn't turn my head to greet him. I just kept staring outside. In front of the window, my mother had hung a pop bottle upside down, with a feeder tube. Sometimes hummingbirds came. Ralph approached me. "You must be Julia." I nodded. His voice sounded kind. He looked out the window with me, and we stood like that for a while. I was very aware of where Mom was. She had gone into the kitchen and opened the refrigerator door. She was removing items from the fridge and putting them on the kitchen counter. April was downstairs. The house across the street was over one hundred years old. I knew that because our house was also over one hundred years old. Many houses in Harmony were. It was settled, and since then rarely disturbed, in 1810. After a few minutes, Ralph spoke. "Do you see how wide the wooden boards are on that roof? Underneath the shingles?" I nodded. I hadn't noticed, but they were about two feet wide. "You can't get boards that wide anymore," he said. I wondered why not. "No trees left that big." I turned to look at him, finally.

His beard was so neat it looked drawn. He smiled at me and raised his hands in the air. "Where'd all the trees go?" he asked. An adult asking me a question.

"We cut them all down?"

Ralph nodded. "We cut them all down.

☯

Smirks and I entered Kootenay National Park of the Rocky Mountains the next day, through a gateway of sheer cliffs, exposed sedimentary rock there since the Pleistocene era. A family of mountain goats scaled the walls of the north cliff, causing a traffic jam. Smirks and I rode past the amateur photographers, greedy for a shot of the wildlife to take home to their friends. No one seemed to notice, or care about, the multiple signs peppering Highway 93 that politely, Canadianly, asked tourists not to take pictures of the fauna. "Please keep our wildlife wild." You could expect to see bears, moose, lynx, bighorn sheep, caribou, elk, coyote and wolves, but you weren't supposed to get out of your car and take their picture. The animals shouldn't become accustomed to human presence. That would only lead to trouble.

Around a bend, Smirks and I rode past a group of white-tailed deer. "A group of deer is called a herd," he said.

"I heard."

"Come on, girls!" Smirks shouted, and the deer took off, running alongside us. "Come on! Come on! Let's go!" He pumped his arm like a windmill. A dozen deer, does and bucks and fawns, their shaggy strawberry coats about to moult. They ran so fast, thin legs launching their bodies through the air, they passed us, leaping and bucking through the grass, their white bums flashing as they disappeared, one by one, into the trees.

I had forgotten to buy cigarettes after leaving Radium, and about an hour into the park, I ran out. We weren't due to arrive in Banff, 136 kilometres away, until the next day, and I'd assumed there'd be a store open before then. But every little shop we passed was closed for the season, not due to open until the first of June. I tried hard to concentrate on the scenery, to appreciate the pristine river flowing beside us. But without nicotine, the colour of the water unsettled me. An unnatural iridescent turquoise, thick and opaque as paint. "It's the silt suspended in the water," Smirks said. "The rock-flour erosion. They call it Glacial Milk." Every time he stopped to take pictures, I looked for cigarette butts on the road. Smirks frowned. "That's really gross."

"Don't judge me."

Around the next bend in the road, we saw a log cabin in the distance surrounded by cars and motorcycles. As we got closer, I saw people enter and exit the open front door. We rolled up, locked our bikes, and I ran inside. A wholesome-looking teenage girl smiled at me. Her hair, eyes and teeth all had a healthy sheen. "Do you sell cigarettes?"

"No, sorry." Chirpy voice, bright smile. She didn't sound sorry. I narrowed my eyes. Next to the cash register sat a pile of gigantic chocolate-chip muffins. I held one up. "Five dollars." She looked very happy about everything.

"Five bucks," I muttered, and bought one anyway. Sugar, the poor woman's nicotine. I took the muffin outside and joined Smirks at a picnic table. He was looking up at the roof of the cabin and laughing.

"Look at that crow!" he said. There was a big, fat, shiny black crow on the peak of the roof. I shrugged. "He's just really fat," said Smirks. I sat down at the picnic table and put my muffin in front of me. Smirks pointed at it. "Whoa. That muffin is as big as that crow." I squinted at him. "No cigarettes?" I shook my head. I swivelled my butt around on the bench, shielded my eyes and scanned the parking lot. A nuclear family of redheads—mother, father, son and daughter—stood by a sparkling electric SUV, loading a miniature decorative totem pole into the trunk. Rental company sticker on the bumper. Not local. Too wealthy to smoke. The next group over, a slew of Asian tourists, the adults wearing capri pants and wide-brimmed hats that covered their faces. Children giving each other the peace sign through camera lenses. No curls of smoke wafting up from them, either.

I turned my gaze toward an older couple, a man and a woman,

each leaning against the seat of a Harley-Davidson. How adorable, their matching leather suits, black with purple flames lucent up their legs, and in the man's mouth, tucked between his curly grey moustache and his long grey beard, sat a cigarette, burning bright. Jackpot. I heard Smirks whoop behind me. He'd spotted the smoke as well. I started walking across the parking lot toward the cigarette. Smirks shouted, "Uh oh!" My eyes still on the cigarette, I saw the smoking biker break up into a thunderous, wheezing laugh. He pointed up into the sky.

"Looks like your lunch got away!" he hollered. I turned. That fat-ass crow landed on the peak of the roof, my chocolate-chip muffin clamped firmly in his big, stupid beak. Smirks was laughing, really playing it up: slapping his knee, buckled over, eyes watering. I felt like smacking him. Beardo was still laughing too, and I stomped over to him and his partner and glared at them in their matching leather suits. They were both in their sixties, both grey hairs, both with easy smiles. "Those birds are some fuckin' smart," he said. He puffed his cigarette. "He waited until you got up, you know. And then—" the old man put his cigarette between his lips and stretched his arms out like a bird, swooping down. He clapped his hands. "Bam! Lunchtime!" His partner, a slight woman with a broad nose and shiny hair that curled at her chin, giggled behind a cupped hand.

"You guys brother and sister?" I asked. They looked at each other and the woman squealed, clasping the man's shoulder.

"I sure hope not," she replied, and dropped her head against his chest, her eyes closed. He wrapped his arm around her. He reminded me of a beluga whale. His skin was smooth and white, soft folds at the neck. His knowing, cetacean smile. The way he tilted his head to look at me out of one eye and then the other. But he had a deflated look to him as well, not in spirit, but in size: his jacket and pants hung loosely on his belly. His thick, grey beard like a mould, long and furry, on his otherwise hairless head.

"You got a cigarette?" I asked him.

"Where you pedalling to?"

"Nova Scotia."

"Ha! You're fucking crazy." He reached into his pocket. He pulled out a pack of cigarettes, half-empty. Half-full. "Here you go, honey." I felt the weight of all the cigarettes and the darkness lifted. Suddenly, I found the crow funny like everyone else. I put a cigarette in my mouth and laughed. Beluga-man handed me a lighter. "You need those smokes more than I do."

I invited them over to our picnic table for lunch. Their names were Bruce and Rhonda, and they lived in Kingston, Ontario. One of Dirtbag's cities. Smirks looked at me in recognition and I subtly shook my head. Nudged him under the table. I didn't want him to mention our intention to ride through there. "It's about three hundred kilometres east of Toronto," Rhonda said. "We've never been west of Toronto. We've always wanted to ride to Vancouver and see the Pacific Ocean."

Bruce lit another cigarette. "And since I'm off work now, we have no reason not to do everything we always wanted."

"Retired?"

"Nope. Chemo. I'm supposed to go three times a week." He shrugged.

I looked at Rhonda. She was watching Bruce. "You're not going to?" I asked.

Bruce leaned into me, conspiratorially. "I'm not going to." He winked. I looked at Rhonda again. Her lips were in a half smile, and she looked as though her thoughts were very far away. Half smiles can make the eyes look so sad. How odd it is to step into a stranger's private life for a moment. We were both making voyages across the country, both carrying our reasons as baggage and both the centres of our own universes, colliding with and bouncing off other particles along the way. When Bruce asked what the hell we were pedalling to Nova Scotia for, I put a hand on Smirks' thigh and said, simply, that I was going home to see my mom. "Come visit us in Kingston when you pass through," said Bruce, giving us a phone number. Maybe it was easier to feel a connection to a man who was dying. Maybe the closeness I felt was purely sentimental. But sadness for Bruce ran through me in that moment like a river. I felt it clean out my guts, as I imagined glacial milk would. Cold and exfoliating with the ancient, cleansing rocks of mountains.

We hugged our new friends goodbye and rode east. We curled through a pass and came upon a dozen cars parked on the narrow shoulder. About thirty tourists standing in the road. Smirks grunted. "Must be more wildlife up there." He'd grown increasingly annoyed with the tourists in the park. His hidden penchants for order and obedience, for etiquette and rules, became more obvious the longer we spent together. The conservative pedophile. We approached the cluster of people snapping photographs. The black lumps in front of the mountain face had the plodding air of bears. Next to the animals, a sign. "Please keep our wildlife wild. Do not stop to take photographs." Smirks biked faster. "No one holds anyone accountable," he called to me over his shoulder. As we rode through the crowd, he yelled at the tourists. "Stop taking pictures! Can't you read? You're not supposed to take pictures!" His voice got louder and louder and I started laughing. The big laughs. The deep belly laughs that made it impossible to breathe. Difficult to stay upright on Shelley. The tourists started to exclaim, to shout back. I feared retaliation.

I managed to work my vocal cords for one syllable. "Smirks!" I wanted him to stop his scolding, but I accidentally made eye contact with one tourist—florid cheeks, stunned eyes—and the laughter swelled up again.

Smirks continued shouting. "Buy a postcard, you idiots!" He waved his arm up and down in front of their faces. "Get back in your cars, morons!" Parents exclaimed and pulled their children in close to protect them. And then, as we approached the last photographer at the end of the crowd, a heavy-set woman with frizzy brown hair and a giant camera plastered to her face, I saw Smirks gear up for the final blow.

"Smirks!" I straggled behind, my throat tight, my stomach muscles sore. He rode right up to the fat lady and jammed his face into her fully extended zoom lens.

"BOO!" he shouted, and the woman screamed and stumbled backwards, dropping her camera to the ground and falling flat on her wide bottom. This was too much. I could barely see straight. We biked as fast as we could through the twists and turns of the winding, rocky roads. I kept swerving too close to the edge of the road, too close to the yellow line. Our laughter echoed off the canyon walls. Every car that passed, I worried would pull over and seek vengeance. It wasn't until we'd pulled over safely into the Dolly Varden campground that I realized with disappointment, I hadn't even paused to look at the bears.

The next day, Smirks and I found ourselves marching down a busy, tourist-filled sidewalk of Banff, Alberta. We trailed Lark as she made her way through the weekend crowd to Cascade Plaza. She called over her shoulder, "I just have to exchange some belts! And then we can go back up to the room and you guys can change." Her smile tinged with distaste. We couldn't blame her. She looked as though she'd just stepped out of a *Vogue* editorial, and we looked like shit. We hadn't done laundry since Christina Lake and sweat stains ringed our Spandex shirts and shorts. Salty, crusted dirt lined our foreheads and our jawbones and I couldn't smell either of us but I knew we reeked. She had hugged us tightly anyway, in the lobby of her hotel, giving Smirks a big kiss on the cheek, her dark purple lipstick leaving an imprint there like a bruise. She'd run her hand across his chest. "Mmm, a real man!" Looked at me. "No more skinny twits." Rolled her eyes. In Banff for only four days, Lark had already bedded a young designer only to find out the next morning he had a girlfriend. A model on his runway. "I hate fashion people," she said to us, hoisting five Holt Renfrew bags over her shoulders. "Follow me!" She navigated deftly through the streets on her leather flatforms.

"Flatforms?" I'd asked.

"Flatforms. They're huge right now, Julia. I'll lend you a pair for tonight." When Lark's Blackberry rang, Smirks and I fell a step behind her and listened to her animated conversation. I'd always envied her public irreverence toward social mores, such as the volume at which one should speak on one's cellphone. I didn't know who she was talking to, but she was relaying the story of the cheating designer from the night before. After she'd found out about his girlfriend, she'd gotten a bit too drunk with an editor from *Chatelaine* and had stirred up some trouble at the hotel bar.

"Dude, it was hilarious!" she exclaimed. She marched adroitly, dodging pedestrians while wielding her bags and managing to look like a model in a photo shoot. "I suddenly turned into an African-American farmer from the south. I said—" Lark's voice took on a hearty twang, slow and swinging—"You don' think ah willed it inta being..." she paused, waited a moment while the person on the other end spoke. "Oh no, wait. It gets better. I said—" she assumed the accent again, "You don' think ah willed it inta being...did it?" With that, she burst into her honking laughter, and I did too. "Did it?" she asked again. I heard and saw her pronoun foul over and over in my head. The error tweaked some sort of existential, linguistic quandary in my brain. *You don't think I willed it into being...did it?* Language doing somersaults. Lark laughed, and I laughed with her. Nothing held her down for long.

Smirks was chuckling too, and he watched the back of Lark's head with what I interpreted as affection. I felt a spring of hope shoot up my belly and into my throat, cool and spreading. Could Smirks be attracted to her? Look at her perfect bum through her sheer cream skirt. Round in her black body suit, like a lollipop atop strong, thin legs. And then, suddenly, Lark was screaming. Her hand flew up to her eyes and her bags fell to the ground. An old man with a dirty face and a tattered army jacket swooped down, picked up Lark's bags, and looked inside. "I GOT BELTS!" he screamed and took off running down the street. Smirks chased after him. Lark had no idea; she couldn't see. She still had her Blackberry pressed to her ear. "James!" she screamed into her phone. "James, I think I just got *maced*!" I grabbed Lark's shoulder and spun her to face me. Her eyes were squeezed shut, water welling out of the corners and running down her cheeks, leaving long streaks of black mascara across her porcelain skin. "Julia?!" she shouted, reaching blindly toward me.

"I'm here!" I yelled. "What happened!?"

"I don't know! That man ran by me," she screamed. "I didn't really see, but I think he pepper-sprayed me! I can't open my eyes." I took her hand and led her into a pizza parlour. Lark was moaning, announcing her pain to everyone, though she couldn't see anyone. We approached the front counter.

"Can we use your washroom?" I asked.

"I've been *maced*!" Lark added, swinging her head wildly, like a fast-motion Stevie Wonder. The teenager standing behind the counter didn't bat an eye. He just shook his head slowly and pointed to a sign that said "Washroom for paying customers only."

"Oh, Jesus," I said. "Make us a pepperoni pizza."

The teenager handed me a key and I led Lark into the washroom. She continued to cry.

"Where are we?" she groaned. "It smells awful."

"We're at Shangri La," I said, and guided her head down to the sink, where I proceeded to splash water into her face, frantically and ineffectively, and we stayed like that in the bathroom for twenty minutes, until she could open her eyes, wild and bloodshot, her perfectly smooth hair now a frizzy ball around her face, her previously flawless makeup hanging in clumps and drips of black and beige and purple all over her neck. We looked at each other, my eyes betraying perhaps a bit more fright at her appearance than I'd meant to, and she turned toward the mirror and, upon seeing her reflection, burst into another bout of honking laughter, keeling over at the waist, holding the edges of the sink for support. She swung her arms around me and whispered in my ear.

"You don' think ah willed it inta being—"

"Did it?" I finished for her. We nodded solemnly at each other and left the bathroom. We found Smirks by the front door, holding Lark's bags of belts and my pizza, the lid splayed open, revealing a large pepperoni and cheese, already a third eaten, and, for the first time, he had a big smirk across his cherubic face.

Back at Lark's hotel room, she emerged from the bathroom looking, somehow, a superlative more perfect than when we'd greeted her that morning. She walked to the closet and began pulling out garment bags, mysterious and dark and zipped up tight. I knew what was in them would be beautiful and luxurious and far more expensive than Shelley, the most expensive thing I owned. Lark was excited, smiling at each bag. She laid them on the bed and then stood on her tiptoes to reach the top shelf of the closet. She pulled out an old film case and shook it in the air like a rattle. Pills. "Shall we?"

Before we'd left Vancouver, when we were planning our rendez-vous in Banff, Lark had convinced Smirks and me to try MDMA for the first time. My mother, having counselled her fair share of dead-heads in prison, had always warned me that one mistake with chem-ical drugs could make me schizophrenic. And Thierry had always been firmly against party drugs, so I'd abstained over the years, but now I felt I had no reason to. There certainly wasn't anything left for me to find in alcohol. We'd all agreed that we'd arrive in Banff and Lark would have the drugs waiting. She had promised we'd do the first round in the hotel room to make sure nothing went disastrously wrong. "It'll be fun. We'll listen to music, get ready for the night, have a little love fest. Trust me."

And there we were, one month later, Lark sprinkling a cap into each of our palms. "Cheers," she said, and we bumped our pills togeth-er like martinis before swallowing them down. Funny how you can imagine how drugs will feel. Before I'd ever done MDMA, I'd guessed how it would present in each part of my body, and I had been right. The tingling began in my thighs. "One cap of Molly will be a slow burn," Lark said right after we swallowed. She floated over to her iPod dock and played something light and mellifluous. "Sometimes," she said, looking at me, specifically, "if your perspective is stuck at a certain angle, and no amount of thinking can dislodge it, a chemical catalyst can help."

I knew the buzz in my thighs couldn't be the pill yet. I knew it would take at least thirty minutes, closer to an hour. But that's where it started, for me: the tops of my thighs. My body remembering what hadn't happened yet. Remembering what was to come. Remembering the future. "Go have a shower," Lark said to me. I headed toward the bathroom. "There's a new razor in there!" she called. "And leave the door unlocked in case you start rushing."

I stepped into the tub and pelted my skin with the hottest water I could stand, until I was as pink and tender as a scar. I wanted to give Smirks and Lark some alone time. To allow whatever might be revealed to show itself. I started to shave. I shaved my legs and my armpits. My bikini area. Usually I left a triangle of hair, but I wasn't ready to turn off the water, so I kept shaving. Rinsed and re-rinsed the razor, pressing it against my pubis, removing hair, cutting hair, razing hair. I had never gone completely bare before. I hadn't seen this skin in, what would it be, thirteen years? Hello, skin. I sat down to finish the job, to get intimate with it. The steam, thick and wet, made my head feel weighty and my actions significant. The triangle beneath my belly got smaller and smaller, but always equilateral, working inward, removing strip by strip, until, suddenly, I was naked. Bare, like a child. I rinsed the razor again, watching the drain as curls of my pubic hair circled downward. I rubbed the smooth skin, slippery and sensitive. Nothing left.

I looked at my forearms. Light dusting of sand hair, golden with my bicycle sun. I went to work on this down. This hair gave easier: a few strokes and my left arm was bare. Like stars through parting clouds my freckles emerged. Did I always have that many? Had I acquired new ones on the long Canadian road? Freckles were like supernovas of the skin: black holes of dying flesh. The peripheral world rushed away in streaks. The bathroom door opened. Lark said, "Is it happening?"

"I think so."

She sat down on the toilet. "You shaved your crotch." I looked at her. Lark. All her different parts in layers. The beauty and the perfection. Riding on top of a radiant pain. The source of her love. I nodded. Tears pricked my eyes.

"I love you."

"I love you, too. Are you shaving your arms?"

I nodded again.

"Smirks and I just had a good conversation."

"What did he say?"

"Well, nothing."

"Did he mention—"

"We didn't talk about pedophilia."

I started shaving my other arm.

"He said you want something from him that he can't give you."

"What does that mean?"

"He said you were expecting a different bike ride, and he knows he's not who you want him to be."

"Why is he speaking in code?"

"I don't think he is."

With my right hand I touched my left arm. Grabbed it. Moved it through the air. I could make my body do anything I wanted. I could go anywhere. My body was solid but my spirit was free. I had ridden through the Rockies. I could do anything. "I had this fantasy that we would come to Banff, and he would see you and want to be with you."

Lark laughed, raised her eyebrows, threw her hands up, like: *oh well.* "Or, maybe you had a fantasy that Smirks would go on this bike trip and want to be with you."

Maybe she was right. Definitely she was right.

Lark smiled. "I am still going to try to fuck him, though." She looked at her fingernails then at me. Her eyes said: *what do you think of that?* "Why not? I've fucked a gay guy, a straight woman, and a blind man. Now a fashion designer with a fucking supermodel girlfriend. Why not a pedophile?" I nodded. Kept shaving. I didn't like the word *fuck.* It made my chest tight, breath shallow. I wanted a cigarette. I wanted to swim in an ocean as warm as bathwater. "I just feel bad for the guy," she said. I nodded again. She touched my shoulder. "How are you doing?"

I started speaking, and that's when I really felt the shape of the drug. The words were solid forms in my mouth, each one round and whole, and I felt as if the letters created perfect representations of the things I was trying to say. I had never had this feeling before—that what I was saying was one hundred percent the right thing to say—and it was very seductive, this feeling. It echoed between my cheeks and on my tongue.

I told Lark about Sally. The canoe and the sunlight. How their bodies moved together and apart like beads of oil. How I couldn't see. How I swam. What I had thought, and what had been true.

Lark let out a long, low whistle. "Julia—"

"I know."

"What were you thinking?"

"My mind felt like a crazy mind. I just blocked all consequence from my awareness. All for the sake of experiment. I thought it was research. I was imagining, seriously, that I'd go back to Christina Lake in ten years and ask Sally her memories of that day."

"Oh, Jules." Lark reached out and rubbed my arm, now smooth and hairless and soapy. "Get out of the tub before you shave your head." She handed me a towel. I dried off and Lark stripped out of her sheer skirt and black top. From the door hanger she retrieved a silk maxi dress, hanging limp from the steam. She slipped it on. It was the colour of metal, with two large cut-outs revealing her slender waist. We stepped into the room. Smirks lay on the bed, still in his bike shorts with his shirt off, and I noticed how muscular his legs had gotten—two smooth and rippling tree trunks. His hard pale chest and stomach sprouting irregular tufts of wiry hair that gathered at his belly button and funnelled down under his waistband. I resisted the urge to go lie on top of him. Lark pranced into the room, twisting and turning in front of him to show the skin of her belly. "Smirks! What about this dress?"

He shrugged. "I like that one, too."

"Geez," she said, looking at me and pointing to Smirks with her thumb. "With this one, it's like pulling teeth."

"Sometimes," I said. Lark pointed to the other bed where she'd laid what was meant to be my outfit. A high-waisted denim A-line mini and a sheer, iridescent tank top. I checked the tag. Paco Rabanne.

"Oh, Lark, I don't know."

"Just try it on." Her favourite tagline. *Just Try It On* was the name of her first blog and now her column in *Flare*. Years ago, when she worked at Front and Company, a trendy hipster consignment boutique on Main Street, she was the top-selling employee the store had ever had. It was the middle of the decade, an important time in hipster-wear, and Lark had been the lady to graduate many fledgling fashion-istas from boot-cuts to skinnies. Myself included. I'd gone to visit her one day, wearing my old jeans, and Lark had refused to let me leave without trying on the strange, tight pants. "Just try these on," she'd said, holding out a dark denim pair.

"No, Lark." I'd sidled toward the front door.

"Just try them on." She pushed them into my hands and ushered me into a change room, where there was, horrifyingly, no mirror, and where I begrudgingly pulled them over my hips, confounded by their grip at my ankles and calves. "Come out!" Lark called, and I was morti-fied. I stepped outside the change room feeling as if my body was on fire. She led me to the full-length mirror. I hated them. My hips were too big, my thighs like stumps, my stupid knees. I wanted to disappear. But Lark had made me stay there for almost ten minutes, talking me through the silhouette. "It's like when the lights suddenly go out," she explained. "And at first you can't see anything. Your eyes have to adjust to the dark. That's how it is with skinnies. Your eyes aren't used to the shape. You have to adjust. Just wait. Just watch." I stared at myself in the mirror, watched as the foreign body in the reflection became my own. "Just wait," she'd said. "Just watch."

I picked up Lark's Paco Rabanne and headed toward the bathroom. She stepped in front of me. "We're all friends here, Julia. Don't be shy." I looked at Smirks. He was surfing on his laptop. The prospect of see-ing me naked didn't titillate him at all. But with the drugs, I didn't care. I turned around so my ass was facing them and dropped my towel. Lark whistled. "Nice bum!" I dressed. "Tuck in the shirt." I did, and before I could look in the mirror, she sat me down, blow-dried and soft-waved my hair and covered my face in makeup. Finally she let me stand up and look in the mirror. The skirt, which sat about mid-thigh, revealed my bike-shorts tan line. My knees so brown they looked as though they'd been dipped in caramel. And just above, a glaring white bar of flesh. Lark tossed me a pair of beige pantyhose. "Tights," she corrected me. "No one calls them pantyhose anymore."

❂

Banff was the first place Dirtbag had called from, four years after he disappeared. I was twelve years old. In the basement of the house we'd moved into with Ralph, practising my alto saxophone. Fireplace hot beside me. The school jazz band was playing "Louie Louie," and I had a solo, for some reason. I think the conductor saw potential in me, though I wasn't a musician. The notes came out in choppy honks. I didn't have the lung capacity, couldn't make the music smooth. I'd pleaded with the conductor to give the solo to someone else. "You'll never outgrow your self-consciousness if you keep thinking everyone's watching you," he'd said. But everyone was watching me. It was a solo. He'd shaken his head. "You just don't get it."

When the phone rang, I froze. Sometimes the body picks up on things the brain doesn't yet know. I heard Mom walk over and pause, look at the caller ID. She let it ring two more times before answering. I couldn't make out her words, but her voice was low and careful. Stern. As if she were talking someone down from a ledge. I waited for her to call my name. I knew she would. I knew it would be Dirtbag. I felt it all through my body. "Julia." I took the long, solemn hike up the stairs. My saxophone hung heavy around my neck like a noose. She held out the phone to me and silently mouthed, "It's your father."

I took the receiver. I hated how small and weak my voice sounded. I wanted him to think I was powerful. The fingers on my right hand still rested on the brass keys of my instrument. It wasn't mine. We'd borrowed it from the music department. Only the truly talented had their own. I pressed the keys down and released them while he spoke. The empty, tin-can sound contrasted Dirtbag's voice. Thick and sloppy. I thought of pea soup spilling from its bowl. He asked me if I'd read the Dylan Thomas books he left behind. I told him I didn't like poetry. I wanted to be a psychologist like Mom. "If you really want to be a psychologist, you have to read Thomas," he slurred. "Find my Dylan Thomas books and read them. Then you can figure out the human brain." Mom puffed on a cigarette over my shoulder and I kept turning away from her, away from the smoke. Dirtbag began reciting a poem. About being young and easy. A lilting house. Green grass. I handed the phone back to Mom and walked away. I felt as if I was going to vomit, but I didn't. I looked up the area code later, after Mom had gone to bed. Banff, Alberta. A million miles away.

In Banff with Lark and Smirks, I was supposed to spend the afternoon doing Dirtbag reconnaissance, but instead I spent it doing drugs. I put his phone number in the pocket of my mini skirt, imagining that at some point in the evening I would get drunk enough to dial it.

Lark was on the phone ordering more party favours for us for the night. "Molly and Kate," she kept shouting into the phone. Molly meant MDMA and Kate meant coke. "We're hanging out with Kate tonight FOR SURE," she yelled. I could hear music pumping through the speaker on her cellphone. Smirks was lying on his back, staring at the ceiling. "If Molly can make it, that would be fantastic!" Lark looked at me and winked, smiled. Then she frowned. "No! No! I've seen enough of Mary Jane to last me a lifetime. Get back to me. Okay. Get back to me." She disconnected the call. "We have an hour. How are you guys feeling?"

"I'm high," said Smirks.

"Me too," I said, flopping down on the bed beside him and the bags of salvaged belts. "Tell us again about the homeless man."

"He was just homeless. I think. I grabbed the belts, and he kept running."

I rolled onto my back. "I go through periods when I stare at older street men on East Hastings, expecting to see Dirtbag."

Smirks looked at me. "That makes sense."

"And then I just forget about him completely for weeks." He nodded. "What about your parents?"

"I do not expect to see them on East Hastings Street. Unless Dad's rescuing someone." His eyes were bright, and he looked at me with an open face. I felt my chest go soft. I wanted to touch his cheek, where the light didn't hit, where there was always a shadow. Lark moved away from us, to the music. She turned the volume down and put on something ambient and dark. She spun, slowly, in the chair, around and around, not wanting to be a part of this conversation, I could tell. Lark and I had different strategies when it came to discussing personal issues. Hers were usually exponentially more successful. When I saw her in action, getting to the root of someone's deepest insecurity or inhibition, it reminded me of a YouTube video I had seen where a mother bird fed her young. Except the video was in reverse and in slow motion. It showed the lark pulling long strands of food out of the throats of her young. Insect viscera and little green worms coming back up from the hatchlings' depths. Back into the mother's beak. Lark was the mother bird. She pulled things up from inside us. There was a pair of sunglasses sitting next to the speaker. She put them on and swung the chair toward us, the dark lenses reflecting the room.

I touched Smirks' knee. Knobby bone. "What are they like, your parents?"

"They're nice."

"Do you blame them for anything? What do you blame them for?"

With that, Lark swung toward the computer again. I could tell she disapproved. She had said to me once, "People are like Magic Eye pictures. If you just watch, they will eventually show themselves to you." I hadn't learned that yet.

"I don't blame them for anything."

"Bullshit."

Lark looked at me, her shiny aviators showing me my face, still foreign and glossy with makeup. She shook her head. Don't push it, she was saying. He'll crawl inside himself.

"My mother used to take me on these long walks," Smirks said. He held a beer bottle up to his mouth like a microphone. "Every day after school, we'd go on these long walks before Dad got home."

"What did Dad do?"

"Dad is a minister."

Lark whistled.

Smirks smiled. "We'd walk for hours. She just needed someone to talk to."

"To confess to," said Lark. Smirks looked at her. "She needed someone to confess to. That's how it works. Your father was busy with the sins of others. So hers fell to you."

Smirks nodded. I could see the drugs in his eyes. "It felt like the weight of the world on my shoulders." He said it slowly, as though he meant it.

We were all quiet. Lark had chosen the perfect song. We listened to it and I swear we all heard, under the chords, Lark's low, southern voice, whispering to us, asking us, *who did it? Who did it? Who did it?*

Then Lark spoke, slowly, realizing. "She was the first one to call you Smirks, wasn't she?" As if she had just figured it out. As if it made perfect sense. Smirks brought the beer bottle to his lips and blew the low b flat of a foghorn. Lark walked toward him, stood behind him, pressed her hands into his shoulders and forced him down to his knees, leaning all her body onto his. "This is the weight of the world," she said. "The world weighs exactly one woman." Then, Thomas' prose in my head, loud and insistent and unwelcome. In a letter to someone, he'd written about unborn children. Banging their fists on the wombs of their mothers. The womb as a prison. The world as a snugger prison. Dylan Thomas had been a sickly boy. Too weak for the war. I'd always thought *snugger* was some Welshman's pejorative term, like bugger. But it was a superlative: more snug. Snugger. The snuggest.

Lark spread her arms, her chest pressed into Smirks' back, and she floated there like a bird for what seemed like a long time. I bent down to look at Smirks' face. He was smiling. Lark jumped up onto her feet. "Any vase can look like an urn if you turn it the right way," she said. She changed the music to something with more beats per minute. It was time to go downstairs and party.

The night floated by on a bass line. We found ourselves in a club full of eighteen-year-olds. I danced on top of the music. I thought: with weed, the world crawls on top of you; with ecstasy, you crawl on top of the world. There was a boy, I remember, thin and twisty, and I could see the top of his head because he was shorter, and we danced together for a long time, me gazing at the top of his head, where his cowlick spun like a whirlpool.

At one in the morning I checked my cellphone. Five missed calls from April, one voicemail. I listened to it. "Jules, everything is fine, everyone is okay, but you have to call me." Her voice, usually frantic and high-pitched, very notably wasn't. I sat down on the dance floor. I felt the drugs behind my eyes fighting. The drugs said: everything is great, remember? They punched my eyeballs from inside my head. The drugs, stuck in the jail womb. Me, stuck in a snugger prison. Lark pulled me up laughing. There was a bubble around me made of blown glass. I could hear the music outside, and I could see many colours swirling. Inside, my eyes were closed. Everywhere else was wind, but I was in the slipstream. The rushing velocity of air that I rode as I rushed made the world feel as still as an empty closet.

April picked up the phone right away. "Well, they got in a car accident," she said, that thick valley drawl, as though someone was grabbing hold of her A's and stretching them. "Mom broke her back in three places, but she's fine." Broke her back in three places. But she's fine. What did that mean? Could she walk? Was she paralyzed? "No, no, she's fine," said April. She knew. She worked with old people. She knew that Mom would be fine. Mom would walk. And Ralph had walked away. Hurt his arm a bit or something, but had walked away. "Where *are* you?" April asked. I told her about all the drugs. "Ew," she said. "You should go to bed, Jules. This isn't the right time for any of that."

When I went back into the club, I found Lark and Smirks in the corner. Her body pressed into his, his body pressed awkwardly into the crook of the walls. Both their arms hung at the their sides, and their fingers intertwined. They were kissing, or Lark was kissing him, throwing her mouth on his with sloppy urgency, like a child throwing eggs. I watched them for several seconds, then pulled Dirtbag's telephone number out of my pocket. The digits blurred together like words do in a dream.

I went back outside. Two-thirty in the morning. I stood beside a cluster of smokers. Their high-pitched drunk voices and lack of balance comforted me. I dialled the number and waited. Long-distance charges may apply. A twinge of futile anger, paying money to get a hold of someone who had never given me a dime. Never given me anything good. I expected it to ring and ring. I expected an answering machine to pick up and inform me that a happy couple lived at that number now, so go back to Vancouver and get a life. But then a man picked up, and his voice was gravelly and raw, as if a snowplough had gone by and torn up all the grass.

"Dirtbag?" I asked. That had been my plan, if a man answered, to just say his first name and see what happened. Catch him off-guard. Catch him.

"This is Dirtbag."

I buckled over at the waist and threw up on the sidewalk. A chorus of disgust rang out all around me. High heels and pantyhose ran away. I kept retching. I could hear the man's voice. "Hello? Who is this?" When I finally stood up straight and wiped my mouth, all of the kids were gone.

Daddy

Of course, it wasn't Dirtbag. He just had the same first name. What were the chances? Another Irishman in Dirtbag's old apartment. This man had a shock of white hair and eyes as blue as Santa's. He opened them wide and leaned close to me. "Your dad had those black Irish eyes, right? I remember. As you can see, mine are true blue." He waved his hand beneath his face.

"I know," I said, assuring him. "I know you're not my father."

He told me to call him Moore, his last name, so I did. I sat in his living room the morning after my drug-filled night, drinking coffee that tasted like pencil shavings and pushing his cat off my lap. Moore had a strong, solid body and a stooped neck. From years—twelve, apparently—of ducking the low ceilings of this apartment where Dirtbag used to live. He shuffled over to his worn oak desk, weighted down with years of paperwork. The apartment was shabby but highly organized. Within seconds of my arrival, he had the lease agreement in my hands. Dirtbag's signature, shaky and scrawled, real live ink underneath my fingertips. My signature of our last name, Hoop, was the same as his. How was that possible?

I dropped the lease on the coffee table. "Was this furniture his?" Moore hesitated. I assured him I didn't want it. "I live in Vancouver. I'm just curious."

He sighed. "Yes. It's all his. Everything. I came with nothing. I expected to acquire furniture as I went. You know. It was just a dream to live in the mountains. But he asked if he could leave his furniture. He didn't seem to have much else. A couple of bags packed up by the

144

doorway. All the shelves were bare. He seemed a bit desperate. Like he needed to get out of here fast."

"He needed to get out of here fast because he'd just contacted me and forgot to screen his phone number," I said. I ran my hand along the coffee table in front of me. Moore was quiet. I understood that driving impulse to hide from those you've failed. Dirtbag had passed that down to me. I imagined, sitting in his old apartment, that I could feel what he must have felt. Packing his bags. Eyeing the phone. I got up and walked over to the large oak bookshelves. I recognized his work. Heavy, oppressive pieces moulded exquisitely with the most delicate patterns. His favourite was the egg-and-tongue moulding that seemed so sexually symbolic. Those round, ripe eggs interspersed with phallic darts. Dirtbag had wanted to be a poet, but instead, he was a woodworker. His talent was undeniable. Unfortunately he denied himself the fulfillment that comes with mastery and, instead, suffered for his poetry. He tried so hard to twist words into phrases that no one had said before. But it was only wood he'd left behind. It was wood that showed the world who he was, not his words. Not his actions. "He built all of these, you know," I said to Moore.

Moore nodded.

"He taught me how to use a lathe when I was six years old."

I was six years old. Dirtbag had carried me into his shop and sat me on the counter. My feet dangled, and I stared at the woodchips on the floor. Dirtbag touched my arm. "Watch." He attached a block of wood to the spindle of the lathe. Then he turned on the motor and the spindle rotated. "Should we make a bowl?" he asked me. "A candlestick? A vase?" He took a thick, blunt chisel and held it to the spinning block, carving out his basic shape. Then, with a thinner, sharper chisel he got more specific. Soon, a bowl appeared. A coarse bowl, the wood still rough and raw. Dirtbag completed this entire process in less than seven minutes. He then, however, spent hours sanding the bowl. I grew sleepy watching him. The sun travelled from one window to the next before it disappeared altogether. Finally, he finished. "Touch it," he said. He gestured to the bowl. "Touch it." I ran my fingertips across its curve. I expected to feel wood. Instead, I felt sand. The softest sand, like the inside of an hourglass. As if I could push my fingers, my palm, my entire arm inside. "It's very sensual, right?" I did not know what sensual meant. I guessed that it meant something soft, melting and warm. He removed the bowl from the spindle and turned it over. He pointed to a jagged crack in the bowl's centre. The scar ran about an inch long, a yellow scratch against the otherwise soft pink maple. "But it's broken."

"Not broken," I said.

"Yes, broken." He put the bowl back on the lathe. "But it works."

After Dirtbag left, our house was filled with unfinished bowls. Inside their bellies existed imperfections that he could not sand away. I looked at the photographs adorning a shelf that Dirtbag had built.

Moore stood behind me. "Those are my kids," he said. "I can't imagine not knowing where they are."

I looked at him. "I suppose it is strange not to know."

"It's sad." Moore filled up my coffee cup though I'd hardly made a dent. The drugs from last night had left a calm inside me. A wide-open space that words fell into and hardly caused a stir.

"Do you know what he was doing for work?"

"Construction. Like me. That's how I heard about the apartment."

"You knew him?" My voice cracked with hope.

"No, sweetie. We were on different sites. I just got his number from the boss and set up an appointment. He seemed fixing to get out of here awful fast. Left in the middle of the month but didn't make me pay half the rent."

"Did he say where he was going?" Moore shook his head. "Did you ask?" No, again. I must have looked disappointed because he said he was sorry. "It's okay," I said, touching Dirtbag's signature on the contract. His last name, Hoop, identical to mine. Back in my first year of university I'd taken a graphology class for the express purpose of performing party tricks in the dormitories on Friday nights. I only remembered the letters of my own name. According to my and Dirtbag's "H," we had strong intuition which was inhibited by a sharp sense of self-doubt.

"You can keep that paper if you want," Moore said. He looked a little nervous about losing a piece from his stack of documents; his offer was kind. I shook my head. I asked him if he still worked for the same company. No. But he gave me the name and telephone number of his old boss, just in case.

"Did he say *any*thing else? Girlfriend? Future plans? Family?" I'd always wondered if there was another child floating around out there, by-product of my father, Radon son or daughter, half-life of Dirtbag.

"Nothing," Moore said. "Except…" He walked back over to his desk and opened the bottom drawer. He shuffled through some things and pulled out an old writing notebook. "I wasn't going to keep this around. Felt a bit funny keeping another man's journal. I flipped through it a couple of times. Seems he was a bit of a writer. I don't know poetry from Adam, but I read a couple and they made me think, feel, a bit different." He handed the journal to me. I opened it to the first page and read. It was Thomas. *In My Craft or Sullen Art*. Words I'd read a hundred times. He wrote by candlelight, singing candlelight— which I had always heard, cleverly, as *singeing* light, and imagined a candle flame licking at Dylan's arm, igniting his self-important elbow, a combustion which he, idiotically, would move to extinguish with whiskey, causing a greater conflagration. I turned the page. More Thomas. Thomas all the way through. So sullen. I closed the book.

"These aren't his."

"Oh. I'm sorry. I thought it was his handwriting." ˙

"It is. But these are another poet's."

"Oh. That's strange."

This made me laugh, which confused Moore. I shrugged. "You don't know the half of it." I put the notebook in my bag and stood up. "Is that all he left?" Moore nodded, but tilted his head back and to the side, as if pointing to the other room. His eyebrows were high and uncertain. "Are you sure?"

He shook his head. "One more thing." He gestured for me to follow him. He opened a door next to the fridge. It opened to a small room. Inside, one object: a model ship. Sails as high as the ceiling and a hull as long as the room. It was as though the room were a display case, existing only for the ship. My father built that, I knew. "He couldn't bring it with him," Moore said, standing behind me. "He wanted to, but he couldn't." I walked into the room. The mahogany gleamed in the dim light like the eyes of an old aquatic animal. Moore must have polished it, taken care of it. Thousands of intricate interlocking pieces created the sweeping sails. I touched my finger to one.

"How many—"

"There are twenty-one sails. This is the flying jib, here's the jib, the fore topmast staysail, then the fore staysail." Moore worked his way all the way back to the mizzen topgallant. "I knew nothing about sailing ships until I moved here." He walked around the boat, his eyes wide. The dust blown off. He looked at me, hesitated. "He asked me to look after it." He pointed out various parts, pointed to them until I came closer, leaned in, examined their complexity. "You see, these pieces are all real. Real chains, real shrouds. Look at these gunports. Hand carved. They have to be." The ship was big enough to house a small animal.

"Does your cat ever hole up in here?" I asked.

Moore looked appalled. "No," he said firmly. Tried to explain. "There are five different types of wood here. Do you see?"

I nodded. It was important to him, this ship.

"Mahogany, maple, poplar, beechwood and tanganika." I could tell he wanted me to study the ship. So I did. I walked all the way around it. The room was as quiet as a museum. Finally Moore spoke. His voice sounded defeated. "This should be yours."

I laughed, again unintentionally. It just burst out of me, the ludicrousness of it all. Again Moore looked perplexed. How could I be so obtuse? He'd grown attached to this leviathan. Had spent hours with it, maybe days, polishing its wood, cleaning the silver chains. Removing and washing the linen sails, replacing them with the care of a surgeon. I shook my head. "What would I do with this?"

"You would take care of it."

This must have been the kind of person my mother had fallen in love with. The person who would take care of a model ship as though it were a child. I said goodbye to Moore. When I stepped out onto the street, the sun flashed across my eyes like a bomb. I imagined Dirtbag leaving twelve years ago, looking left, looking right, then heading east toward Ontario like a madman. Like me.

❂

I met Lark at a coffee shop. She looked awful. Hungover, remorseful. The café crowded with clean and healthy tourists. Lark had scrubbed herself bare. No makeup. Plain cotton clothes. The belch and gush of espresso machines. Squawks of international names called out for coffee orders. Monique? Yuki? Pablo? Katya? I sat down in front of her. She looked at me. "Did you find him?"

I shook my head, took a sip of her cappuccino.

She moaned. "I feel like a bag of smashed assholes." So did I. I hadn't slept yet. After calling Moore last night, I'd wandered around Banff, waiting until the time in the morning when the hospital in Halifax would finally connect me to Mom's room. "How is she?" Lark asked.

"Fine, apparently. Very confused and disoriented, physically broken, but everyone keeps saying she is fine." I wanted to tell Smirks what happened with Mom, with Moore. Wanted him to pull my head into his chest, press his lips to my head. And then I remembered: Lark and Smirks, kissing.

My voice shook. "Tell me about your night."

Lark breathed in deep, let it out slowly. "It was fucked."

"Where's Smirks?"

"Still sleeping, I guess. Where I left him."

"Tell me everything."

"When did you leave the club?"

"You guys were making out in the corner."

Lark frowned with her eyebrows, trying to remember the details. "We made out on the dance floor for awhile. He was really resistant." She looked at me, eyes panicked. "I feel like a rapist." She lowered her head to the table. "I kept telling him I could be whoever he wanted.

I told him I had a bare pussy, and I grabbed his hand and stuck it up my skirt so he could feel."

My face crumpled. Smirks' hands on her. I gripped the table. "Did he like it?"

"Not at first."

"But you kept going."

"I thought if I could get him hard, get him horny for me and give him good sex, then I could, like, cure him or something." She looked at me when she said this. Her lower lip quivered. She swallowed deeply. Shook her head again. "Fuck, man. It was brutal. We cabbed back to the hotel. I don't really remember that part. I kept calling him Daddy. I remember looking in the review mirror and seeing the driver's eyes looking back at me. Pure disgust in his eyes. Or fear. Or both. Smirks said, 'Don't call me Daddy, don't call me that,' but he kept kissing me harder and harder, and his dick got hard and I knew it was working. We got up to the hotel and I asked him what he wanted. Like, what fantasy. I told him I would do anything, be anyone. I told him he must have a million fantasies that he never got to play out, and that even though I wasn't a little girl, I was a damn good actress. He kept shaking his head. He looked really sad. And then..." Lark trailed off. Her face puzzled, as if she was trying to piece something together. I waited. "And then, something changed. He let go. He went for it. He told me to go to the bathroom and take off my makeup. But he said it all commanding-like. In a deep voice. 'Go to the bathroom, little girl, and take off your makeup. I want to see your face.' So I did. And he said, 'Don't call me Daddy, call me John.'" Lark stopped here. "Is that his real name?"

"No."

"Okay. So, I called him John. He asked me to put on my little baby-doll dress." Lark paused, cocked her head. "It would actually look really cute on you." I scowled. "Anyway, he told me to put my hair in pigtails, too. So I did. And then we acted it out."

"You acted what out?"

"Sex."

"You had sex."

"Yeah. Sex between a man and a child. He had all these rules. I wasn't allowed to pretend it hurt. I wasn't allowed to pretend I was afraid. I wasn't allowed to pretend he was forcing me to do anything."

"And he wasn't forcing you. To do anything."

"I know. But I thought he would get turned on by me pretending to be afraid. Like a child would be afraid. I don't know. I don't understand pedophiles. Obviously."

I laughed, though I still felt awful. I was jealous. Jealous she had felt Smirks inside her. I wanted that. I wanted him to want me. "And then what happened?"

"I came. And he came with me. We both came really hard." Lark looked at me.

I tried to smile. "Well, that's good. Right?"

"He wasn't wearing a condom."

"Okay."

"I'm not on the pill."

"Okay."

"So, Smirks and I may have a lovechild." She took a sip of her coffee. I became aware of people sitting near us, listening. Lark whispered, "Maybe in ten years he'll want to fuck her instead." Lark tied her hair in a knot. "I'll pick up the morning-after pill on my way back to the hotel." Her hands were shaking.

"What happened next?"

"Dude, as soon as he came, he was, like, overwhelmed with this sickening guilt. I could see it in his eyes. I could feel it in his body. We both were. It was so weird. What we did was so wrong."

"Why? You were two consenting adults."

"Were we?"

I didn't answer.

"He hadn't wanted it. As soon as he came, he pushed me off. He didn't mean to. It was just impulse. But he literally pushed me off him and rolled away. I think he was crying." Lark's eyes filled with tears. "I feel like a rapist," she said again. My jealousy evaporated. I just felt sick.

Images flashed through my mind—Lark in a white dress, Smirks gripping her wrists. Pulling her pigtails. I tried to push them from my mind. "It was fucked," she just kept saying. "It was so fucked."

I left Lark at the café and went back to the hotel to retrieve Smirks. It was time to get the hell out of Banff. I found him standing in the front lobby. He looked sad, but not sad enough. There was something different there. A satisfaction. A wholeness. As if he had gotten something he needed. A heat lit in my chest. My vision blurred. "She wants us out of here," I said. Smirks nodded. I had the urge to pinch him. The soft skin under his arms. Make it hurt. He dragged his foot along the grout between the marble tiles. A little kid being punished. Lark thought she'd taken advantage of him, but I knew he'd taken advantage of her. Molested her. I wanted to scream at him. And then he put his fingertips to his pale cheeks. The skin beneath his eyes quivered. His lips pulsed red. The anger left me, abrupt and forceful, like a flock of frightened birds.

He wiped at his eyes. "I wanted to tell her I'm sorry."

"She knows."

I left Banff still looking for my father. We rode our bicycles along the Trans-Canada Highway through Dead Man's Flats. The name had given us hope: flat land. Dead land. Nothing. False hope, though. Nothing is flat on a bicycle. The name came from a story of First Nations beaver trappers who, spotting a Caucasian warden patrolling the land, covered themselves in beaver blood and lay flat on the ground, pretending to be dead in order to avoid punishment.

Punishment, indeed. The vacant death after Banff, before Calgary, felt intensely personal. As though we deserved it, this purgatory. The first fifty kilometres felt like a trip on a treadmill, running forever and going nowhere. Though the sky, having shed its mountains, would finally be open, we still felt trapped. Inside something massive, but contained. We hadn't brought enough water and we ran out about thirty kilometres before the next gas station. We didn't think.

The air was hot and dry and I was hungover and dehydrated. I tried to empty my brain and focus on pedalling. *You need to shear your head. You mean* clear *my head? Whatever.*

Smirks stayed far ahead of me, pulling his slipstream out of my reach. I didn't know what energy reserves he was running on. I watched his body grow smaller. As I pedalled I became aware of a series of grooves in the road that were causing me to thump, thump, thump with each revolution of my wheels. I looked down. There were no grooves. The thumping sound was my rim on the pavement. A flat rear tire. "Fuck!" I screamed loudly, but Smirks didn't hear. He kept going. My rape whistle blasted through the air. He turned and made his way back. By the time he reached me, I was tucked into a ditch several metres from the road, smoking. Grateful for an excuse to give up.

Smirks inspected my tire. "Where's your patch kit?"

I shook my head. "I'm not doing it. I can't. I'm hitchhiking. We're out of water. Look at all these trucks." They blew past us, thundering engines, honking horns. I felt too small for this road. "Let's get a ride into Calgary. Please." Smirks looked relieved and sat down beside me. A huge transport truck roared by. The driver honked and waved. Funny how highway people liked to include us in their day. A honk, a wave, a "Way to go!" out the window. Everyone was supportive. They would go home and tell their families or friends they saw two cyclists with Nova Scotian flags on their panniers, heading east. Isn't that something, they would say. I hope they make it. What could stop them? Physical tragedy. Mental breakdown. Emotional defeat. Smirks picked up a pebble and threw it toward the road. I did the same. We threw pebbles in silence.

A few minutes later a big, black Dodge Ram drove past and screeched to a halt a hundred metres away. The driver threw the truck into reverse and backed up toward us. A tiny, compact, brightly blonde woman hopped down from the cab. Her energy and size belied her age, which, judging by her wrinkled face, had reached at least fifty. Her friends probably called her Mighty Mouse. Her eyes buzzed with endorphins. Probably a fitness instructor of some sort.

"Where are you headed?" A bright, sunny voice.

I stood up. "Nova Scotia."

The woman squealed. "I knew it! I did that! I did that two years ago. It was the best trip of my life!" Smirks and I looked at each other. Neither of us so far could say the same. "Do you need anything? You have enough water? What do you need?"

I looked at her huge truck with its big, empty cargo space. "We need a ride."

She frowned. Smirks laughed. Put her hands on her hips. "To where?"

"Calgary. I've got a flat and I'm out of patches." A lie.

The woman did a little hop. "You won't believe it. I've got a patch kit!"

I stared at her. She stared at me. Smirks kicked at some dust. It was a standoff.

Finally, she relented. "Okay, sure." Her cheeriness returned. "Yeah! Okay! Load 'em up!" I sat in the middle with the giant stick shift between my legs while she talked for the whole hour about her tour across the country. She'd gone with five other divorcees and they'd stayed in hotels the entire way. "But I suppose if I was with my honey I wouldn't mind roughing it like you." She winked at us.

"We're not together," I said.

Her voice became flirty. "You should stay with me tonight. I've got a spare bed for you, Julia." She leaned past me to look at Smirks. "And a king-size bed for the two of us?" Her laughter, too loud. Startling. Smirks looked at her, his mouth open. I was so tired of meeting new people I could scream.

"Smirks doesn't like women," I said. Let her assume whatever she wanted.

"Oh. Oh. Okay." Smirks stared at me in wonder. She composed herself. "Well, I don't know of any campgrounds."

"Could you just take us to a hostel?" I asked. "I'm tired of watching out for cougars anyway." Smirks pressed a finger into my ribcage. "Animals in general."

"Of course," she said.

Smirks leaned past me, looked at her. "That'd be great." His voice was sweet and apologetic. We watched the scenery in silence. The foothills of the Rockies peeled away like dead skin. The earth flattened and the sky widened. The world became two-dimensional. We flew through it at a dizzying speed. My motionless legs felt strange beneath me. Strange to be carried. Strange to have someone else do the work for me. We entered the ticky-tacky suburban corner of the city and she pulled over at the first hostel, grateful to be rid of us. Her tires actually spun as she pulled away.

Smirks gaped at me, bemused. "Why did you say I don't like women?"

"Did you want her hitting on you? She was fifty."

He shook his head and we went inside. A pretty young woman with a pink rhinestone Monroe piercing served us at the counter. We booked a private room. "Separate beds," I said, which made her smile.

She leaned over the counter as Smirks signed for the room. "I'm left-handed, too!" she announced. I rolled my eyes. Weeks of cycling in the sun had made Smirks even more hale and hearty-looking. These poor women across the country didn't stand a chance. We went upstairs and unloaded our gear.

I undressed for the shower. "Did you know that thirty percent of pedophiles are left-handed?"

He nodded. He reached into his handlebar bag and pulled out one of the many texts of pedo-lit I'd pushed on him back in Vancouver. He started flipping through the pages and I continued to undress. He read. "The part of brain organization that determines handedness happens before birth." He closed the book. "It's a birth defect."

Naked, I turned to him. "Left-handedness?"

"Pedophilia." He held up the book. "I've been reading. Like you told me to." I crossed my arms over my bare chest. "It's a dysfunction. The white matter in my brain is screwy. I don't have enough of it. Grey matter does the thinking, the information processing. White matter controls the signals between the information, their connections. When you look at a child, your white matter connects the child to a nonsexual being, and sends a signal of nurture. Love. Care. My white matter signals sex. Pedophilia is not a sexual orientation. It's a birth defect."

I sat down beside him. "Potato, potahto."

Smirks closed the book and looked at me. "What would you have happen? If you could solve the pedophile problem, what would be your solution?"

This was a question I had thought about endlessly. "I would create an island for all the pedophiles. There I would send cloned, fertilized eggs that would develop into babies. You would have to wait a few years, but eventually you would have a population of prepubescent children who had no idea that sexual relationships between adults and children were supposed to be traumatic. You could love the children openly, and make them feel good, openly. You could impregnate them, and make love to the children of others. There would be so many, you wouldn't have to worry about incest."

"And what happens to the sixteen-year-old girl who gives birth and is no longer attractive to any of the men or women on the island?" Smirks asked.

This is where my utopia always fell apart. You couldn't keep the women on the island, obsolete and loveless. You couldn't send them back to the mainland, where they wouldn't understand all the new rules, the new conventions. The laws. I took the book from his hands. Flipped through it. Placed it beside me. "You'd kill her," I said.

Smirks nodded. He lay down beside me and closed his eyes. With his leg, he urged me off the bed. I stood, my skin splashed with goosebumps.

"You'd have to," he said. "Wouldn't you?"

Mama

Time passed. Summer heated up. Set us like curlers under the beauty-salon dome of the sky. I made promises to Smirks about the humidity that would find us in the east. Sauna-like conditions. In the Prairies, we baked like earth. Terracotta. We pedalled on, out of Alberta and into Saskatchewan, where we discovered several falsehoods and misconceptions about the province. The first was that the wind there blew east. Not that summer it didn't. The wind blew west, into our faces and chests, into our panniers fat with food and camp gear. So powerful was the wind, we could be pointed downhill and still have to pedal lest we stand still.

The second falsehood was that the province was flat. Not that summer it wasn't. It rolled and undulated like a sick belly, the highest point 1,500 metres above sea level in the Cypress Hills. Maybe you wouldn't notice that in a car. But on a bicycle, that long stretch in the prairie heat, echoing *dust bowl, dust bowl, dust bowl* as we climbed to Lookout Point, we could feel the elevation in our legs. Beneath us, the trains sounded like gasps and sighs of the land.

The third falsehood was that the Cypress Hills were hills of cypress. They weren't. The Métis used *cypres* for all evergreens, and termed these hills *les montagnes des cypres,* the Cypress Hills. I kept looking for cypress trees, but found none. We rippled east along Route 13, passing towns with names like Forget and Forward, Limerick and Horizon. I tried to draw literary connections between these towns but I couldn't find a thread. Whenever I stopped for a cigarette, and Smirks got out his notebook and scrawled into it, I imagined the poetry possible for a writer on this road. But my mind was prosaic and clinical. As soon as we left Forget, I forgot. There once was a town called Limerick.

In the mornings, Smirks would always rise before me. He would make coffee and use his compass to determine east. I didn't speak to him when he meditated. When he lowered himself into the lotus pose, our site grew silent. I watched him, though, with his eyes closed. His long, deep breaths lifting up his barrel chest, laying it down. I wondered what he thought about. What he tried not to think about. When he finished, he echoed calm like a gunshot. Everything around him silenced. Birds scattered far away. "Why do you always face east?" I asked him one morning. We were at a campground in Milestone.

"It's important to look where we are going, not where we've been." When he said this, it occurred to me for the first time that we might not make it to Nova Scotia. I'm not sure why I realized it at that moment, but I did.

That day we biked to Parkbeg. We rolled into town late, past the magic hour into twilight, when the air is milky-purple and calm. "The lavender haze," Smirks said. The sun had sunk and left its gloaming, and the blue grama grass crawled thick at our feet, inflorescence like thousands of shiny insects, living and then at once asleep with night. I would learn later, after I had finished biking and had made it home, that Parkbeg was a ghost town. But we didn't know that then. We just thought everyone had gone to bed. Everyone except a woman we found outside her mobile home, watering her garden by moonlight.

We rolled up beside her. "Is there a campground in town?"

She laughed. A port-wine stain covered the entire right half of her face, and she was very pretty. "I saw you coming down the street. I thought you were an apparition," she said. We laughed too. I lifted my hand to wipe the sweat off my forehead, but there wasn't any. "You're dry as a bone." She arched the hose toward me, dousing me from head to toe. I was suddenly so thirsty, and I opened my mouth to catch the stream. "Close that mouth, girly. The water around here is poison. Didn't anyone tell you that? There's something in the wells."

I could smell the sweet, hot oil of hot dogs cooking through the open trailer window. A voice squeaked through the screen. "Who you talking to, Missy?" A woman's face pushed up against the mesh. "Oh. Hello, kids! Would you like a hot dog? You look half-starved."

The woman with the hose, Missy, rolled her eyes. "Mama's making hot dogs again." She looked at her mother, who smiled brightly, eyes sparkling, a beautiful Kathy Bates. "You made hot dogs two hours ago, Mama. Why're you doing it again?" The hot dog sweat was making my mouth water.

"'Cause I knew company'd be coming." Mama left the window. Missy hustled us inside as though we were guests late for dinner. Empty boxes blocked the doorway. Missy pushed them aside, frowning, and I looked at her port-wine stain. Later, I would learn the Latin term for it: *Naevus flammeus*. In the Middle Ages, women with port-wine stains were burned at the stake. It was thought to be the mark of the devil, Missy said later. Hers was a deep, glowing purple on exactly half of her face. Her eyes shining like wet, black stones. My mother had always said it was better to have your disfigurements on the outside of your body where people can see them. It makes you more honest. "Why do we hide what's wrong with us?" she would ask. "What good does that do for anyone?"

Mama gestured at the boxes. Grunted. "They're pushing us out of town. You know this used to be a plantation?" Mama swept her arms wide. "This used to be a *house*. A veranda all the way around."

Missy told us the various ways Mama'd been delaying her packing. How just recently she'd started setting her hair in curlers every morning. She was sixty-eight years old and had never used curlers in her life. All of a sudden, she got a rack of curlers from the thrift store in the next town over, and she twisted them into her voluminous mane every day. "But she never leaves the house!" Missy said. "Sure, she's allowed to, in her old age, acquire vanity." As though vanity were a taste, like horseradish. "But here's the kicker." In the afternoon, when the curls started to fall out with heat, and sag with humidity, and stink with cigarette smoke, she marched right back into her bedroom, plugged that rack of curlers in, and started the process over from the beginning.

"But she won't pack a single box. Isn't that strange?" Missy asked.

Mama watched us—an eager grin on her face—for an answer.

Smirks shrugged. "I understand. Change is hard."

Mama snorted. "Change is impossible." We ate our hot dogs and listened to the interminable squawking of the pet parakeet whose cage hung from the ceiling. Smirks and I kept looking at each other, stifling giggles. Where had we landed? Mama watched us with keen eyes. "How long have you had that ring, girly?"

"Me?" I pointed to myself. Mama nodded. The thin, gold band had been mailed to me ten years before when my grandmother, Dirtbag's mother, had died. It had belonged to her, and I'd been wearing it ever since.

"Perfect," she said. "I'm gonna read it. Hand it over."

"Mama, really?" Missy sounded tired.

"Hush," said Mama, holding her hand out to me. I slid the ring off and she placed it in the centre of her left palm. When she spoke again, her voice had lowered an octave. "This ring is heavy," she intoned. I looked at Smirks, his mouth open wide in a delighted smile. Mama lowered her palm down to the floor, and then lifted it up toward the ceiling. She did this several times. Then she raised her right hand several inches above her left and moved it in a circular motion. She moved her hands toward each other, then apart. Toward, apart. I was embarrassed by the pageantry. Finally, she cupped her palms together and shook them ever so slightly and I imagined my ring was a tiny earthquake between her fingers. Her eyes closed, Mama spoke. "Someone in your life has chronic pain."

I thought of April's migraines.

She continued. "You value this person's opinion, but you believe that the physical disconnect—her pain and your lack of pain—impedes your understanding of one another."

Mama was good, but I knew what she was doing. I interrupted her. "I could probably say the same to you and in some way, I'd be right. Correct?"

Mama looked at Missy and they smiled knowingly at one another.

Smirks looked interested and leaned in closer. Mama slid my ring onto her pinkie and touched the nape of her neck. "The pain begins here, at the back of the neck." She was right.

"I'm sure many people have pain in their neck."

Mama took the ring off her finger. Smelled it. "You sympathize with this person's pain. But you feel it disconnects you. You feel the main reason you cannot understand this person is the pain." The parakeet squawked. Mama stared at me. Missy nodded. Smirks touched my hand.

"You said that already. Anything else?" I asked.

"Just one thing." She took the ring off and placed it on the table in front of me. "You're looking for someone." She stood up and walked over to the stove and started boiling more water. I looked at Smirks and he looked at the table. Mama put a hand on her hip. "I don't think that person wants to be found."

"Mama—" Missy said.

"Who wants another hot dog?"

Smirks and I stayed up late on the pull-out couch, whispering into the night. "When you're travelling," he said, "you try to attach meaning to everything that happens." He paused. The parakeet squawked. "Well, we always do that, actually. But it's more noticeable when you're travelling. Because there's a literal journey. A narrative arc. A beginning, a middle and an end."

"So where's the meaning here? Why witches?"

Smirks looked incredulous. "You really don't know?" I shook my head. He scrambled to the end of the mattress and reached into one of my panniers. He rummaged through some texts, chose one, placed it in my lap. *Pedophilia: A Modern-Day Witch Hunt*. "They're witches. And remember Lark's book. The law's the thing."

"The law's the thing wherein we'll catch the conscience."

"Yes. You think pedophiles are scapegoats for twenty-first-century anxieties."

"Yes."

"Like witches in the past."

"Sort of."

"There's a theme here. Of law and order. Controlling the un-known, the other."

"You think we can learn something from them?"

"Absolutely. Let's stay another day. Where else do we have to be?"

We were spinning our tires, I knew. Smirks was acting odd. He'd been different since Banff. Looser, funnier. Less serious. As though he'd stopped caring about something. It worried me. The bird bit the wires of his cage with his hard beak. An aggravating, painful sound. Smirks burrowed under the covers and once he had fallen asleep, I curled into him. A little spoon.

❂

The next afternoon, Smirks and I found ourselves with the witches hours north of Parkbeg in a mosquito-infested forest, our sweat mixing with the warm light rain. We'd been pulled out of bed at dawn. Mama had sung elaborate, convincing arias about her reoccurring nightmares. "You need to help me banish the bad dreams." I felt like I was dreaming myself. I slapped my skin and sprays of blood sprouted where bugs had been. Mama'd had the dream every few weeks for years. A dead baby visited her and told her to come to this forest and dig for his bones.

"We come even in the winter," Missy whispered. We traipsed over fallen logs and rotting leaves. "The baby tells her that until we find him, and move him, he won't rest." Smirks was sombre and made a mocking show of looking behind trees. I showed him my arms smeared with blood and he reached into his pocket and handed me a small bottle of bug repellent. Always prepared. We edged our way up a steep embankment and Mama panted heavily, stopping every minute or so to catch her breath. I noticed for the first time the magnitude of her physical heft, her stomach drifting beneath her dress like a wave. I imagined her having a heart attack right there in the woods, collapsing to the ground and tumbling down the hill, scratching her bare arms on broken branches and rocks as she rolled.

When we reached the top, Mama walked ahead of us toward a pond and then stood still, her chin tilted up toward the sky. She waited to hear something, to sense something, to be shown something. Walked a little farther. Missy stood next to me swatting mosquitoes away from her face. Mama ventured into the sludge and disappeared behind the tall grass. Smirks looked worried. "Where is she going?"

"The water," said Missy. "The baby is in the water." We waited and listened to the sounds of the forest. Smirks pulled his notepad out of his pocket and started writing, pausing once to spray bug repellent in his ears. The forest took me then. The mosquitoes' drone in my ear. The way the canopy shifted and scattered the light and the rain. Smirks with his pencil, always, like an insect's flight. I wanted Mama to bring something back, anything. Even if it weren't the bones of a baby, I wanted a story. We were not supposed to be there. We were supposed to be heading east. We were supposed to be riding, looking for the living, not the dead.

Smirks sidled up beside me and whispered. "Did you know it's illegal to pretend to practise witchcraft in Saskatchewan? To pretend. Isn't that funny?"

I nodded. Why was he so amused these days? I was waiting for Mama to bring something back. I prayed she would bring something back. The grey matter in my brain had galvanized and pushed outward, exacting control over the scene and willing bones to rise from the earth. But Mama came stumbling back through the bushes alone. Wet up to the shoulders. The ends of her hair plastered to her breasts. I thought of newspaper strips soaked in flour water, pasted to balloons for papier mâché. She was shrugging and empty-handed. Smirks went to her. "Nothing?"

"He's down there. I can feel him. I think we need a dredge."

Smirks leaned in closer. "Where do we get a dredge?"

"I don't know. I—"

"Let me try." Smirks took off his t-shirt and started undoing his pants. Held his wallet and notebook out to me.

Dazed, I took it. "You're not going in that pond."

"Why not?" He slipped through the bulrushes.

I followed him. "Smirks."

He looked over his shoulder. Wide, expectant face. Clear, open, unburdened. Happy. He laughed. "Julia. It's just a lark. Relax."

A lark. He waded into the swamp and I was hit with the noisome smell of rotting eggs. He raised his arms, squeezed them against his head, his hands clutched each other and he dove in. Missy ran up and stood beside me. "He's crazy."

"Not usually." We waited for him to emerge. He was under for almost a minute before he came splashing up in the centre of the pond, covered in weeds and mud. "Smirks!" I yelled. But he plunged back in.

Mama tugged on my shirt. "Why is he doing this?" Her voice had an edge. Panic? Fear? Smirks dredged the bottom like this, up and down, back and forth. Mama paced back and forth, her feet sinking into the wet ground. I smoked cigarettes to keep the mosquitoes away. "What's he got?" Mama asked. "What's he got now?" Missy watched her mother, lightly touching her port-wine stain as though it were braille. In about fifteen minutes, Smirks had covered the entire pond. He'd pulled up beer bottles, empty gas cans, lengths of rope. But no bones.

He joined us on the shore, filthy and stinking. "No baby, Mama."

Mama's eyes filled with tears. She slapped him across the face. Missy jumped toward her. "Mama!" She grabbed her arm. Smirks looked down at the ground.

Mama stuck her face in his. "Why would you do that? Why did you do that?"

Smirks wiped sludge from his body, shook his hair out like a dog. "I'm sorry."

I tossed his shirt at him. "Really?" He looked at me. "You don't seem sorry."

He laughed. "What am I sorry for, exactly?"

"You're an asshole," said Mama.

Missy stepped between them. "Wait, what's going on? I don't understand. He was trying to help, Mama."

Mama spat. "No, he wasn't."

Smirks pointed to the pond. "There's no baby there. You can move on. You're free."

But she couldn't move on. Where would she go? She panted, wrung her hands. Messy anger followed swiftly by remorse. Shame. She grabbed at her own neck. "I'm sorry I hit you."

"I'm sorry I didn't find a baby."

Mama shook her head. "I'll find him. I know it."

❂

The next day, Mama and Missy drove us to Redvers, the town where I had heard from Dirtbag years before, the town he might have moved to, or had at least stopped in, after Banff. They dropped us off at the town's entrance in front of a statue of a giant red-clad Mountie perched atop a giant horse. "The law!" Smirks said in greeting. "Julia, take a picture of us." I reached for his camera. "No, with your phone." He put his arms around Missy and Mama, and they stood beneath the maw of the horse, the frowning Mountie. Only Smirks smiled. He trotted over to look at the shot. "You should text that to Lark."

"Why?"

"She'll think it's funny." He pointed at the Mountie. "The law? The book? *You Can't Do That in Canada.*"

Mama put her hands on my shoulders. "Good luck finding who you're looking for." She hugged me.

"You too," I said. Mama hugged Smirks too, but I could tell she didn't want to. He'd upset her. His act of searching for the baby had been aggressive. Unwelcome. A mean-spirited suggestion that Mama was wasting her time. Mama stepped away from Smirks and looked to the road. Missy looked apologetic. We waved goodbye. Their rusty Jeep puffed west toward the ghost town.

Smirks smiled at me. "That was fun."

"You're acting strange."

"I'm happy. Can't a guy be happy?"

Not really, I thought. The air was flat and hot and even though it was the golden hour, when the sun's oblique angle should have lit the trees on fire, nothing shimmered. Everything stayed matte and muted. We pedaled as if on autopilot toward the campground we knew would be just around that corner and down that lane, even though we had no idea where we were. We could always find a campground. Sniff them out. They pulled at us with invisible drawstrings.

"Those ladies were so sad," said Smirks.

"Why?" Down the town's main drag, I slowed to pick up a copy of the local newspaper, *The Optimist*. I wanted a memento. Redvers marked the two-thousand-kilometre point, as well as the second town that Dirtbag had called me from. I stuffed the newspaper into my bar bag and we continued down the road.

"Just stuck. Delusional."

"Delusional?"

He looked at me. "They're looking for a dead baby Mama dreams about."

I shrugged. "They seemed happy to me."

When Dirtbag called from Redvers, I was fourteen years old. I had never left Harmony, was tied at the hip to Lark, and under the impression that Lark's mother, a sculptor from Latvia, was the coolest person in the universe. Her name was Sofia, and when she caught us doing something bad—raiding the kitchen cupboards after bedtime, trying on her costume jewellery without asking—she would throw her hands up in the air and laugh, shouting "Glasnost! Glasnost!" Which Lark told me was Latvian for "kids will be kids."

Sofia was Buddhist. In their home, everywhere I turned, I'd en-counter a blinking Buddha. His profile adorning the bathroom wall, loving and accepting me while I peed, so much serenity in the simple strokes of his eyelids. Or the little mini laughing Buddha she'd glued to the dashboard of her old Mazda. His belly protruding in front of the speedometer, his face dopey as if he'd just smoked a joint. I was a shy child, hesitant to perform the simplest tasks in front of grownups,

and whenever we climbed into her car, Sofia would shout my name—
"Jeeeeewlia!"—above the Beach Boys, drawing out the syllables as
though each one were important, and I would lean into the front seat,
praying she wouldn't notice the shaking of my hand as it reached toward the Buddha's belly and rubbed it for good luck. I'd feel silly at
first, desperate for the attention to shift off me, my whole body one
knot. "Keep rubbing!" Sofia trilled. And eventually an arabesque of
calm would unfurl within me, and the atoms of my body would feel
farther apart, and Sofia would sing along with the music. *I'm picking up
good vibrations. She's giving me excitations.*

Sometimes though, because she was a human being and subject
to the cloud-like nature of her own emotions—"they come, they go,
they come, they stay, hovering in the sky for days, no one can blow
them away, Julia, you must wait for them to dissipate on their own"—
sometimes Sofia felt cloudy. That was her word for it, and on those
days Sofia would take Lark and me on walks through Harmony, and
as we passed people in the street, Sofia would look directly in their
eyes and say, "I give you my love and compassion." She spoke loudly,
insisting that the clouds evaporated quicker if people returned her
eye contact. On these days Lark would trail behind her, mocking her
mother's actions, dramatizing Sofia's subtle bows and earnest namastes.
Lark would pull me close, whisper in my ear, a twist of anger in her
voice. "Buddhists aren't perfect, you know. They've attempted geno-
cide. Just like everyone else."

Back at their house, Sofia gave us exhaustive tours of her pottery
workshop and taught us how to throw bowls. I loved just the idea
of that—throwing bowls that didn't break. How disparate the movements of pottery. Against a thick wooden bench she would pound
the soft brown head of clay, then slap it onto the spinning turntable
where suddenly it liquefied, became spinning, swirling chocolate,
and Sofia's hands a magician's, forming shapes out of shapelessness
with the quirk of a thumb or the slide of an index finger. I was mes-
merized. She encouraged us to experiment at the wheel, her voice
over my shoulder like music, her soft instructions the chorus to a song:

"find the centre, find the centre, find the centre." Every attempt, failure or success, was placed on a gilded shelf behind a glass door on the far wall of her workshop, where it would stay until long after Lark and I had moved to Vancouver. Then, one day a burglar broke into that workshop, dismantled the cabinet and took the gilded shelves to sell. Sofia sent us photographs of our wobbly, childhood vases smashed to pieces across the workshop floor. "How wonderful!" she'd written joyously across the back. "A new beginning for us all!!!"

Sofia smoked us up for the first time after finding soda bottles full of her own homemade wine under Lark's bed. We'd siphoned it from her glass jugs, and planned to drink it at a barn party that weekend. "Ladies," Sofia said, dumping the fetid liquid down the kitchen sink along with our teenage dreams of drunkenness. "Don't start with booze. Booze is dirty. Booze is angry." She brought us into her pottery workshop and put Patti Smith on the stereo. She removed a joint from an urn on the top shelf, lit and inhaled deeply. When it was my turn I sucked at it like a straw, gulping the weed down. I felt the smoke spread out like a starfish, rays stretched into every corner of my body.

Ten minutes passed, but it felt like three hours. I felt my heart whirl on its axis like a spinning top. The workshop appeared to me in descending Tetris blocks. Where had I gotten all this extra time? It struck me that I might be punished for stealing Lark and Sofia's hours if I didn't apologize. I looked at Lark. Sounds were happening one at a time. One chord of music. One lyric. *Girl in white dress. Boy shoot white stuff.* Lark stood in the corner. Her laughter. Sofia behind me said my name, her voice sliding over the back of my neck and down the front of my shirt like a snake. Above was the music, as though it might fall on top of me. "I am so sorry for stealing your time," I whispered to Lark and Sofia. "I don't know why I took it. I didn't even use it, I just stood here."

"Oh, dear," said Sofia, turning the music off. "She took too much. Lark, sweetie, come here, look. She took too much."

Lark walked me home. Mom and Ralph were out and Sofia had thought I would sober up more quickly in my own bedroom. The canopy of trees above us blinked. Lark's voice sounded hollow, canned.

I couldn't tell if she was being nice or mean. I couldn't tell if every-thing had fallen apart, or if everything was perfect. The duality of all things revealed itself. I didn't think I'd ever be able to feel just one way ever again. I didn't like weed, I decided. And once I'd decided this, the colour of the trees popped brighter. The air smelled sweeter. A sum-mer evening, and the angling sunlight pooled in the grass for a few minutes, then left behind a shadow. "Nothing stays the same," I said. "Even this feeling."

Lark did a cartwheel in the middle of the road. "You sound like Sofia."

When I opened the front door to my house, I could smell the pasta sauce Mom and Ralph had heated up for dinner. Out the back window, I saw laundry hanging on the clothesline. A load of white towels, white panties. The telephone in the kitchen was ringing and the idea of speaking to someone excited me. What new thing could be said, with this new brain I had? I looked at the caller ID. An area code I didn't recognize. I knew it was Dirtbag. "It's Dirtbag."

"Julia, don't—" said Lark.

I picked up the receiver. "Hello?"

"Julia?"

"Yes."

"It's me."

"I know."

"How did you know?"

"Because my pussy got wet when you said my name." I heard a click. I waited. Dial tone. I turned to Lark and she had the funniest expression on her face. "He hung up."

She took the phone from my hand, put it back on the receiver. "Why did you say that to him?"

I had heard my sister's friend, a promiscuous eighteen-year-old, say something similar. About her pussy juice dripping onto a picnic table during outdoor sex. I hadn't thought about it. It just appeared in my mouth. I picked up the phone and hit redial. The ring drone buzzed in my ear like a bug. I started laughing. I laughed so hard I could barely see. No answer. I dropped the phone and walked over to the kitchen cupboards, opening one and slamming one so hard a screw knocked loose and the hinge fell off and the door slapped onto the counter, cracking the Formica, then fell to the floor with a boom.

That was the first time I saw the spots. The first time the anger rushed to my head like a fist, cracking blue, red and orange phosphenes—a Greek word that meant "light show"—into my eyes. When I told Mom about it later, she smiled and nodded. "The Prisoner's Cinema," she said. When inmates in the jail were kept in solitary confinement, they could be left in the dark for days at a time, causing the inmate to hallucinate colours bleeding out of the black. When you're stressed, she told me, the arteries in your brain dilate, causing rushes of blood, putting pressure on your optic nerve, creating spots of colour. "Don't worry about the light show, baby. It just means you're alive." My Internet search that evening for Dirtbag's phone number turned up Redvers, Saskatchewan, a town whose name I'd never heard. A town whose name sounded small and angry and possibly even fake.

"Like Dirtbag's heart," I'd said to Mom as she assessed the damage to the kitchen counter.

She laughed. "Oh, to be fourteen again." She took the money for the cupboard incident out of my allowance. All of this—her laughter, her blame—sparked an anger inside me, which Mom suggested I needed to expel, as though it were a demon. She encouraged me to punch pillows and bought me a rubber baseball bat to smash into the oak tree out back. The self-defence classes served as another outlet. Mom watched sometimes, hands clasped together. "Doesn't it feel good?"

I'd nod. "Good," I'd say. The wrong word, I knew even then. How it really felt was involuntary, the way I imagined a seizure would feel. Was this my only option? Exorcism by force? I never felt purified afterward, just exhausted. I knew the anger was still there, sleeping. It could wake at any time. If I didn't have the bat or a pillow within reach, I'd break something else. A porcelain doll. An ashtray. *Bad girl. Clean it up. Pay for it. Don't do it again. Get it out. Get it out. Get it out.*

❁

In Redvers, the campground evaded us, but we knew we'd find it. We cycled down a rutted road between white birch. To our left and to our right we passed three baseball diamonds, a football field, and one tiny, dilapidated school. Horse rings and lots full of tri-drives and excavators. The water tower loomed above and short, simple bungalows huddled below. Did Dirtbag hide behind one of these storm doors? Did he drive one of those oversized pickup trucks? Did he work at the sagging grain elevator, its four storeys tilting south, peeling paint, but still a formidable backdrop to this prairie town?

It was a long road to the campground. I remember thinking: why is this road so long? In small towns like Redvers, right off the highway, campgrounds were usually close to the turnoff, close to the gas station and the convenience store. Close to the road, because that's what people really wanted. People didn't come to Redvers to see the giant Mountie on the giant horse. Tourists weren't there to soak up the culture or partake in wilderness activities. People were there to eat and sleep, to do the things they had to do in order to keep moving. They had to be off the road just long enough to get back on the road again. Because what they really wanted to do was drive across Canada. Everyone wanted to drive across Canada.

For me, it was the pillow lava in Ontario. Just the name—pillow lava—sounded like the most exotic, sweetest fruit. Or perhaps a drug that promised something better and more salutary than heroin. Pillow lava. Two billion years ago, tongues of lava—tongues! Of lava!—were extruded from the tight-lipped, hot mouth of the earth and licked their way into the world. The tongues pushed into frigid ocean water, and their skin froze, like wet flesh to a metal pole in winter, while inside the tongue stayed molten, pressuring the skin like a blister until—pop! Thousands of popped blisters, lobate like puzzle pieces. Nature's first cobblestones, revealed when the ocean drifted elsewhere. I wanted to lie on a bed of pillow lava, curl my body into the Temagami greenstone belt, and fall asleep atop the oldest rocks on earth. Ancient, petrified mouth of the mantle.

Pedal

But in Redvers, there was nothing to see. And the road to the campground was endless, a narrowing promenade through a birch-tree corridor. We cruised slowly, my speedometer reading ten kilometres an hour, enjoying the empty road. And then we saw them, the children, up ahead maybe about a hundred yards, off the road, in a ditch, by the treeline. Their blonde hair flashed in the sunlight, and I remembered thinking: it looks like a mirage of fairies.

We got close enough to make them out. They were not fairies. Three boys, all white-blondes, all wearing faded, oversized t-shirts and ripped jeans. The oldest was maybe thirteen, the youngest eight, and the three obviously brothers, not only for their similar features but their comportment. The way they stood, their reaction to strangers. The boys eyed us with a sort of embryonic suspicion, the harsh looks of children just beginning to doubt the goodness of others. Dirty hands. Each boy's coated with chain grease from the youngest boy's bicycle. They stood on guard, watching us with frosty blue eyes.

Smirks pulled up. "Damn. Looks like your chain is pretty jammed in there." I saw the coach come out in him. "Need a hand?" The boys remained silent, shooting oblique glances at one another, eyes hardening into steel. Noses that curved down at the end like beaks. The youngest boy lifted his bicycle out of the ditch and leaned it toward Smirks. He kneeled down to the chain. It had lodged itself tight between the boy's cog-set and his seat-stay.

I handed the boy my hand-rag soaked in citrus soap. "For the grease," I said. He took it. "What's your name?" He looked to the oldest boy, who shook his head. The young boy looked back to his bike, his chest rising up and down quickly, and I realized that these boys did not speak—or did not choose to speak—English. As soon as I understood this, the oldest boy started talking in a foreign language, looking up at the sky. He could have been saying, "Looks like rain." But what were those words, that language? I'd heard it before, in a valley named after me, Julia Valley, in the country where Thierry was from, Switzerland. The language, Surmiran, meaning *above the wall*. He took me to Julia Valley because it was the most beautiful place he'd ever seen.

The trees there were so dense you could almost hear them. Feel them breathing. And the mountains, sheer concrete, rocketed up to the sky, dividing the land absolutely, and with the land the languages, so that a person living in Julia Valley might not understand a person living in Tiefencastel, only fifteen kilometres away. At least, that's what Thierry had told me, because he knew I was seduced by romance like that. The fourth official language of Switzerland, Rumantsch, a dying language, a descendant of vulgar Latin, spoken only in enclaves of the Alps by people who looked like gypsies.

The boys must have been tourists, but they looked unlike any European tourists I'd ever seen in Canada. These boys were poor, their bicycles rusted, and their faces distrustful. I wished I could re-member one word of the language, one phrase Thierry had taught me when were camping around the eastern outskirts of Switzerland, so close to Italy I imagined we could smell it. But I remembered nothing. I stared dumbly at the boys and each of them fidgeted, mut-tered, grew cagey. The older boy spoke again, words that sounded mean, though his brothers made no move to respond. My chest flut-tered. The situation focused in on itself and an edge of danger came into view.

Smirks freed the chain from the seat-stay and smiled widely, accus-tomed to his handiness garnering approval. But these boys seemed an-noyed, not grateful. I wondered where they were staying. Swiss tourists usually rented large motor homes and stayed in places like Banff and Jasper. Were they staying here, at the campground? Would we have to be with them all night? The older boy grabbed the bike from Smirks and handed it to the youngest. "You're welcome," I said, unwilling to believe that these boys didn't know the phrase "thank you" in English. The oldest coughed and looked at the ground, a string of black words falling from his mouth. He spat. The three boys stared. Smirks and I mounted our bikes and continued down the road. I looked over my shoulder. They stood, a row of three, watching us ride away. "Those kids are freaking me out."

Smirks laughed. "They're fine." But I could tell he was tense, too.

I looked over my shoulder again. The boys had climbed on their bikes and were trailing us.

"They're following us."

"They're fine."

But they were catching up. I didn't know if I should go faster or slow down. I felt as if I was pedalling underwater. Everything was silent. The sun on the edge of the horizon cut a gold knife through the scene, illuminated the boys' white hair like halos. The oldest boy flew ahead of us, and the two others flanked us, creating a crude, roving triangle.

"What are you doing?" I asked. My voice shook. The oldest spoke again, asking a question, the same question, over and over. The children beside us laughed, manic, looking in all directions, behind, ahead and beside them. They were keeping an eye out. They were planning to hurt us, otherwise why would they care who saw? The oldest continued to ask his question. What did those words mean? My chest hurt and his brothers laughed and the fear swept through me, a vertiginous panic. "Smirks," I said. They wanted money. They must have wanted our money. But Smirks was looking at the oldest boy, who had reached into his pocket and pulled out a rock. It was a smooth rock, the size of a heart. If we died there, who would find us? We never wore our helmets once we'd turned off the highway. We thought being off the highway meant we were safe. How sweet it was to take off our helmets after seven hours of captivity. How sweet everything had been, before these boys came along.

The oldest boy's voice got louder and deeper, and his face grew older, and what I had initially imagined to be a thirteen-year-old child was aging, in front of me, into a man. I tried to turn around on my bicycle, a move of blind panic, but my panniers threw me off balance. I crashed into the pavement, and as I crashed I heard a shot ring out in the air so loud it must have been the rock. The rock must have smashed into my head. I lay on the ground. My eyes closed and I thought: if it isn't over yet, it will be soon.

But then, my face to the pavement, I heard the soft whoosh of tires speeding back toward the highway. No one spoke. They just rode. The vulgar Latin ceased. They were gone. I heard an eagle screech. Then nothing. Smirks above me, nodding. A gun in his hand. He nodded frantically in my direction. "You were right." Nodding. "You were right. They were going to hurt us."

I scrambled to my feet, staring at the pistol. Small and dainty. Old-fashioned looking. A gun. "Why do you have a gun?" For bears and cougars? Where had it been? He'd been carrying it all this time?

"I've had this gun for years." He opened his bar bag and placed the gun inside.

"But why do you have it here?"

"What if I hadn't?"

"I can't believe you have a gun."

"Let's go."

"I need a minute." My legs trembled. I looked in the direction of the kids, toward the highway, but they were gone. I waited for someone to show up: a scared farmer. A cop. The giant Mountie from the statue. But no one came. My legs solidified and I climbed back on my bike. We rode forward, sensing the children were gone. A lightness in the air, as though the gunshot had cleared the sky like thunder. Had those children existed at all? Preternatural and nightmarish, a vision conjured collectively by the two of us, to reveal what had, up until that point, remained hidden: the gun. I thought of Thierry. What would Thierry say? He would say this: no story with a gun has ever ended well.

We finally reached the campground. It was empty. It was our custom for Smirks to roll over to the taps and fill our water bags while I unpacked the cookware. But I wasn't hungry. I tried to think of things to say to him, but nothing came. The silence between us felt impenetrable. I'd held a gun once, last summer in Fort Nelson. On a beach with a man named Rusty. We were both drunk, and he had driven me there to teach me how to shoot. He stood behind me and put his hand on my belly. Whiskey breath in my ear. Told me that when he could feel my heartbeat in my stomach it meant I was ready to pull the trigger.

I felt his dick get hard against me. I locked the front sight in between the rear sights. Hit three empty beer cans in a row, and then missed the next thirty.

The Optimist newspaper stuck out of my bar bag and I opened it and sat down on the picnic table. Beneath me, peeling red paint pressed into my thighs like ragged fingernails. I read the headlines, but none of them mattered. I was supposed to call Dirtbag, but it could wait. I wanted to get rid of the gun. Where could we safely dispose of a gun? The Mountie statue at the entrance to Redvers must have signified an RCMP station. We could go there. We could ask them to take our gun for us. We could make it their problem. Smirks kept staring at me.

"I had a relationship with a girl, once," he said. I looked at him. He had an air of confession around him. He sat down on the grass in front of the picnic table, so I had to look down at him. I didn't move. "I was twenty-five and she was ten." But this was not a confessional. I was not there to take in his sins. I was no expert. There would be no punishment. All I could do was listen. "I worked at a basketball camp coaching kids. For some reason, I was assigned to the girls' team. I didn't ask to be. I'd never mentioned any preference. Of course, at that time, I put myself in those sorts of situations willingly, hoping to be placed with girls." He looked me in the eye. "Her name was Maria."

I tried to imagine I was talking to Lark, and that Lark was telling me about a man she used to love. "What was she like?"

"Funny. She was a really funny kid." It made him happy to remember her. "Her mother was a professor at the university. She'd given Maria this catch-all book of philosophers for children. Confucius, Descartes. Nietzsche. It had a purple cover, green font. *For Thinking Kids,* it was called. She carried it around, read it on the bench during basketball practice. I remember the first thing she said to me. 'Nietzsche was misunderstood,' she said. I found the line later in her book. But she really did get it. She said to me once, 'People thought he was bleak, but he was actually really flamboyant.'" He looked at me. "Somebody must have told her that, right? That Nietzsche was flamboyant?"

"Or somebody told her he was bleak."

"I suppose. I suppose she could have figured it out for herself. She was very bright."

I wanted to ask so many questions, like: What did she look like? What did you love about her? What did you do to her? Where is she now? What's her phone number? But I could ask none of those things. I was the enemy. I was the person whom Smirks did not want to face, the person trying to figure out what was happening to these women, later in their lives, how they had absorbed the molestation into their bodies. Did it curdle inside them? Make a part of them rotten. Was there forever one piece of them sad and broken? Or could it sometimes be good? Could it sometimes be right? Could it sometimes be better than if it had not been?

Of course, Smirks hoped he had made her life better. Because he loved her. And that's what you want to do when you love someone. "She had behavioural issues. Problems at home. You can tell. Right away."

"Tell what?"

"If there are problems at home," he said.

Was that true? I thought back. My grade one teacher, Mrs. Cartwright, asked me to stay after class sometimes. Everyone would leave, and I would walk up to her big tidy desk, and she would have my latest book report sitting in front of her. She would hand it to me and tell me to smell it. The first time, I had no idea what to expect. I thought maybe it smelled like candy. So, I smelled it and all I smelled was paper.

And she told me that was very disturbing, because the book report actually smelled very strongly of cigarettes. "Do you know someone who smokes, Julia?" Both my mother and Dirtbag did. "Do they smoke in the house?" Where else would they smoke? In someone else's house? "I want you to ask your parents to please not smoke around your homework. When I brought that—" she pointed to the sheet in my hands—"out of my bag last night, it stunk up my entire living room." I stared at her. She had big brown eyes like marbles. "It was really quite disgusting." I guess she wanted me to apologize, but I didn't know that then. Three more times she did that in the course of the year.

*Pedal*

The year Mom was in and out of the hospital for broken ribs and teeth. The year Dirtbag was in and out of my bedroom for sleepy-time story hour. But the only thing Mrs. Cartwright could smell was the smoke.

I shook my head at Smirks. I didn't think you could tell, right away, if there were problems at home. "Children are just smaller people. They can hide things. They can hide things as well as any adult."

"Children are not just little adults, Julia. If they were, they would come out of the womb speaking." Smirks tore at the grass. "They have to be taught things. They have to learn things before they can be adults." He stretched his legs out. "That is what is so wonderful about them. They aren't adults at all."

I thought about this. "So what were her problems at home?"

"From what I could glean, her parents weren't abusing her, per se. They were just ignoring her. Which is terrible for a kid. She never said it, exactly, of course. Kids don't have the language for that yet. That's what makes them so helpless. They don't know what's being done to them. It's just the water they're swimming in."

"So how could you tell?"

"To get a camp counsellor's attention, she would do one of three things. She would be mean. Like call them stupid or even hit them. Or she would act erratically, like throw her book at my feet, and then pick it up and throw it down again. If I asked her what she was doing, she would look at me like I'd smacked her." Smirks got quiet.

"And the third thing?"

"She would flirt. With me. I know it's taboo to suggest that a ten-year-old girl can flirt, but of course she could. Everyone can. Even children are capable of playing at love."

"Like adults."

"No. Adults know they're doing it. Children are just learning while they do it."

"How did she flirt with you?"

"She liked me right away. Probably because I understood her behaviour. I treated her as an equal. When a child acts out, most adults get angry. But with Maria, I just asked her what was wrong, like I would

178

an adult. Of course she couldn't really tell me what was wrong. Kids don't have that vocabulary. If we think someone is ignoring us, we can say it. 'You're ignoring me and it hurts my feelings.' But a child doesn't understand those causes and effects. They just feel emotion. So I would talk to her about her philosophy book. She asked a lot about Nietzsche's *amor fati*. Do you know it?"

"The love of fate," I said.

"The idea that idealism is dishonest, and the only truth is to view everything that happens, even suffering, as good. Even beautiful."

"And Maria liked this idea?"

"She was confused by it. The idea of suffering. She talked about it all the time. Tried to figure it out. Asked questions. About homeless people. About kids beaten by their parents. About prostitutes killed by Johns. She couldn't figure out how to see it as beautiful." Smirks stopped speaking and ripped at the grass. I waited. "She wanted to understand the philosophy, because her mother taught philosophy." He spread his hands wide and pressed them into the earth. "Children want to please the adults they love."

"Adults want to please the adults they love."

"No." He looked at me. "Adults want to please themselves."

I wanted him to tell me everything, particularly whether or not they'd been physical. But these facts were untouchable, it seemed. Locked in the adytum of his memory, as if revealing them to me, saying them out loud, would in itself cause damage. He didn't speak again and I thought he was finished. I climbed down from the picnic table. He said, "We spent the summer together. Three months. And then, in the fall, she had a brain aneurysm." He looked up at me. Voice cracking. "She died." I sat back down. He was quiet for a long time. Crickets chirped. "If she had grown up, what would her life have been like?"

"There's no way to know."

"Many experts would disagree."

"Experts, schmexperts. How do they know?"

"She would have hated me," he said. I knew this was not necessarily true. But maybe it was better for him to believe it. Smirks stood, brushing grass off his lap. We weren't going to eat that night. We each set up our own tent and crawled in wordlessly. At some point I fell into a dreamless sleep.

❂

I woke up the next morning to find that Smirks had left. His tent was gone, his gear was gone, his bike was gone, and he was gone. I paced up and down the campsite, calling his name. He wouldn't leave me alone. He couldn't do that, not now. Any minute he would peek his head around that corner. *Gotcha.* The sky was clear blue and mocking. I stood where his tent had been, tried to sense his heat. I replayed last night's events in my mind. Eventually, the realization that he'd abandoned me surfaced in my mind like a repressed memory. Surprising, but inevitable. Did he go east or west? Would he go home to Vancouver, or would he keep travelling on? My insides plummeted fast toward the earth, while my body stayed upright. From the outside, I imagined I looked very still. Unmoved. Fine. But inside I was falling away. What would I do without him? I didn't want to be alone.

I sat down on the ground and my bike tipped over, crashing onto the cement patio of our campsite. I needed to tell Lark. I opened my laptop and hugged my knees. Activated Skype. Her name with the green light beside it. She was online. Probably working on a story for *Flare*. After one ring, she picked up, and I told her everything while she sat in her apartment in Vancouver, blowing cigarette smoke into the screen. She barely blinked, except when I mentioned the gun, at which point she gasped and clutched at her throat. When I finished, she butted out her cigarette. Lit another one.

"This is part of your journey. You know he went east. So go. Just ride. Follow him. This is the hard part. Everyone thought it was going be the Rockies, but it's now."

"How are you?"

"I'm fine." She took a long drag from her cigarette. I did the same. "Just waiting for my period."

"You're late?"

"Not yet," she said. Her tone indicated a change in subject. "I've been researching this story on fast-fashion. Consumable clothing. Sweatshops. Holy fuck, is it depressing." She put her cigarette down on her ashtray, pressed her fingers to her temples, massaging first her head and then her eyes, pressing her palms deep into her sockets. I realized I wasn't the only one with a problem.

"Are you okay?"

"You know, we eat clothes now." Her eyes were damp. Blotchy skin. "We eat cheap, poorly made clothes. And then we shit them out."

I didn't want to talk about clothes. I wanted to talk about Smirks. "Lark—"

"The woman I interviewed yesterday wore this beautiful knit sweater by a local Vancouver designer. Perfect linen pants. The sweater was three hundred dollars and the pants were three hundred dollars and she had owned both pieces for three years and wore them at least three days a week and they looked fresh off the shelf. When you wear quality clothes, it changes everything. It changes the way you look, for one. You look like you care about something. Like you care about yourself. And about the world. And when you look like you care about something, and you act like care about something, guess what? You actually start to care. You've willed a conscience inta bein.'"

You don't think I willed it into being. Did it?

Banff. Smirks and Lark fucking on the hotel bed. Smirks with a gun. Why did Smirks have a gun?

On the road adjacent to the campground, a procession of dump trucks drove toward the highway. Ten massive vehicles, diesel engines blasting, rumbling like beasts. I pointed to my ears. "I can't hear you." But she kept talking. I started to gather my things. I had to leave. I had to find him.

Lark shouted. "Why don't people understand this? Why do people say, 'Ugh, fashion? So superficial. Who *cares* about clothes? Who cares about what we wear? I'd rather think about politics.' Are you kidding me, morons? Are you fucking kidding me? What do you think politics are?" Her face filled the screen. Imploring me.

I froze, tent half disassembled. "What do *I* think politics are?"

"Clothes are the first decision we make in the day and the last part of our identity we cast off at night. Clothes don't matter? You're kidding me. Clothes are one of the only things that actually do matter. They cover our body. We wear them." She sat back in her chair. Breathed deep. Softer, now. "We wear them." She cocked her head, listened to the riot of revving engines in the background. "What is that noise?"

"Are you done? With the clothes?" I shovelled some granola into my mouth. Stuffed the bag into my pannier. "I'm kind of in crisis here."

"I'm sorry, Julia. But this isn't a problem. Don't start wallowing."

"It's not a problem?"

"No. It's just what's happening. You are close to something. Go find Smirks. Go find Dirtbag, or whoever it is. Just don't stay still. And do not go backwards."

We said goodbye to each other. I loaded my panniers onto my bike. Out of the corner of my eye, I kept seeing snatches of blonde hair. I kept hearing swells of Rumantsch. I looked at my watch. On the relatively flat surface of the Prairie, with the tailwind we had that day, Smirks could travel at approximately thirty-seven kilometres per hour outside the slipstream, which meant I could travel at thirty. I had no idea what time he left, but I knew he would probably stop in the next town to get food for the day. I looked at the map. Pipestone. I would bike to Pipestone. I would find him.

The road unrolled before me. A blur of CN trains, purple wheat, salt fields. I tried to listen to music on my iPhone, but the sound of piano and strings in my ear frightened me. Too strange. Ear buds like walls in my cochlea and I worried he would yell my name and I would miss it. All I could see was pavement. All I could count were the dashes of road lines. They blinked at me like animals. I was on a treadmill, cycling in one place, while Saskatchewan rushed backward, behind me. I searched for Smirks in gas stations, grocery stores, churches. He evaded me.

"Have you seen this man?" I held up his photograph. Smirks. Every time I looked at his picture I wanted to cry. He was much too beautiful to be a pedophile. He was the perfect pedal-phile. His hair was the colour of the gold flecks in Lark's eyes. His hair was the colour of a wheat field in Pipestone at dusk in early June. His hair was the colour of the third carriage back on the freight train that followed me. Every time I thought of the train, it appeared, above or below me, pleached into the landscape like a roving ribbon. The conductor waved at me. Hello again! Hello! The third carriage back was the exact colour of my lost friend's hair. And in the photograph I had to show he was smiling, which he didn't often do.

"You wouldn't see him smiling," I said to the gas station attendant, a dusty man with coal-black eyes and a chin that looked like a block of wood. "He'll look more like this." I showed him a picture of Smirks I'd taken with my phone. The photo was of his profile and in it he was in Banff National Park, staring at a mountain that had been decimated by a forest fire. The trees growing there were bare and withered and grey, but if you squinted, they shone like silver scar tissue against the snow. The sun and the water at their feet. I thought: how tragic, how devastating, this black welt across this mountain's back, surely caused by humans. Maybe a cigarette butt. An unattended campfire.

But Smirks knew better. "This fire was intentional." And I'd looked for the placard I figured he must have been reading, but there wasn't one. "It's called prescribed burning." He looked at me and shrugged. "I've been using it as a metaphor in a story I'm working on." Oh, right. Smirks was a writer. He worked on stories. He crafted other worlds out of concrete images—ash—and their abstract concepts—loss. "Trees absorb carbon dioxide and become, essentially, living fossil fuels. The longer forests grow unrestrained, the hotter and more destructive their potential fires."

"We destroy some trees now to save more trees in the future."

"Yes. And some cone trees have evolved over the millennia to require the heat from fire to germinate."

"Another male species just burning to spread its seed," I quipped. Silence from Smirks. I looked back to the grey forest. The bald trees, limbs twisted and crippled, looked like metal sculptures shaped by an artist trying to express something sad. You couldn't see the trees in the photograph of Smirks, but you could sense them.

The gas-station attendant shook his head. Each one shook his head.

From Manitoba, I called April. I had just passed St. Claude and was angling toward Winnipeg. Though the myth of the flat Prairie had long since been dispelled, I still felt displaced being able to see miles and miles ahead of me. As if I'd landed on a different planet. A smaller planet. Like if I could only bike fast enough, I would finally reach the horizon, and tip over to the other side. However many times a day I wanted to, I could watch the sun set.

"That's from *The Little Prince*," said April. April used to read *The Little Prince* to me when we were young. We'd huddle together on her bed when Mom and Dirtbag fought, or screwed, or both. When I recalled those times, it wasn't the fighting or the rape that I envisioned. It was the walls of April's bedroom. Dirtbag had insisted on adorning them with Manet and Renoir. While she read to me the heavy, lamenting words of Saint-Exupéry, I stared at the mournful eyes of the barmaid at the Folies-Bergère. Years later, when I started studying memory in my psychology courses, I remembered those paintings in April's room, which had disappeared when Dirtbag did. I Googled the barmaid at the Folies-Bergère, and discovered the woman in the painting was in fact not sad at all. She was tired, a bit pissed off, somewhat resigned. But I saw nothing as weak as sadness. What else from my childhood had I misremembered?

"Manet wasn't a full Impressionist, Julia," April said. "He was a Realist with a wound that bled *into* Impressionism. You always bring up art when you're trying to make me forget what we're talking about."

Did I? It wasn't intentional. Anyhow. *The Little Prince* was, ostensibly, a book about art. The story began with the narrator's inability to communicate, through his art, his sense of wonder. I was ashamed that Smirks had left me, that I wasn't able to keep him near. "Has he been writing on your trip?" asked April. He had. He wrote every night. He wrote every time we stopped on the side of the highway for a granola bar and a cigarette. He wrote as I lay on the banks of the icy rivers that crashed through the Rockies flowing west or flowing east, depending on which side of the continental divide we had paused. On the divide itself, cresting the spine of the Rockies, the rivers flowed in all directions eventually draining into the oceans. I imagined squatting on the divide and peeing. Which way would it trickle down?

"Or straddle the divide and feel the direction of your blood," said April.

"My menstrual blood?"

"Yeah."

The Continental Divide was also called the Great Divide. When Smirks and I passed over it, he stood on one side and I stood on the other and we set up the automatic timer on his camera and took a picture. April laughed. "The Great Divide. Therapist and mental patient." April had this theory that all artists experienced some degree of mental illness. Fixation was a form of nervous tic, she argued, and in order to be an artist, you must have some high degree of fixation. "Imagine, Julia," she would say, "imagine sitting in a room for hours a day inventing an imaginary world! That's insane! Well, not insane. But anti-social, yes. Detached. Dissociated from reality."

"This, coming from the art therapist."

"The art I counsel intends to release the patient from the fixation. The art does not intend to replace reality, but act as a key to the door of reality."

"This, coming from the artist."

I didn't tell April about the Dirtbag diary, the journal full of Dylan Thomas poetry, because, surely, this would only prove her position that all artists are mentally ill. Was Dirtbag an artist? He did, allegedly, according to Mom, write his own poetry, his own fiction. But no one had ever found it. *Look behind the Manet,* a voice whispered in my head. *Behind the trapeze artist's feet at the Folies-Bergère.* Since Smirks had left, the voices were getting louder. "I'm telling you, Julia," April continued, "he's probably about to kill himself. And if you do happen to find him before that moment, if you do get lucky and stumble upon him before he ends it all? Tell him to stop writing and start living. Tell him about the men you know who went down that tortured-soul road. And tell him how it ended."

"First I have to find him." How stupid I had been to have no contingency plan. Who to call in case of emergency? I had no idea. I supposed I could have contacted one of Smirks' friends in Vancouver, but I felt that would be a huge violation of his privacy. I knew most of them did not know the nature of his vacation, whom he was with, where he was going. It was normal for his friends to have no idea where he was. It was normal for his parents not to hear from him for months. Silence wouldn't be any cause of alarm for his coterie back home, especially now he was on the road. So where did my responsibility lie? Should I contact someone about the runaway? The pistol-packing pedophile?

"No. Just look for him. That's where your responsibility lies," April said. Smirks was like the little prince. How April and I had envied him as children! His rootlessness, his liberty. He had no parents, how lucky! The freedom to move from planet to planet, visiting kings and geographers and lamplighters and drunkards. The ability to *leave* the drunkard. He drinks because he is ashamed and is ashamed because he drinks. Let the drunkard drink alone, little prince, there are one million other worlds to see, lessons to learn, artists to inspire. Anything essential is invisible to the eyes, anyway. "Keep looking for him," said April.

In gas stations, I held up Smirks' picture to fat women scratching lotto tickets behind counters. I held the photo up to brown men wielding wrenches with grease-stained fingers. I held it up to children, apparently parentless, scrambling amok in the grassy fields beside parking lots, where families let their car-crazy kin run wild and their car-crazy dogs pee freely. "Have you seen this man? He's riding a bicycle like mine." Every last one of them shook their head no.

At nighttime I hurried to set up my tent. I hadn't told Smirks, but the newspaper article he had read to me in Thompson, Saskatchewan, had haunted me. Coyotes there were such a problem that the government was offering a $20 bounty for every wild dog killed. For proof of carnage, one had to submit the severed paw of the dead animal.

Front leg, left paw. Smirks was left-handed. I couldn't help envision this process. The bullet entering the animal. The body collapse. The hunter grasping its paw, the most slender and smooth part of the coyote, thin and downy like a child's wrist, miniaturized in the giant, rough hand of the human. And the hacksaw biting into the flesh and then bone, the sound it would make. It seemed ghastly to me, this sanctioned massacre. But it was necessary. Coyotes had been sneaking into farmer's fields and destroying their livestock. One woman told of her sheep being eaten by a coyote in a particularly macabre fashion: six of her purebred ewes had had their udders sliced open around the edges with the precision of a surgeon. The contents had been removed—eaten—and the skins of the udders left hanging from the torsos of the dead ewes. "Ewe," I'd said to Smirks. My pun went unacknowledged.

After he left, in my tent alone at nighttime, I dreamt of the footless, dead coyotes. I saw them reanimate, their limp bodies rising, their stumped legs oozing, scraping on the ground, leaving streaks of gritty blood where their footprints should have been. I dreamt of Smirks' gun, cold and heavy in my hands, aimed at the circling amputees. But I was unable to pull the trigger. My finger was poised but wouldn't engage. My eyes fixated on those bloody stumps. Snarling dogs surrounded by flies. Their lifeless bodies slinking, skulking, toward me.

Part 3

Baby

I'd been alone for four days, but it felt like much longer. I needed external stimulation, some noise and some bustle. I needed to see crowds of other humans doing other human things, like arguing and sneezing and eating food from McDonald's. Also, the spasm in my back made it difficult to ride. The pain had started in my lumbar region and radiated north, culminating in a pinch at the nape of my neck. It felt as if every time I looked up, someone grabbed me there and squeezed. I'd first noticed the discomfort when we left Banff, but had ignored it. Now the pain had grown so strong that it took over. I couldn't think of anything else out there on the road alone. I'd promised myself I'd stick to the back roads, knowing Smirks would avoid the cities. But heading east along Route 2, the road signs drew me north toward Winnipeg.

I snaked my way into the city. The sounds of demolition and construction comforted me, intoxicated me: jackhammers and chainsaws and sanders. The gruff, expedient shouts of men. Do this. Drive there. Stop that. Traffic lights. Enchanted by the traffic lights. Never noticed how huge they were. I sat in crowded intersections letting the signals pass by. Green. Yellow. Red. Green. Breathing in the steam and buzz of engines and exhaust. Marvelling at the colours, bigger than headlights, hanging from the sky.

On the rural Canadian roads I had stood out, marring the landscape, a conspicuous intruder, invasive species. But in Winnipeg, gridlocked city, I blended in. Faded. Lost myself. But the pain in my back pushed me forward. I knew I needed to find a bike shop to adjust the height of my handlebars. I could do it myself, I had the tools, but not the motivation. The first two or three flats I'd had to change and gear cables I'd had to adjust had thrilled me. Endowed me with a sense of accomplishment and control. But that energy had left. I wanted to pass Shelley and some money to a professional. The massive sporting goods store in the distance, corporate and generic, beckoned me like a cathedral. I pulled into the parking lot and took in its size. Roof as high as a warehouse, its walls spread so far apart you could run from end to end and lose your breath. What decadence, what wanton anonymity. There, I was just another cyclist heading home from work. No grand journey. No hunting down demons from my past. No lost pedophile with whom I had fallen stupidly in love. I could be from anywhere. I could be from Winnipeg.

The skinny teenager eyed me from behind his thick, shiny glasses. "You're not from Winnipeg, are you?" He removed the head tube from my crossbar. "Where'd ya come from?" I couldn't see his eyes because they were obscured by the glare of the fluorescent lights.

I fiddled with a rack of handlebar accessories that hung beside me. "Vancouver." Turning away from him, I pretended to be very interested in what they had to offer in the department of bike bells.

"Oh! Cool! I just fixed up the bicycle of another Vancouverite yesterday."

My fingers froze in front of the rack. I looked at him. The white glare of his lenses flashed.

"Same bike, actually. Maybe you know him?" He laughed, as if this were improbable.

I reached into my pocket and pulled out the photo. "This guy?"

He stood up and took the photo. "Yeah! That guy!" He looked at me and faltered, realizing just a moment too late that there had been a reason I didn't know where he was. A reason we were no longer together. A reason Smirks had left me. He handed the picture back to me and continued working on my head tube.

Something struck me, knocked me off balance. I gripped the counter, leaned toward him. My head flooded. I lied. "It's an emergency."

He looked up at me. "I'm sorry."

"Do you have any idea which way he went?"

He sighed, wrenching my new, higher crossbar into place, the one that was going to straighten my back and eliminate the pinching in my neck. He frowned. "No."

He was lying too. "You do."

"I shouldn't—"

"You should."

"It's really not my place."

"I'm pregnant. I need him."

He took off his glasses. "Jesus." His eyes were wide and blue. He was a sweet kid, and I had shocked him. "I took his bike apart for him. He asked for directions to the Greyhound station. I saw him write on the bike box. 'Toronto.'"

I reached out and put a hand on the boy's wrist. "Where is the Greyhound station?" My thumb touched the articular disk of his ulna, that dainty ball of bone that separates the forearm from the hand. Another part of the body I had to look up in the dictionary because I'd fallen in love with somebody's. Thierry's ulna. I used to press my thumb into it as if it was a button, and he would make a sound with his mouth like a robot. In that mammoth bike shop in Winnipeg, quite unexpectedly, a fit of homesickness swept through me. My stomach curdled and I missed Thierry's ulna then so sharply and hotly that I felt my own limb had been removed, sawed-off at the wrist, tossed away. "Just take it apart."

He looked at his wrist.

"The bike. Can you take it apart and pack it up?"

The Greyhound was full. Diverse clusters of people had hopped on at different junctions and the bus felt lived in, homey, thick with fast friendships, instant community. Passengers compared travel times, number of days without sleep, amounts of processed foods.

"I've been here since Calgary!"

"Yeah? Try Nelson, motherfucker! I don't even know what day it is."

Chocolate bar wrappers littered the aisle and the scent of toilet chemicals lingered in the back of the bus. Lithe, dirty children crawled on top of their parents, reaching for their iPads, their cellphones. A group of senior ladies in shiny blue baseball jackets chanted sports cheers. A cluster of beautiful healthy teenagers scattered around me. They spoke mellifluous Spanish and sang American pop songs and wore fluorescent necklaces and bracelets as if they were headed to Mardi Gras. Water bottles full of juice and rum passed back and forth across the aisle, and the teenagers shouted and laughed above the chronic wheezing of the bus engine. I inhaled their sweet, drunk breath when they leaned over me. I felt their liquor buzz behind my eyes and in my belly.

A girl with a wide face and soupy brown eyes, spiral ringlet locks, looked at me. Pulled an extra bottle from her backpack and kneeled next to me. A thick wave of her hair fell onto my arm. "You want?"

"Thank you." I took it and drank deeply.

"Keep it!" She had a languorous smile. Gratitude and alcohol flooded in. My body sank into the booze and my anxiety around Smirks softened, just a bit. I hid my bottle from the others so they couldn't see how quickly I was drinking. I did everything fast: ate, smoked, drank, biked. Made decisions. A bus all the way to Toronto. Goodbye, Canada. Goodbye, road trip.

We entered the rocky hills of Northern Ontario and I realized with a start that I would not see the pillow lava. I would not get to rest my head on the fossil of a tongue of lava. I'd be three cycling weeks closer to Kingston, Ontario. Three weeks closer to Dirtbag. Or what was left of Dirtbag. Or all I would ever know of Dirtbag. That made me feel a bit faint. I'd never been sure if I'd make it all the way to Kingston. Kingston, where it was illegal to take worms from a park without permission from the town. Mythical land of Kingston, with the royal street names and the ivy on the university brick. The famous old prison. Had Dirtbag ever made it in to that prison? When I arrived in Toronto, I'd be three days by bicycle away from Kingston. By embarking on this bus trip, I'd jettisoned two thousand kilometres from my cycling. Twenty days.

I'd catch Lark in Toronto. Unless her plans had changed. I texted her. "Have fun in T dot this weekend. Why are you going again?" I watched my iPhone for her ellipse. It appeared within seconds. "Goya's fashion show."

"I love his frescoes," I texted.

"Goya from last Canada's Project Runway! Debuting Fall Collection at Pride. Floral vanguard." More ellipses. "Any news from Smirks?"

"Nope."

No response.

I pressed my head into the back of my seat and bit my lip. I tried, very hard, to contain my exultation, to ignore it, to pretend I didn't feel it. I should feel ambivalent about cutting over a quarter off my trip. But I didn't. I'd been dreading Northern Ontario alone. Cycling deaths occurred on those tortuous roads through the Canadian Shield. It was through the Canadian Shield that a person needed to carry food portions for more than one day, just in case. It was through the Canadian Shield that one really grokked how big Canada was. *Can you grok it, Julia?* I heard my mother whisper. My mother had used the verb *grok* liberally and, despite her loyalty to the true-crime genre, remained insistent that *Stranger in a Strange Land* was her favourite novel of all time. To grok meant, literally, to drink in, and figuratively, to love, to understand, to empathize with. *Do you bear Fair Witness, Julia?* I could hear my mother whisper. Again, in homage to the novel, Fair Witness being a profession invented by Heinlein. A Fair Witness' job was to observe and record exactly, without extrapolating or assuming. I wanted to bear Fair Witness to Smirks. Somebody had to. I was grateful to him for giving me an out. The perfect excuse to skip Northern Ontario. My pride would never let me admit that I was too weak or too afraid or too lazy to do it myself. Now I could just blame it on Smirks. *Smirks left. I had to chase him.*

The Spanish kids had all turned in their seats and were looking past me out the back windows, exclaiming and pulling out cameras. Behind me was the most beautiful sunset of our bike tour, maybe the most beautiful sunset I'd ever seen. The sky swelled a hot tangerine-orange against massive purple trees and a fiery red lake. The colours were shocking, overbearing, and soon everyone on the bus had turned to watch the western sky simmer. iPhones snapped pictures that would translate nothing. I wished for Smirks' fancy camera, and then I wished for Smirks. For my bicycle, for the road. Why was I on a bus? I should be on the road with that sunset. Smirks would watch it until the sky turned dark. My stomach turned. I had left the road and missed the most beautiful sunset of my trip. What did it mean? Did I make the wrong choice? Was I doomed?

The girl with the wide face grabbed my wrist. "It's so beautiful, no?"

"But I'm missing it."

She laughed. She pointed outside. "It's right there!" Shook her curls. "We are so lucky!"

I looked back to the sky, already a different colour, already fading. "I missed it."

The girl frowned. "How can you miss a sunset?" She laughed again. Turned to her friend, a tall boy—no, a man, at least eighteen years old—with black curls that fell into his eyes. She said something to him in Spanish. He smiled and reached over to me, clinking his bottle to mine.

"*Salud!*" He pressed his bottle to his thick pink lips and took a long swig and I watched the bottle's rim sink into his juicy mouth. He kept his eyes on mine. I felt a twinge deep in my stomach. The girl laughed again. They were so happy. They didn't think anything was wrong. I envied people like that. I sank back into my seat and willed gratitude. Gratitude, at least, for the shrinking of the sky. The encroachment of treetops and mountaintops. I didn't know how much more infinity I could stand, that endless prairie ceiling, like an eye that just opened and opened, wider and wider, seeing everything. The Ontario sky sizzled around the edges. Fat eastern clouds in front of us puffed up like fresh bruises. I finished my rum, every now and then feeling the eyes of the boy—the man, the young man—on me. I curled my body toward him and eventually fell asleep.

❂

In Ontario, the trees and the hills contained the sunlight like the walls of an oven. The bus's air conditioning had broken down that morning, and I was sick with heat. Sitting on a moving vehicle, flying up hills and around bends through which I would otherwise have crawled on my bicycle made me feel like a character in a video game. Speed had become a special feature, a novelty, but it made me dizzy. Lark's book *You Can't Do That in Canada* informed me it was illegal in Wawa, Ontario, to show public displays of affection on a Sunday. On a Sunday, the Greyhound bus pulled into the parking lot of an A&W. The asphalt shimmered with the midday heat. The Spanish-speaking boy stood beside me, looking up into the sky. He wore a long tank top, the armholes low, exposing his slender brown ribcage. He stretched his arms up and I wanted to bury my face into the tufts of hair in his armpits. I wanted to lick his chest. He smiled, enjoying the fact that I was watching him. He must be at least twenty, I thought. So virile-looking. Teeming with kinetic energy. His eyebrows were thick and dark. I grabbed his hand and pressed it into the small of my back and when he bent his head down toward mine I opened my mouth for the kiss, which was long and urgent. I stood on my tiptoes and pressed my hips into his, felt him get hard through his thin basketball shorts. His hand inched toward my ass. I turned around and walked toward the restaurant. We had fifteen minutes until the bus left. He followed me. In the family bathroom he let down the diaper-changing station, lifted me up on to it. He pushed my panties to the side and I asked him how old he was. "Twenty," he said. "Why? How old are you? Who cares? It doesn't matter." He pushed into me and it felt perfect, I felt full, and then that feeling passed and he moved rhythmically and then it was over. The awkward dismount from the plastic shelf. He watched as I squeezed his cum out of me into the toilet. "You on the pill?" he asked.

I laughed. I had an IUD. "Does it matter?" We left the bathroom together and didn't speak. On the bus, I felt woken up, horny. He hadn't given me time to get off and I was frustrated. I spread my sweater over my lap and thought of Smirks, my fingers under my skirt, my panties still wet. I envisioned him coming into my tent and unzipping my sleeping bag. Putting one hand on my neck and with the other pushing my legs apart. I came very softly, my eyes shut, trying not to move the muscles of my face, hoping no one was watching. When the flexing subsided, I looked up. The boy—the man—was stretched out across the aisle, asleep. No one was looking out for me. No one was watching me. I was all alone. I felt that old anger stir. Thin doilies of light bloomed in my vision, dripping down as though against a pane of glass. I imagined finding Smirks in Toronto. In a park, watching children. Watching a little girl in a skirt. I would walk up to him and grab him by the neck. I would dig my fingers in and hurt him. I breathed deeply; my heart pounded. I couldn't believe he left me. The lightshow exploded, ferocious, and then tapered off. The storm passed. I fell asleep.

❂

I woke up as the bus pulled into the Coach Terminal and the driver announced over crackly speakers that we'd reached the terminus station. It was my first time in Toronto. The boy I'd had sex with in Wawa was already halfway up the aisle, still drinking from his pink water bottle, tapping out a beat on the head of the beautiful girl in front of him. She laughed and reached back, pressed her palm into his stomach. My head ached and I needed a drink. Out the window, I watched the Spanish-speaking group of kids grab their bags and leave. As they turned a corner, the tall boy looked back, scanning the tinted windows for my face, maybe. His expression never changed.

I stepped off the bus and was smacked in the face with a thick, putrid stench of garbage. The air had a tinge to it and I thought of all the cartoons I had ever seen where green fumes wavered stinkily above overflowing garbage cans or from the meals of terrible chefs. "Wafterons," Thierry had told me. "Those squiggly lines in the comics are called wafterons." Toronto, where it was illegal to cause damage to a tree's roots. Toronto, where you could be charged and fined for touching a bird's nest. The Greyhound depot looked like an old Art Deco bank and the surrounding buildings popped up red brick, blue glass and multi-coloured spandrel panels. Unfamiliar languages and skin tones; mellifluous patois and deep blacks. I inhaled the smell of old garbage, noting that all the bins were overflowing with waste. *Thank God*, I thought. *A city*.

My boss, Elaine, was from Toronto. Her family had moved to Vancouver when she was a teenager, thinking it would have more wheelchair accessibility. Elaine had always resented the abundance of green space and natural landmarks on the west coast. She'd point to the northern skyline outside her apartment window. "What am I gonna do with a mountain?" The surfing and the skiing and the old-growth trees bored her. "Highway 401," she had told me, "now that's the heart of a city. Eighteen lanes of traffic. The only river I'll ever need." Less than three minutes off the bus and I could already sense that Toronto was tougher, older, more confident than Vancouver. Neighbourhoods etched like tattoos. A resilience that comes with age.

The bus driver set my bicycle box down on the sidewalk. I was exhausted and sore and the prospect of piecing Shelley together infuriated me. Twenty hours on a bus had left me with more painful kinks in my body than weeks of cycling. I was pissed off at Smirks for having brought me there. I dragged the box toward the windowed concrete wall of the station and began to unpack.

A middle-aged man, fat and sallow and wearing an expensive suit, watched me while he smoked a cigarette. His buzzed hair crept along the sides of his head like tiny bugs. "How much all that stuff cost you?" he asked, gesturing to my bicycle and panniers and camp gear.

"All together? About $1,000."

He burst out laughing, clutching his cigarette between two fat fingers, squeezing so tight the cherry broke off and fell to the concrete. "You could have bought a car for that!"

"How much did your suit cost?" I asked him, lighting my own cigarette.

He looked down at himself. "All together, about $1,000."

"You could have bought a treadmill for that." His eyes went flat and his pupils widened. Tunnel vision. Rage fascinated me. Preverbal and precognitive, it has no foundation to stand on so it flies in all directions. Anger is focused and has a target: protect myself, protect others. Anger has intelligence, whereas rage has no ability whatsoever. I knew rage. For me, like the fat man, it came too fast and easy. "You know why they call it 'dressed to the nines'?" I asked, stepping closer to him. This threw him, diluted his rage. "Because in order for every thread in your suit to be running the same way, the seamstress must use nine whole yards of fabric. Using nine yards of fabric for one suit is incredibly wasteful. Hence the price you paid."

The fat man threw his cigarette down to the ground in front of my feet. "Bitch." He thumped away, the back of his neck wrinkled and jiggling with each thunderous step. Threat removed, my muscles slackened. My eyes welled up. I caught the bus driver staring at me. I pointed to the garbage can that sat between us, its contents seeping out, brown banana peels and coffee cups and cigarette packages and candy wrappers. An unsuccessful attempt had been made to contain the refuse: someone had wrapped a thick choker of packing tape tight around the mouth of the bin, but the rubbish still spilled out, uncontainable.

"What is going on?"

The bus driver laughed. "Waste removal's on strike." He had a comic-book twinkle in his eyes, glinting through the wafterons. He laughed. "Nobody's collected the garbage for almost two months." Still giggling, he sauntered away.

I assembled my bicycle and meandered through the blocks of Toronto half-heartedly searching for Lark's hotel. The streets were narrower than in Vancouver, and engraved with skinny trenches for the streetcars to slide through. Toronto, where it is an offence to bring your bicycle on a streetcar during rush hour. The air was thicker with humidity here than in the Prairies, striking me with a sensory memory of my hometown in the summer. A summer day, no school, bare feet on brown grass. Horseflies landing, biting, eating. That hot pant of the Annapolis Valley breathing down my neck. My mother in the garden, scraping at the earth with sharp, metal fingers. I thought that day, as she scraped, that her flowers had the colours of disease. How if you cut a sick person open, you would find their organs stained and blossoming those aberrant yellows and purples. Those oily blues. This, before Mom got sick. When her eyes still had the sharp bite of a Venus flytrap. That was the extent of the memory: wanting to run, but knowing if I ran, I would trigger a giant, poisonous stomach to snap shut around me.

I parked my bicycle outside the Cosmopolitan Hotel. Inside, the concierge looked horrified at my appearance. I'd done my best. I'd changed out of my Spandex and into a sundress which, granted, was wrinkly and stained with chain grease but it was all I had. I'd even put on mascara. My resources were maxed out. "My friend is staying here. She's staying here all week. I think she's giving a lecture today. And she's writing a piece on Goya." When I mentioned fashion, the concierge's eyes lit up.

"Ms. Hoop, I know exactly who you're talking about. I believe she signed in under a different name, however." That was Lark. If the room wasn't on her credit card, what was the point in going by her actual name? What fun was that?

"Who is she this week?"

The concierge punched some keys. "Well, if she's the woman from *Flare*, then she's here as Sparrow. Sparrow Spranch." Once she'd said it out loud, she burst into laughter. "That's so funny," she said. "Sparrow's branch."

"Great. Is she here now?" I was impatient. I wanted to drop off my bags and comb the city to find Smirks. I assumed there had to be an MAA meeting somewhere. That must be why he had come. Like an alcoholic in search of a sponsor. I imagined it would be easier to find the MAA crowd in Toronto than in Vancouver. This city seemed to have a bit more balls to it, a bit more in-your-faceness. More solidified history.

"Yes, she's here. She's just about to start the Textiles Talk in the auditorium. You should go watch. I'll waive the entrance fee."

"I don't want to distract her."

"If you go in the back entrance she probably won't even notice you. It's dark in the back of the auditorium."

"The auditorium? How big is the audience?"

The concierge looked at her computer screen. "As of this moment, there are three hundred and seventeen registered guests." I was shocked. Over three hundred listeners for a lecture on fabric? I left my panniers in storage and headed to the auditorium. Holding my breath, I very gently pushed open the door and peeked through the crack. Lark, or Sparrow, stood in a wash of light at the front of the room, a slim, dark line cutting up through the pale of the whiteboard and the white lights. Her voice over loudspeakers filled the space.

I could infer so much about Lark from the sound of her voice. I knew she was smoking too much. Her voice cracked at the high and low pitches, like sparks snapping off a campfire. I knew she'd had a liquid lunch. She took lazy somersaults over consonants that, when sober, she tended to march across. I knew she was interested in her subject matter, but distracted, and annoyed by that distraction, and trying to ignore it, trying to throw herself into the lecture despite whatever else was going on. I was tempted to run down the steps and make my appearance known. I thought it would ease her, somehow. If she knew I was there perhaps she would stop worrying and be happy.

But I stayed back and listened instead. Lark was speaking about silk. "Most people don't even know where silk comes from. I mean where silk really comes from." She was alone up there, no power-point presentation or images of any kind to aid her. Usually she relied on her own appearance as the visual feature of her presentation, but today her outfit lacked lustre. A plain, loose denim tunic and wedge sandals. "Sericulture is a grisly process. We plant silkworm larvae on mulberry trees where they consume the highest-quality leaves in order to produce the highest-quality silk. The larvae moult and moult and then spin their beautiful silken cocoons. If the moth is given time to emerge from the chrysalis, however, he will damage the silk fibres, so just before he's set to take flight, we steam the chrysalis, killing him. Then we throw the whole lot into hot water mixed with detergent to 'de-gum' the silk, which essentially means to strip the dead body of his valuables, in a macabre post-mortem larceny."

The men and women in the audience shifted uncomfortably in

their seats. Something was wrong with Lark. For her, appearance and quality were the most important elements of a textile, not how the textile was reared. Silk was magical, she'd told me once. She'd drawn a magnified silk fibre for me. Multi-faceted and rainbow-striped. The triangular-prism structure. Thousands of strands of prisms, breaking up light into colours. This was why silk shimmered. Had depth and motion. Of all the fabrics, Lark argued, silk was the most communicative. And wasn't that what fashion was about? Expression?

It seemed Lark's Eco-Fashion show in Banff had impregnated her with a heavier conscience than I'd thought possible. I left the auditorium, slipping through the swinging door unnoticed. My footsteps echoed through the shining hallway of the Cosmopolitan, and I had the urge to run, to break out of the contained, white, cold hotel air and into the heat of the summer. I found Yonge Street. *Yonge Street, where it is illegal to drag a dead horse.* The sidewalk teemed with business suits and cellphones and sunglasses and brisk walks. Meanwhile, the garbage still poured from the bins into the streets and onto the sidewalks. I kept walking.

At an intersection, I watched a group of people standing at the corner of Wellington, waiting for a green light. From where I stood, with my head tilted just so, it appeared to me as though they were all holding hands. About twelve of them, staring straight ahead, various races, various ages, various facial expressions, male and female. Some plaintive, some perplexed, some ponderous. But all of them with their arms at their sides in what appeared to be a group hand embrace. *Don't call attention to it,* they seemed to be saying, as they all stood there holding hands. But then the light went green, they all took a step, and the angle was broken. They were at once separate people, on separate journeys, inharmonious and alone.

❁

I wanted to hear Mom's voice, so I called home. The telephone rang and my worry for Lark twisted in on itself. Became lighter, wispier, like a scarf a magician flutters to divert your attention. I felt it loosen and leave and then Mom picked up and I could tell from her voice that she was in pain but I could also tell that she didn't care. She was finally out of the hospital and at home, healing slowly but surely from the car accident. She tried to describe her back brace to me, but the painkillers mixed with her neuropsychiatric drugs and caused more confusion. Synapses misfired and brought words to mind that were poetic and absurd.

"Well, there's a halo," she said, and I imagined a glowing nimbus pendent above her head. "With branches, no, sticks, at my sides…" she trailed off, and I remained silent, knowing that eventually the description would come. "They've tied a bullet around my waist," she continued. I said nothing. "I mean, a belt. I don't know, Jules. It's a lot of stuff. I can't move that well. That's the point, I guess." There was a long pause between us.

"I should be there with you," I said. My voice cracked, guilty. Selfish.

I wanted to touch her skin. Like mine, it was so prone to dryness and peeling. Someone would have to bring her her Keri lotion. Someone would have to rub it into her hands, or else the creases of her knuckles would turn hard and red, like subcutaneous rings of blood. "I'm fine, Jules," she said.

She and Ralph and April had determined a new pattern of existence, a new normal. Ralph would help her out of bed in the morning and bathe her. At seven-thirty, April would arrive to blow-dry Mom's hair and apply her makeup. Then April would rush off to work, and Ralph would sit Mom in front of her crossword puzzles or her latest true-crime book. She would open it to the first chapter and start it again. "It's actually kind of nice, to be honest. It's like a vacation." She was lying. A vacation from what? She hadn't worked in a long time, and the only thing that gave her any tangible pleasure, any real stimulation, was gardening. Which she couldn't do anymore. Probably wouldn't be able to until the fall, when it was too late. When the flowers had already been dispatched by an early east coast frost. But we didn't talk about that. Why talk about something you cannot change?

That was my mother's mantra. The mantra of a psychologist for criminals, a psychologist for murderers and rapists—rapers.

In my second year of university, I had told my mother I was following in her footsteps and going into psychology. I couldn't afford a cellphone or a land line, and I'd co-opted the payphone in the hallway of my all-female dorm. In the phone's alcove I sat on the uncomfortable metal stool and propped my bare feet up on the wall, leaning my back into the cool, rippled concrete behind me. "I'm going to study trauma."

"Why in the hell would you want to do that?" Mom had asked me. "Have I taught you nothing?" Mom had always said that psychology, in the classic sense, was a dead art. So why was she a psychologist? If psychologists were so obsolete? The secret, she told me, was no childhood stuff. Don't even let them mention a family member, unless the family member was into the prison to visit them that day. "We can't change what happened to us in our childhood, Julia," Mom always said. "So why do we talk about it? It doesn't work. We know that now."

I assured her I wouldn't go into traditional psychology. No couches, no hypnotherapy, no modalities of the talking cure. "The talking cure is bullshit," she'd said over the phone that day. "Doing is the only cure." That was Mom BD, Before Dementia, a woman I never got to ask for an opinion on my Molestas, or Smirks, or my graduate research in trauma theory. I could only ask Mom AD, a different Mom, a softer, less jagged Mom, who cooed and purred at the stories I told her, whose response was never sharper than a soft sigh or hum.

"I still haven't found Smirks," I said to her now. I had wandered into Berczy Park and was standing on the lip of the water fountain, feeling cool drips of foam spray the backs of my legs. I faced the red-brick flatiron building. A strange mural took up almost the whole back façade and seemed to protrude from the wall on some sort of armature. The painting used *trompe l'oeil* and depicted magnificent white drapes revealing an art deco façade underneath that was both a different colour and style than the actual building. The mural disoriented me. I imagined tugging the dangling corner of the formidable curtain and watching the whole armature crash to the ground.

"Well, Jules, if he wants to be found, he'll be found, I guess."

"I know. I'm just worried about him."

"I understand."

Mom AD was mostly a receptacle for information, and rarely a dispenser. She listened and listened and listened, and one sensed that the reason she listened so well was because she did not have anything left to say.

Her doctors said it would be like that. Layers of her personality slowly taking their leave. You didn't notice while it was happening, like the greying of a white wall. Not until you remove the painting that has hung there for years do you see: the wall isn't the same colour anymore. When was the last moment Mom was exactly Mom? Who was there for it; who saw? I stared at the artificial façade on the flatiron building, the fantastical snowy cloak set to fall to the ground, and I listened to her breathe. "I understand," she said again, and I believed her. Very soon, she wouldn't understand. Very soon, it would feel as though Mom were reaching out to me from the back of a speeding truck, and I was chasing after her on my stupid useless feet. The gap between us would keep growing until the truck was gone and I couldn't see her anymore. The fountain bumbled behind me. In front of me, that monstrous façade painted on top of a façade. I considered telling her. I opened my mouth to tell her. *Mom, I have to tell you something about Dirtbag.*

But what would she say? How could she know? It was such a complicated story. Too long a story. No beginning, no middle, no end. The spectacular thing about Alzheimer's was how it left the story behind. No longer pain plus the story of suffering. Just pain. No longer joy plus the story of attachment. Just joy. Pain plus nothing. Pleasure plus nothing. I heard her wince, a sharp intake of breath. "Ouch," she said.

"Stay still, Mom. Try not to move too much."

There was no point in bringing up injuries of the past. This became the moment. The last moment that Mom was exactly Mom. I froze this replica of her. Hung it forever in my mind.

✿

I still wanted to surprise Lark. I hid behind the corner of the hotel hallway and watched her approach the door to her room. She looked sad and tired, as though lifting her arm to slide her keycard through the lock was an arduous task. Toronto wasn't good for her, I decided. Not enough trees, not enough ocean, not enough daily rubbish removal. I was about to jump out from my hiding spot and yell "Surprise!" but something odd stopped me. Frightened me. She swung her door open and didn't move, just stared inside her room. For about ten seconds she stayed like that before girding herself and stepping inside.

I waited a bit, unsure of how to proceed. I'd seen Lark this morose exactly once, after the Stanley Cup riot in downtown Vancouver, when the Canucks lost and all those fuckhead suburbanites lit the city on fire, tipping over police cars and smashing storefronts and designer clothes from The Bay. As if that weren't bad enough—the gross destruction of a city she loved, for no worthy cause whatsoever—when Lark had returned home that night she found her apartment broken into and her laptop and half her wardrobe gone. She called me, sobbing, nearly incoherent, and I raced over to Main Street on my bicycle, swerving around upended garbage cans and fizzled firecrackers and the busted, scattered street signs littering the roads.

Lark was inconsolable for a while, and then the cleanup of her apartment began. I pulled her blanket taut across her bed and she stood on top of the mattress and swept broken glass into a dustpan. We made eye contact at a perfect moment and both burst into laughter at the absurdity of it all. The next day she wrote what would become her first published article: *The Night Hockey Stole Fashion,* by Lark LaRoche. A penname, of course.

I knocked on the door to her hotel room and then stepped away from the peephole. I still wanted to surprise her. But then the door opened, and instead of Lark, there stood Smirks. Back from the dead.

I blinked. The world stuttered. Stalled. It took my brain a second to catch up to my eyes. For a moment I felt sweet relief. A cool stream of glee. Smirks, my love. He was okay. The space between us shrank and my head pressed into his chest, my hands at his neck and then I remembered: he'd abandoned me. I pushed his shoulders away. "What the fuck."

He wouldn't look at me.

"What the fuck, Smirks?"

"Julia—"

"What are you doing here?"

A panic in his eyes. He teetered on an edge. I heard Lark's voice. "Smirks?" She stepped into the doorway, saw me. "Oh, shit."

I laughed. "What is going on?" No one answered. "I just spent the past week looking for you."

Smirks shrugged. "I came to Toronto."

"Yeah. Obviously. Why?"

"What are you doing here?" asked Lark.

Smirks rubbed his temples. "How did you find me?"

"I wasn't trying to find *you*. I came to see you," I said to Lark. To Smirks, "I had no idea you were with her." I flailed my arms. "You just fucking left."

"I'm sorry."

"I biked hundreds of kilometres alone," I said. A pain coursed through me like electricity. As if I'd been hit by lightning. It made me dizzy, rushed up from my groin and belly into my chest. Galvanized into steel in my jaw. "I thought you were dead." Smirks stared at the ground. "Don't you care?"

Lark touched my shoulder. "Julia, come in." I pushed her hand away.

"No. What the fuck, Smirks?" He didn't look up. I pushed him, hard. He stumbled backward into the hotel room and I followed him.

"Julia—" Lark grabbed my shoulder and I shrugged her off.

"What the fuck, Smirks?" I said again. He still wouldn't look at me. "You don't care about me." I pushed him harder this time, but he was prepared. He stood rooted, didn't move. I started beating on his chest and I reached up and grabbed his hair.

"Julia!" Lark yelled, and clamped onto my arm with both hands. I saw the lightshow. I whipped around and knocked my body into hers.

She fell backward and landed between the bed and the desk. I moved to help her, but felt myself lifted up and pressed firmly into the wall. My feet grazed the floor. Smirks' face less than an inch from mine.

"Don't touch her."

I looked down at Lark. She was curled up in a ball on the floor. "Her?" I shifted, tried to wiggle out of his grasp. Orange splashes of light blurred my vision. "You'll protect her? What about me? Do you know what could have happened? What if those kids had come back? Don't you care about me at all?" I was shaking, my hands still gripping his hair. He wouldn't look at me and he wouldn't let me go. I started banging my head backward. Heavy thwacks as my skull hit the wall.

Smirks reached up and put his hand behind my head. "Don't."

Lark stood up, her eyes ringed black with melting mascara. "Push me again," she said to me, standing behind Smirks. "Punch me."

"Lark, what the fuck is going on?" I asked.

Lark fell back and lay sprawled on the bed. She stretched her body long. "I'm pregnant," she said. The lightshow ended. My muscles loosened and my body melted. Smirks let me slide to the floor. On her back, Lark spoke to the ceiling. A blue column of cigarette smoke exhaled above her. "Push me again," she said. "Let's kill it."

Smirks sat on the bed. Wrung his hands together and looked down at Lark. Full cheeks now sunken, pale. Red eyes. Three-day scruff. Lark jumped up and opened the minibar, mostly depleted. Held a tiny bottle of white wine toward me. "Have you eaten?"

❁

Lark sipped the wine and smoked a cigarette while Smirks tried to explain why he'd left Redvers. Those blonde kids speaking Rumantsch had terrified him. He'd lain awake the whole night frozen. Not afraid they would return. He was afraid at what he had felt. He'd wanted to kill them. When he'd pulled out the gun he'd pointed it at the youngest one first. His finger on the trigger. His whole life, the whole world, collapsed into a metal point. How did his arm swing up to fire at the sky? He didn't know.

I tried to absorb this. To excuse it. "They were going to hurt us."

He looked at me bitterly. "No, they weren't."

"You don't know that."

"They were kids, Julia."

"Why didn't you tell me?"

"What's the point?"

He'd shot the gun in the air when what he'd really wanted to do was shoot the kid. Then he'd wanted to shoot himself. "There was so much relief in that thought. Almost joy. But mostly just this intense, overwhelming relief. In the idea of dying. It was as though I had been sick, and the prognosis was terminal, and then I recovered. I wasn't sick anymore. That's how it felt. The idea of dying."

He'd had the idea before, but only when he was looking for a way out. Only when he was trying to imagine what would make him feel better. "In Redvers, it wasn't about fixing a problem. It wasn't about protecting a child. It was just the perfect next step. The inevitable unfolding. Remember, Julia, at the bicycle workshop, with Grandpa? How he got us to look at our bikes as machines? He said that everything happens in steps. The perfection of mechanics."

"Yes."

"This was the next step. Ending it. The perfect next step. The only way to go."

With the echo of the gunshot in his mind, he imagined the bullet entering his brain, and he thought: now that makes sense. He'd watched the blonde boys scatter, pedalling for their lives. They didn't look back. He'd looked at me, crumpled on the ground and he knew that it was time to put an end to the pain. His and mine.

"Mine?"

"I look at you, Julia, and I feel responsible."

"Responsible for what?"

"For what you're going through."

"What am I going through?"

"I don't know. But whatever it is, it was caused by someone like me."

And so he left. And he planned to bike far away. Far off the path we'd set for ourselves so that, when he did do it, I wouldn't find him. He wanted me to keep going. He wanted me to make it to Kingston. He'd biked north for three days straight and made it to Swan River. He went to the water. It wasn't emotional, he said. It was just the next step. He was calm. He wondered about his mother. Should he write a note? He wrote a note.

He thought about Maria. He thought about how she'd made him feel: normal. Fine. He thought about how it was not her body that he had loved, but her age, and wasn't that everything? Someone said, *age doesn't matter*, but what they meant was *numbers don't matter*. You could not have the young age without the young body. It wasn't immaturity, it was youth, and wasn't that everything? It was youth. It was those words he loved, *nascent* and *inchoate*, loved them because they were beautiful words, and children were beautiful.

"You pretend not to understand children, Julia, but really you do understand. And they frustrate you. Because they are stupid. Because they don't know everything you know, and so you have to teach them. Because you think that somehow having knowledge makes you a better person. A more real person. If you could just get rid of all the children, right?"

He was right. I didn't think of children as real. "They can't help themselves. They can't help what they don't know."

"And so we have to help them. Everyone looks at the pedophiles. Look at the pedophiles, look at the pedophiles! I say, look at the children. What is it about them that is unutterable? What is it about them that we hate so much, and love so much, and why are those feelings the same sometimes? Can adults and children live together symbiotically? Or is the relationship inevitably parasitic? Can we ever be only good for children? Or will we always be, somehow, bad? Damaging?"

Those were the things he was thinking in Swan River. But mostly he was thinking about Maria, and how, even though he had never believed in God or the idea of an afterlife, he somehow knew that when he put the bullet in his brain he would be with her again. "I was only good to her. I gave her only good things, in her short life. I know that."

He had raised the gun. And then his cellphone rang. It was Lark, telling him she was pregnant.

Lark snapped her fingers. "Good timing, right?"

Smirks looked at her. "I would never touch my own daughter." I could tell he had said it many times.

After the phone call from Lark in Swan River, Smirks had ridden his bicycle back to Route 10, and stuck his thumb out for every truck that passed. He was renewed. A new purpose. Something to be good at. *Did you do your best at anything today?* Finally, an older woman named Joan picked him up. She secured his bike with tightening straps and drove like a bat out of hell toward Winnipeg. From Winnipeg, she told him, he could get on the Greyhound and be in Toronto in a day. He had told her: my girlfriend is in Toronto, and she's pregnant. I'm having a baby, he had said, smiling.

The sun had set behind them while they drove. *North of Winnipeg there's more to Manitoba than just wheat, you know. There are forests and lakes up there that the sun hits in a different way.* They drove through white spruce and aspens and fields full of prairie crocus. A soft, aching purple like a newborn's veins. They drove through birch and poplar and stretches of chokecherry brambles, berries gleaming in the sun like drops of blood. And Joan told Smirks several jokes, dozens, probably, in total, because she could tell he was nervous and excited, and she was offering him something to hold onto with the wild prairie winds at their back.

✹

Lark lay on the bed with a cold, wet cloth pressed to her forehead. Since she had found out she was pregnant, she felt sick. "Is it nausea gravidarum?" she kept saying, "Or just the knowledge that I am with a pedophile's child that is inducing nausea gravidarum?"

"You just like saying nausea gravidarum," I told her, and fetched more ice from the box down the hall. Toronto was a sticky city, made stickier still by the garbage sweat and the delicate situation we had all found ourselves in. My memories of Smirks during those few days remind me of a model's photo shoot, with him moving from pose to pose to pose, from chair to bed to floor, trying to find a position that would convince Lark to keep the baby. She smoked cigarettes constantly, which was killing him; every time she inhaled he cringed and his eyes flew to her stomach where he imagined his little spawn's nonexistent lungs turning black. "I'll only be a father to the baby if it's a boy. If it's a girl, I'll disappear. I'll move to Germany. You'll never hear from me again. I'll move to Thailand. I'll adopt a child and make her my wife."

"You think that's funny?" said Lark.

"No."

"See, the problem with pedophilia," she said, as if there were only one, "is that your romantic love and physical attraction depend on their body. You could be head over heels in love with your eleven-year-old, but by the time she turns sixteen, you won't love her anymore. You'll need a new one, a new child. You keep getting older, but you need the girl to stay the same age." Lark eyed Smirks from underneath her washcloth. "That's not normal. That's not how normal love works." The lights in the room were off and the shades were drawn. I sat on the edge of the other bed.

Smirks sat on the desk, facing us. On the desk sat a pile of ripped tissues that he had, one by one, torn to shreds and placed beside him while he spoke. "Yes, Lark. That is the problem."

"So, I suppose, if I had a girl, I could just keep you away from her from the ages of eight to thirteen, yeah? Make it fourteen, just to be safe? Because she could be a late bloomer. I was."

When the darkness swept in fully and we finally turned on the lamp, Smirks left. We didn't ask where he was going. The door closed behind him. I turned to Lark and opened my mouth and she held up her hand to silence me. "Don't even."

"What?"

"Don't defend him."

"Defend him? What did he do wrong?"

Lark snorted. "He's a pedophile."

"That's not his fault."

"Your opinion."

"No, fact." Lark rolled her eyes. "And he didn't rape you."

She was quiet for a long time. When she spoke, her voice was cold and even. "How can you defend pedophiles, when you don't even like children?" She stared at me and lit another cigarette. One of my books was on the desk beside her. Tom O'Carrol's *The Radical Case*. She pushed it onto the floor. "Get this shit out of here," she said. I put the book in my bag. "I want to be alone." I opened my mouth to speak. "You don't get to decide what is right and wrong, Julia."

"I want to help you through this."

"Just leave me alone for now."

I left the room and texted Smirks. "Where are you?"

"Hanging out in a graveyard. I don't know what to do."

I rode my bicycle to St. James' Cemetery on Parliament Street. I found him sitting beneath a tree amongst a cluster of tombstones. "We haven't broken any laws in Toronto yet," he said. Raised an eyebrow at me. "At least, I haven't."

I sat down beside him. "There was that dead horse I dragged down Yonge Street."

He pulled out a deck of cards. "It's illegal to play games in a cemetery in Toronto." He shuffled the deck. Passed a card to me and a card to himself. I leaned against a tombstone, the marble cool on my skin. April and I had played in the Harmony Cemetery as children, taking great care not to step where we imagined the coffins to be buried. Not out of respect, but fear. Bad luck, we thought, to step on the dead. We didn't know the earth beneath our feet was moving, that caskets drifted, bled into the pathways and bumped up against tree roots. If we saw a funeral procession, we'd hide in the bushes and sing. *Never laugh as the hearse goes by, for you may be the next to die. They put you in a big, black box, and cover you up with dirt and rocks. It all goes well for a couple of weeks, but then your coffin begins to leak...* We'd squeal at the disgusting verses about worms and guts. We never thought about the families sitting in the vehicles that trailed the hearse. The people who'd just lost a father, a daughter, a mother. We were children.

"What game are we playing?" I asked. Smirks shook his head.

"We flip our card at the same time. If they're both black, I stay. If they're both red, I go."

"And if they're different?" He shrugged and nodded to my hand. I flipped the card, and he flipped his. Red diamond, red heart. I reached for another card. "Do-over."

He smiled and shook his head. I grabbed his hand. Our fingers intertwined and made one fist in the dark. Small and fragile as a kitten's ribcage. His eyes were full of tears. I didn't know what to say. I wanted to ride my bicycle ahead of him, pulling him along in my slipstream, making it easy for him. Carrying him the rest of the way.

"I'm sorry," I said.

"For what?"

"For bringing you with me. It was selfish."

He nodded. "I knew what you were doing, and I still came."

"Why?"

He shrugged. "Nothing left to do." He opened my hand up and looked at my palms. I shivered. I felt my body opening up to his, my belly stir awake. "And I love you," he said. I inched toward him and wrapped my legs around him. I felt like a child in his lap. He pulled me in tight and hugged me.

"I love you, too."

"I'm sorry I left you in Redvers. I know that hurt."

"I guess it wasn't about me, though."

"That's right," he said. And suddenly he was standing. Pulling me up. "I'll see you."

I nodded. Though we both knew that probably wasn't true. He climbed on his bicycle. His panniers looked lighter. He looked lighter.

Where was he going? I didn't ask. I waved goodbye and he rode away.

❂

It was the only time I had seen Lark in track pants since we were in gym class in grade nine. In fact, years later, I would purchase a magazine for the sole purpose of reading a feature profile about her, and one of her quotes that they highlighted in large, bold print in the margin would say that a woman should only wear track pants on two days: the day of an abortion or the day after a funeral.

I sat in the waiting room at the clinic and I remembered the pact Lark and I had made in high school after her older brother's girlfriend had a miscarriage. The night it happened, we had sat on her bed and Lark had cried. "I wanted a nephew, Julia. I want a baby. I think a baby is the only real thing a person can want. Everything else you can just set on fire."

We'd laughed at this, keeled over, our stomachs stretched and sore. The kind of laughter we had been used to as young children, but how surprised by it we were that evening, surly teenagers in the midst of an actual tragedy. We were new to tragedy. Our brains licked at it like a lollipop. We loved the taste. And Lark swore that night that a child would be the thing that saved her. This, before she knew how she would feel, as an adult, about men. This before she knew that her skin would, just mere years later, grow barbs against them. We swore this: if I got pregnant, she would keep it for me. And if she got pregnant, she would keep it for her. She would be the mother and the father. Be the parents that some children never had.

After we left the clinic, she bled for two days and kept telling me to leave. "The only reason you're still here is because you don't want to go to Kingston."

After Toronto, nothing was the same. What broke between us that day? Something. I have retraced our steps hundreds of times. Could they have been avoided, the losses we suffered?

I heard Elaine's voice in my head about one hundred metres too late: *Don't get on Highway 401, Julia. It's not for cyclists. If you get on Highway 401, they're going to eat you alive.* But in a blur of autopilot, I headed south on Bathurst and hopped on the Gardiner and then Don Valley, not paying attention to where I was and before I knew it, I was heading up the onramp of the infamous Highway 401. Car horns blaring, transport trucks whizzing past less than one foot beside me. I felt as if I'd been asleep and was waking up to a nightmare. The shoulder was nonexistent. I didn't even have enough room to stop cycling northeast and get off my bicycle and turn around. I had to keep going with the traffic flow, fast and hectic and lethal.

That stretch of road was the busiest in North America, ushering over half a million vehicles a day through southern Ontario, and over the years had earned such delightful nicknames as *The Killer Highway*—a bit prosaic if you ask me—and *Carnage Alley,* which was more to my taste, while both could be titles of books my mother would have read. I imagined it all ending there, on the side of Highway 401, Elaine hearing the news from Vancouver, nodding her head solemnly as though, yes, of course, of course that's how she died. Could it have happened any other way? Some might even deem it a suicide. Why else would she cycle onto Highway 401, unless she wanted to kill herself? It would be effective: quick, certain, spectacular.

Finally there was a gap in the traffic long enough for me to turn my bicycle around, which only meant I was now facing the wrong way, head on to the traffic coming toward me, inches away from pissed-off truckers and cellphone-chatting businessmen. When they passed, they looked at me as though I were an alien, eyes locked on me, mouths open, brows crunched. I admonished them with my facial expression and with a shaky arm gesticulated back to the road. Keep your eyes on the road. Didn't they know they were likely to drive directly into whatever they were looking at? Stop looking at me. Keep your eyes on the road.

Finally, I twisted off the onramp and tucked myself into the armpit of the underpass. My body felt like an earthquake aftershock: deep, tremulous nausea, the epicentre in my stomach, the seismic waves radiating to the ends of my limbs and beyond. I lay down on the asphalt slab and through the pavement felt the vibrations of the cars passing above me. Hundreds of tonnes of rubber, metal and glass just metres away from my body. I could feel the weight of each driver, each passenger, pressing down on my chest, all those tires driving over my carapace, pinching my lungs, crushing me.

People had been stuffing trash inside this concrete crevice. The city was bursting at the seams with uncollected garbage. I could smell all of Toronto with one, deep inhalation: oily pizza boxes dripping red and bloody with marinara. Cases of PBR soaked with the dredges of coppery beer. Bags of takeout from the Woodlot, pureed peppered squash and remnants of slimy cabbage rolls that had baked themselves again under the oven of Highway 401.

I grabbed my iPhone from my shorts and opened my SkyView app. I swung the camera up, aiming it at the ceiling of the underpass, the floor of the 401, and saw that Jupiter was up there, directly above me, weighing 317 times as much as Earth. The world weighs exactly one woman, Lark had said. There was Aries, and Venus, and the moon. And Perseus. That was good. Perseus. Thierry's favourite constellation because it held Algol, the famous Demon Star. Algol was Arabic for *head of the ogre,* and translated to English as the Demon Star. Algol had, throughout history, been known as the most unfortunate star in the cosmos. "What does that mean?" I would ask Thierry. But he didn't know. He was a firm non-believer in astrology. Of course the stars we were born under had some effect on shaping our personalities, our trajectories, our destinations. All that mass, pushing and pulling. A teaspoon full of neutron star would weigh 900 Egyptian pyramids. But Thierry's logic was that the stars had no more push and pull over us than every other variable we were born into. Who our parents were, the weather on our birthday, the mood of our delivering doctor. Even our given names had more influence than the planets. It's not that he didn't believe that the stars affected our lives, it's that he knew everything affected our lives, and why should we place more emphasis, more wonder, more blame, more appreciation on balls of gas spinning and churning millions of miles away?

I lay under the overpass and counted the stars. Mirfak. Schedar. Mothallah. Cappella. Menkalinen. Maaz. Eventually my heart rate slowed. Slowly, my breath returned.

Ralph

Ten years ago, I had been fifteen years old, sitting on the living-room floor in Harmony, playing with my dead grandmother's jewellery. She had just passed away. Dirtbag's mom, and my aunt, Dirtbag's sister, had mailed us a shoebox full of her jewellery and some old magazines. Gram had been a model for the Hudson's Bay Company in the fifties. I ran my hands through the strands of beads, turquoise and magenta, fire orange and brassy gold. I tried to attach their colourful plastic hardness to the dead woman who had worn them. To summon some form of grief at her passing.

Gram had always been a bit of a strange character to me. After Dirtbag disappeared, Mom had started paying for Gram's plane tickets from Calgary to Halifax every summer to visit us. Mom and Gram had always gotten along so well, way better than Mom and Dirtbag ever had, and Mom wanted us to have as big a family as possible despite Dirtbag's desertion. So every July we'd drive the two hours to Halifax to pick up Gram at the airport. She would walk through the arrival gate, smelling of sharp, bright notes like orange and lily. She'd hug us and, upon each arrival, ask the same question. "You heard from Dirtbag?"

"Nope, you?"

"Nope."

And then a warmer smell would settle in, something heavier and deeper, that I would later learn was ambergris. Thierry gave me a bottle of perfume that smelled like my grandmother. "Ambergris is made deep in the intestines of sperm whales. It's a sort of palladium against cuttlefish beaks and crab shells. It's like a lube that helps pass the hard stuff. When it floats to the ocean surface and washes up on beaches, it smells foul and briny, like whale vomit. But when it hits the sun, it develops this deep, heavy, sweet-wood smell, like an old-growth forest during a heat wave." Thierry kissed where I had sprayed the whale vomit. His lips pressed into my neck and, each time they pulled away, pieces of me went with him, until I felt as if every sentient part of me was on his mouth.

Gram's jewellery smelled like that, like ambergris. The scent had travelled from the west to the east, stuck in between the glass and wood and plastic, woven into the string and thread. Posthumous smell-braids of my father's mother. The prism-like charlotte beads, colours of the aurora borealis, were my favourite. How they shimmered and swerved like phosphorescence. That necklace was the longest one, and I draped it around my neck once, twice, three times, four, and imagined wearing it to school the next day, an opulent neck brace, how Lark would fawn over it, draw it, plan outfits around it, whole fashion shows. Gram was dead. She wouldn't be in Harmony that summer. In the late mornings, after I'd slept in, I had always found her sitting at the kitchen table, dealing out the playing cards for our daily game of Spite and Malice. We never talked about Dirtbag; she never offered any insight, and I never asked.

Gram's jewellery had just arrived in the mail that day, and as I organized the necklaces and bracelets and earrings by hue and style, the telephone rang, and I knew, somehow, it would be him. I remember thinking in that moment that I could choose how much Dirtbag meant to me. Mom stood at the door of the living room, the phone in her hand, looking down at me while I sat on the floor playing with beads. What must she have been thinking, holding my father in her hand, looking at me, her daughter, on the brink of womanhood. Sitting on the floor, legs slender and bent, freckles running rampant across the bridge of my nose. With one hand she held the phone out to me; the other she dug into her waist, hard. I watched her fingers press deep into her skin, pinching it, as if trying to wake herself up.

Her breathing was heavy and slow, her jaw clenched.

This was during the period when April and I both insisted we were never having kids. Mom had us write it down in ink and sign it: "I am never getting married or having children." Signed: "Julia Hoop." "I am never getting married or having children." Signed: "April Hoop." Mom took delight in these contracts. Showed them to her friends, laughed out loud. Mocked us. When alone, and in cahoots, April and I claimed our choice of childlessness was because we didn't want to fuck up our kids the way our parents had fucked up us. That was our favourite refrain. We must have repeated it thousands of times throughout our childhood. *I don't want to fuck up a kid like our parents fucked us up.* We loved the rebellion of it. The curse and the middle finger to our authorities. What we didn't know at the time, and it would be a lesson hard earned, was that everyone was fucked up.

I shook my head at Mom that day. For the first time since Dirtbag had left, I didn't want to talk to him. I didn't care where he was. Mom raised her eyebrows, surprised, but didn't say anything. I thought she looked a little proud. She lifted the phone to her ear. "She doesn't want to talk to you." And for the first time I had a slight, almost imperceptible moment of insight into my mother as a human being. For the first time I realized that she was a person who, at one point, had absolutely nothing to do with me. "Yes, she's sitting right here. She doesn't want to talk to you."

When she hung up, she typed the phone number that had shown up on the call display into the Internet search engine. Kingston, Ontario. Mom and I looked at each other. That was odd. He was still heading east, in our direction. We had both thought, for sure, that he would end up in Calgary, where he had grown up. The intrigue faded and Mom stood up. "Who gives a shit," she said, turning and stomping back up the stairs. I got up off the floor and opened up the map. Based on its landmarks, it sounded like a very royal city: Princess Street. Queen's University. Kingston.

I opened the Queen's University website. Lots of brick and ivy. Blonde girls with pink cheeks dressed in red, blue and gold. University was a transformative place, I knew. When you went there, you became a different person. You became whoever you wanted to be. You became the girl in the picture, fresh-faced and laughing, the keeper of knowledge that brought happiness. In university, you would meet different kinds of people: black people, Asian people, and people who were from whatever country made their skin the colour of bronze. I started researching universities that day. There were so many things that I had never even heard of—so many things that would be waiting for me when I eventually got to Vancouver. Sashimi. Persians. Pedo-lit. Starbucks.

And now I was sitting, ten years later, again looking at a map of Kingston. I was in a parking lot pilfering Internet from the Bay-Side Motel on Bath Road that curled into Kingston like a finger and eventually became Princess Avenue. There was nothing royal about any of it. I packed away my computer and got back on my bicycle. I would hug this road until I got to the water, where I would rest for lunch in the sun and take in some of the town's famed Busker Fest. Then, after my siesta, I would find a payphone and call Dirtbag. He probably wouldn't answer. I would pack up my panniers and ride another couple of hours out of town. Maybe I'd make it to Perth. The rest of Canada stretched endlessly away. I still looked for Smirks in crowds, in other teams of cyclists. I suspected I'd keep looking for Smirks for a long time.

I knew I should start practising my French. Soon, I'd be in Quebec. And not Montreal, Quebec. Backwoods Quebec, where people don't speak English and they expect you to speak French. I shuddered at the thought. Imagined getting yelled at by leather-faced women with small, beady eyes, standing on their front porches with broomsticks, screaming at me as I rode by, shouting the titles of Roman Catholic symbols that had evolved over the years into obscenities: *Crisse de calice d'ostie Anglais!* Thierry thought it was funny how cultures nominated curse words from the aspects of life that frightened them the most. For the Québécois, it was religion. For the Victorian English, it was religion mixed with sex and carnal excrement. I couldn't imagine biking all that way, another fourteen hundred kilometres, alone. The road felt dry and hard. Inhospitable. I wanted something to happen. I wanted to fall. Break a bone. Fly home instead of ride.

Dusty construction site. I squinted through the powdered concrete. A voice, gruff and familiar. "Well, holy fucking shit!" I swivelled my head in its direction. "It's that crazy fucking foot-pedaller!" I slowed my bicycle and searched through the equipment. There was Bruce. The cancerous beluga. He rested one hand on the end of a shovel while the other hand waved through the air. The moment we made eye contact, the whole time-space continuum seemed to take on different dimensions. I was aware of some large machinery in various states of drilling. There must have been other men milling around, but in my memory of that moment, there was only Bruce, alone on the construction site, being swallowed up by the sounds and shakes of jackhammers. He waved to me from his propped-up shovel in what appeared to be slow motion. Cars rushed by me like flashes of dreams. His long, mouldy beard was gone, revealing a diminutive chin, a soft contrast to his deep, sonorous voice and thick, beluga neck. I started laughing. What were the chances? What were the fucking chances? I was laughing so hard, the way I used to laugh on roller coasters: full-belly, teary-eyed, frightened that I might never breathe again. Bruce started laughing too. Looked behind me up the road. "Where's your boyfriend?" he asked, which made me laugh even harder.

✪

When we got to his house, Bruce put on a giant, steaming pot of spaghetti and a loaf of garlic bread and poured glass after glass of cheap, tart, delicious red wine. I felt as if I was home. Nothing, absolutely nothing, could have made me happier than stumbling upon Bruce. I wanted to call Smirks and share the coincidence with him, but it wasn't our journey anymore. It was mine. I had to stop imagining that everyone should experience all the things I experienced.

I walked around their backyard and took pictures. With Smirks and his fancy camera gone, I was left to record the last leg of the bike trip alone. Smirks had told me, "If the best pictures happen when you're not ready, then you must always be ready." An old, rusted, ripped trampoline. Several mouldy kiddie pools. Two tree houses with the roofs and floors caved in. Bicycles with chains rusted orange, their tires soft and flattened to the ground like sleeping animals. Bruce stood above me on the patio. "We have a lot of grandchildren," he called down. "They're older now. But Rhonda and I don't like to throw anything away." Pretty much the exact opposite of my mother, I thought, who had no use whatsoever for relics from the past, physical or emotional. I looked up at him. His skin was sallow but his eyes were bright.

"How are you doing, Bruce?"

He took a swig of his beer and a long drag off his cigarette. "I'm doing fucking fantastic, girly." The cancer was either still there, or it was gone. But, for that night, what did it matter? Rhonda came home in somewhat of a huff, thrilled to see me, but upset by a situation at work. She was a personal care attendant and had just had one of her favourite private clients put into a nursing home. Her eyes were wet from the ordeal.

"Oh, Julia, I'm sorry to dump this on you, but I'm quite shaken up." She flitted about the house unsure of what to tend to, what small sundry chore would help her feel in control. As she straightened picture frames and tucked in chairs, she told us what had happened. She had been taking care of Ruth for years, in tandem with Ruth's son, Bill. But Bill's care had become erratic. Rhonda would arrive in the morning and Ruth would have been put to bed in her day clothes. Or Ruth would be starving, claiming Bill hadn't made her dinner the night before. Then, last week, Rhonda found the old woman still sitting on the couch where she'd left her the night before. Bill hadn't come home. Rhonda teared up and her voice cracked. "She had soiled her pants during the night." Bruce rubbed her shoulders. They'd been married for almost forty years.

Turns out Bill had a pretty serious cocaine habit he'd been nursing for a while, and it had finally gotten beyond his control. I listened to the story and it made me angry. I imagined my own mother left in her shit for an entire night. I would punch in the face of whoever was responsible for that. "His heart was broken today," Rhonda said, looking up at Bruce, clasping his hand. "He hated putting her in the nursing home."

"Who hated it?" I asked.

Rhonda looked at me. "Bill."

"Are you kidding?"

Rhonda shook her head. "He loves his mother. He loves her deeply. But he can't take care of her. It's very, very sad."

I was instantly suspicious of Rhonda and Bruce. Who were these people? Selfless and non-judgmental and unconditionally loving? Were they Christians? We settled down for dinner. "Are you Christian?" I asked, looking first at Bruce, and then at Rhonda.

Rhonda giggled and her eyes sparkled. "Oh, no, honey," she said, reaching across the table and touching my hand. "I'm Métis." I looked at Bruce and he nodded, shrugged. Bruce and Rhonda, it seemed to me, were examples of those people you heard about, you read about, but you rarely met. Trusting and altruistic without ulterior motives. I looked around me at the walls of their dining room and realized that on each wall hung several photographs of different Christmas dinners. In each photograph, the dining-room table where I sat was laden with a plastic tablecloth patterned in poinsettias. A leviathan, golden turkey as the centrepiece. Bright orange squash and the little green brains of Brussels sprouts. The only recurring characters in each of the dinners were Rhonda and Bruce. Otherwise, their table was surrounded by somewhat bedraggled individuals. Men with patchy beards and sunken eyes. Women with dark roots and the thin, tight lips I associated with drug use.

I stood and walked closer to the wall. "Who are these people?" In the oldest-looking photograph, Rhonda and Bruce looked like teenagers, Rhonda with long, gleaming mahogany hair to her waist and Bruce a long, healthy black beard.

Rhonda rose and stood beside me. "These are our annual homeless dinners." I realized, standing side by side, how infinitesimal she was, the top of her head just beneath my shoulder, her little fingers like a child's. She reached up and ran her finger across the glass. "Every Christmas Day, Bruce and I go down to the homeless shelter and stand in front of the doors."

"The first twelve people who approach, we invite back to our house, where we feed them, give them a shower, and a new change of clothes," said Bruce.

"Nothing fancy, just some pants and a shirt from Zellers."

"But you should see the change in them."

"From when they first enter our house to when they leave."

"Not different people."

"Same people. Just happier."

I walked from photograph to photograph. The anachronisms were uncanny. Rhonda and Bruce were the only ones who aged. Otherwise the tablecloth was the same, the china was the same, the turkey was the same. The guests were of another period, it seemed. A time without fashion or trends or style. Either functional, practical haircuts or none at all. Shapeless, monochromatic garments, no accessories to speak of. But happy. They mostly looked happy. It all seemed very odd to me. I looked at Rhonda. "Has anyone ever stolen anything from you?"

Her eyes showed surprise outweighed by a sort of amusement. She nodded. "Yes. They definitely have."

"Oh, sure," said Bruce. "We lost a ring. An expensive ring, actually."

Rhonda laughed. "Some food. Someone took all the meat out of our freezer one year."

"Shampoo."

"My mother's brooch."

"The most peculiar was when that young man took my paintings," said Bruce, looking into the middle distance, genuinely perplexed.

"Bruce is a painter."

"And one Boxing Day, we woke up, and my workshop was empty and the young guy was gone. I started finding them in pawnshops around the city. I bought most of them back." Bruce chuckled and coughed, chuckled and wheezed. "Strange feeling. Buying my own art."

Rhonda put her hands on my hips and guided me back towards my chair. "Let's eat." I sat down, feeling as if I was dreaming.

Bruce piled slippery white noodles onto my plate. "Seriously, though," he said. "Where's your boyfriend?"

"Seriously. He's not my boyfriend."

Rhonda and Bruce looked at each other in that way that old married couples look at each other. They probably thought we'd been dating and had gotten into a fight on the road. A lover's quarrel. "He's not into women." They tilted their head to the side, in time with one another. "He's a pedophile." They both paused. I reached into my bag and pulled out *The Radical Case.* "I'm studying pedophilia." I pushed the book toward them as proof. "Smirks was kind of my subject." I heard, finally, how awful that sounded. Rhonda and Bruce looked at the book, then looked at each other again, differently this time, a strand of understanding passing between them. Did the capacity for empathy of these people know no bounds?

"We knew a pedophile once," said Rhonda, pushing my pedo-lit back toward me. Past tense: knew. As in: they don't know him anymore. "Bruce worked with him. Became friends with him."

Bruce worked construction. Bruce worked with a pedophile. "When?" I asked.

"Oh," Bruce said, leaning back in his chair. "Met him fifteen years ago, I guess. Knew him for five." He looked at me. "He died ten years ago. Pretty tragic, actually." This was clearly a sad story for them to tell. My spaghetti was getting cold. I could hear two clocks ticking, one fraction of a second after the other. It sounded like a soft, mechanical heartbeat. Smirks' heart murmur skipped a beat in my mind. The rushing in my ears was my own heartbeat coming in like a wave.

On a night in the Prairies during a full moon, Smirks had read a poem to me, not his own this time but someone else's. I tried to recall the author's words then, in the dining room with Bruce and Rhonda. It felt very important that I remember what the poet had written. We believe, Smirks explained to me, that our moon is a chip off the old block. Sundered from our planet during the Period of Heavy Bombardment, when a planetesimal smashed into Earth and sent rocks flying into orbit. "You thought you could hold all of it, but got spinning so fast, part of you pulled away." One of the rocks would become our moon, whose mass would regulate our tilt and sway. The tides of the oceans were the echoes of a collision that took place four billion years ago. "You panicked, said Stay! And it did, and it does, but only for a while. Licking the wound, it slowly moves away."

"Tell me about him," I said. "Start at the beginning."

❁

He arrived on the worksite like most other middle-aged men do. Quiet and tired-looking, dark eyes that said: don't speak to me, and I won't speak to you, and we will stay out of each other's lives, because I have no interest in yours, and trust me, you do not want to know about mine. Bruce got a kick out of his sullenness. Not that he didn't understand what tragedies could lie in the life of a man. But Bruce had always had a penchant for black comedy. His favourite quote was from Garrison Keillor. "God writes a lot of comedy. Trouble is, we're bad actors who don't know how to play funny, or something like that."

Bruce remembered a passage from a book he'd read once, about a woman who was depressed and trying to decide whether or not to go on antidepressants. It seemed the whole world was taking Prozac to mute their problems. Instead of medicating, however, she goes outside in the rain and lies in the grass. She lets the rain fall on her and over her and wash her into the ground. She tries to sink into the ground, to become a part of it, no, to feel the connection between her and it. To feel how she and the ground are one entity, she and the rain are one entity. Her depression is a weather system moving through her. Bruce thought this was pretty funny and he wanted to see if it worked. When he felt sad, he went outside and lay on the ground, and it worked. He laughed.

Maybe this new stranger could be taught to lie on the ground, Bruce thought. And so on their lunch break that day, Bruce sat down next to him and offered him some of his homemade soup. No, he didn't offer.

He poured some soup in a cup and placed it in front of him. "My wife made it," Bruce said. "You have a wife?" The man wore a ring on his finger, but Bruce had learned that a ring did not necessarily mean a wife. The man shook his head. "What's with the ring?" Another thing Bruce had learned was not to beat around the goddamn bush. If you're curious, ask. We invented these notions of privacy and nosiness. Name one good thing that ever came from privacy, Bruce liked to challenge people.

"I can't get it off," said the stranger, pulling at the thin gold band to prove it.

"Why don't you cut it off?"

"'Cause then it'd really be broken, wouldn't it?"

"You can't break what ain't fixed, my friend."

The stranger nodded.

Back at Rhonda and Bruce's house, the stranger looked at photographs of elaborate turkey dinners adorning the walls of their dining room. In each one, Rhonda and Bruce sat in the middle, in front of the large, gleaming turkey, and around them stood a crowd of a dozen or so hobo-looking types. It wasn't their clothes or a lack of cleanliness that gave them away. The stranger could tell the look of a person who had been cleaned up recently, given new, cheap clothes and a toothbrush and a comb. In fact, he'd been one of those people himself. More than once.

"Any of these guys ever steal anything from you?" the stranger had asked. He already knew the answer. Of course they had. People have this misconception, this idealist dream, that if you are good to somebody, they will be good to you. The stranger found this funny, but not in the same way that Bruce found tragedy funny. The stranger's amusement with life had a darker source: a failure, somewhere far back in his history, to connect with other human beings. He had tried. He'd really tried. And it had left him exhausted, completely empty, and on the brink of suicide, much to his dismay, because he hadn't come close to finishing his book of poetry. A book he had been working on for years. Decades, even.

"Oh, sure," said Bruce, gesturing to the last photograph. "This guy. He was young. Maybe fifteen years old. He took off in the night with all my paintings!"

The stranger looked at the child, took him in, skinny and pale, the only one of the bunch not putting on a smile for the camera. "My youngest daughter would be about his age," he said.

Bruce looked surprised.

"You have a daughter!" Rhonda exclaimed.

"Two."

"Great. Where are they?" asked Bruce.

The stranger shook his head and continued to stare at the photograph.

"Do you have their phone number?" Bruce asked. The stranger nodded. "Then you should give them a call." Bruce placed the telephone in the middle of the dining-room table. "I've gotta flip those burgers." He and Rhonda left the room. When they returned, about thirty minutes later, the stranger was still sitting at the dining-room table staring at the telephone. They didn't ask if he had called his daughters, and the stranger didn't offer to tell them.

The stranger continued to come for dinner. Rhonda didn't particularly like him, but she felt a maternal instinct. Although, in this case, she was not protecting the stranger, but was protecting the rest of the world from the stranger. Because she knew. As soon as the stranger told them his secret, she realized she'd already known. She had always known—but the photograph was blurry. How he wouldn't talk about his kids. How he avoided their grandchildren. When he told her and Bruce, the images were brought sharply into focus, and everything was clear, except for how to proceed. Where did their accountability lie? How do you trust a pedophile who's molested his own children and others? He assured them he hadn't offended in Kingston, and that he wouldn't. His libido was gone. He hardly thought about young girls anymore. All he did to entertain himself was write. He didn't have much time, he told them, to finish his book. Of that much he was sure.

Rhonda became very ill after the stranger's confession. Her stomach scratched at itself like a confined animal, and within a month she had developed ulcers so bad the doctors feared for her life. Bruce knew it was the stranger, and the predicament he had put them in. Rhonda's questions. Should they call the police and report him? What about those little girls in Nova Scotia, Banff and Redvers? Should somebody be held accountable? Should somebody be punished? What about those little girls? Bruce didn't know the answers, and he knew the questions weren't going to go away, and that eventually they would tip over, scatter and break something, though he wasn't sure what. And then, one day, it was over, and he didn't have to worry about it anymore.

The stranger had spent the night and didn't come out of the guest room the next morning. Bruce found him, hanging from the ceiling heating pipe. His book of poetry on his desk, with a note. "I hope I have, at some point in my life, produced something good and beautiful. My daughters are in these poems. I hope they find themselves."

❂

I couldn't sleep. I was in the same bed he had lain in ten years earlier. Same pillow, same linens. Same metal pipe in the ceiling. At five in the morning, I rose and went downstairs to use the basement shower so I wouldn't wake Rhonda and Bruce. The water beat down on me, hard and iron-scented, and I stood under the stream of heat while my body reddened and numbed.

The book of poetry and the suicide note were still on the dining-room table, where Bruce and Rhonda had left them the night before. When I'd told them who I was, that Dirtbag had been my father, Rhonda had grabbed me by my shoulders and shaken me hard. "But you're okay!" she'd shouted at me, nodding frantically. "I think you're really okay!"

The early morning light in the dining room was blue like the moon. I could hear Smirks again, reading the moon poem that night in the Prairies. *Something that sounds like that, the waves so loud they pound a pulse that you carry like a portable radio hung from your neck, can only be described as a scar.* I took Dirtbag's book of poetry and the suicide note, and I absconded into the milky morning dawn.

I'd forgotten to ask Rhonda and Bruce what they had done with my father's body. I used my iPhone to look up the location of the cemetery and I pointed my bicycle toward it. My mother had never understood cemeteries. When Gram died, and we couldn't go visit her grave in Alberta, Mom had told me that cemeteries were silly. "What's the point? She's no more there than she is in here." She pointed to her head, and then reached out and touched mine. "Close your eyes and envision her. She's sitting there, on the grass. Take off your shoes and sit down next to her. Talk. She just wants to hear you talk. And you just want her to listen. You can visit her every day if you want."

I found the graveyard in Kingston and rode up and down the rows of headstones in the murky morning light. I read every dead person's name, but Dirtbag was nowhere to be found.

When I left the graveyard, the sun was rising. The sky peeled open like the skin of a red-hot sunburn, roiling with fluorescent oranges and violets. A cartoonist approximating a toxic-waste dump in the heavens. And I hoped those colours presaged a wild tempest, something to take me outside of myself. I rolled along the main drag, slowly, and watched civilians on foot, on their way to work. Postmen and nurses and bakers and construction workers, one by one they stopped heading west and turned to face east, pulling their phones out of their pockets, frozen in the middle of the sidewalk, cameras pointed up at the sky, snapping photographs of the lava churning above our heads.

The twenty-four-hour bus ride unfolded in fits and starts of sleep and consciousness. I was always just aware of the storm we were leaving behind in Kingston. It threatened to follow us, chase us down, crack over our heads and strand us on the Trans-Canada Highway. I had rough, vertiginous dreams of Dirtbag: framed pictures of him on spinning walls would fade to portraits of Smirks. I dreamed of Rhonda's ulcers, that they were mine. I woke in different towns the whole way home, every time missing Smirks so much my chest hurt. There had been other girls in Redvers, Bruce had said. Other girls in Banff as well. What to do about them, what to do. I developed a mild fever. If I kept looking for ghosts, I thought I might die.

Finally I woke up minutes away from Harmony. Before I'd left Kingston, Rhonda had hugged me tight. She'd said, "Practise random beauty and senseless acts of love." Out the window, I saw the elementary school of my childhood. The cemetery where I used to laugh at death. We pulled into the only gas station in town. I took Dirtbag's poetry books and my pedo-lit out of my bag, placed them on my seat and disembarked.

❂

Since I had left Harmony after high school, one traffic light—the first and last—had been installed at the intersection where its presence, added to the grocery store, the liquor store, the bank and the funeral home, made a very symbol-heavy quincunx. The red, green and yellow flashing on the four corners of life and death. Food, booze, money, mortality. I looked east and west up Union Street, north and south down Commercial Street, and could not see one moving car, not one human being. The driver unpacked my bike box and tipped his hat to me and I watched the Greyhound, my last attachment to the road, trundle off into the golden evening light. I went inside the gas station and bought a pack of cigarettes.

Outside I sat down and leaned my back against the side of the building and smoked. I wished for magical elves to come and assemble my bicycle for me. I finished my cigarette and removed my bike tools from my bar bag for what would turn out to be the last time in two years. After the bike trip, I would develop a strong, pathological aversion to cycling. I would gain twenty pounds and forget, for a while, what it felt like to fly across mountain ranges. And then that wound would heal as well.

I assembled Shelley and headed toward April's house. April and Mark lived at the bottom of the South Mountain, and I would stop there first before beginning my final ascent up to Mom. Not one car passed me the whole way. The South Mountain was the home of the notorious Goler clan, a family who made the Annapolis Valley famous for about ten minutes in the eighties when a schoolteacher uncovered a generations-long history of incest, sexual abuse and inbreeding that eventually ended in the conviction of sixteen adults for hundreds of offences. In the years since, the name Goler had become a Nova-Scotian adjective to describe anyone too poor or dumb. *Ew, don't date him. He's so goler.*

I had forgotten about the potholes in rural Nova Scotia. The roads were wasting away, crumbling under years of salt and snow and the reckless driving of bored teenagers with nothing else to do but get in their parents' car and go. There was April's house, with the deck-in-progress that she'd assured me would be complete by the end of August and serve as the platform for my welcome-back party. But the deck in June, like my bike trip, remained unfinished, and there would be no party there for me. April's car was in, but Mark's truck was gone, and I was grateful for that. What I had to tell April, I wanted to tell her alone. I saw her before she saw me. She had set up an easel in the backyard and was painting her sunflowers.

I remembered, years ago, when April was severely depressed, I rued the fact that she had ever discovered art. Artists always killed themselves in such spectacular fashion. Pollock bought an expensive car and wrapped himself around a tree. Van Gogh had shot himself in a cornfield. "Or did he?" April always mused, wistful, eyes squinting off into the middle distance. "They never found the gun." Rothko, with his wrists slit in the bathtub, drawing a final triptych: red blood, white body, red blood, like one of his paintings. But I didn't worry about April like that anymore.

Her sunflowers stood in a row, an amusing tableau, their heads drooped to the sides as if they were tired, their big leaves seeming to shrug and say, *What do you want from me?* Her canvas expressed this more poignantly than the actual plants. She was an artist. "Hello, there!" I called to her, and she spun around and screamed and laughed and we ran toward each other as if we were in a movie. Later, she would tell her friends, "It was just like in a movie!" April often said that about her happy moments. It was a sad thing about her, and also one of the best things about her. She was still holding onto her palette when she threw her arms around me, pressing a rainbow of paint into my back, marking me in yellow and blue and green.

She pulled away from me and jumped up and down. "I knew you were coming today. I swear, I knew it."

"I bet you thought it every day."

She put her palette down on the grass. Looked up at the sky. "Maybe."

I inhaled deeply. The orange tang of her smoketrees. Spicy mink manure from the farm up the street. Wet strawberries.

April watched me. Happy smile fading. She looked at my bike, scanning for damage. Scrutinized my legs, my arms. Had I been injured? Why had I come home?

"I couldn't bike anymore. I wanted to be here."

She nodded. Swatted at a mosquito. I touched her arm, spotted with red bumps. "The bugs are bad," she said. Valley twang like a thumb massaging my heart. "The bats are dying out. There's a fungus killing them." We used to get bats in our bedrooms in the old brick house we lived in with Dirtbag. Summer nights, I'd wake to the sound of their little bodies hitting my window, trying to get out. Their squeaky cries. I'd scream for him, our father, to come catch the vermin. Come save me from those razor teeth, those terrifying wings that could get tangled in my hair forever.

"That's sad," I said.

"It is." We stared at each other. Finally, April asked. "So, what happened? Where's Smirks? Dirtbag?"

"I don't know where Smirks is." The truth. And I would tell the story of him and Lark later, when it wasn't so fresh.

April nodded. Folded her arms across her chest. "And Dirtbag. I'm guessing you didn't find him either." April pronounced it like a statement.

I moved closer to her painting. Those sunflower faces. Weeping and maternal. Tired, but with no concept of how to give up. "How do you do this?" I asked.

April shrugged. "It just happens." Just then, a cloud slid away from the sun. April and I looked at each other and wordlessly set into the sun salutation. It felt so good, reaching up, rooting in. Downward dog. My biceps femoris muscles melting sweetly. We ended in mountain. Bowed to each other. Sister salutation. April shrugged again. "I don't think I want to hear about Dirtbag."

And for once, I didn't care. I didn't care how April responded, if she avoided the issue. It didn't mean anything. It was fine if she didn't want to hear about Dirtbag. It was fine if she didn't want to talk about it. It wasn't a sign of her abuse, her trauma. It wasn't a symptom or a defence mechanism or denial. She grabbed my hand and pulled me to the ground and we lay on our backs and stared up at the sky. A deep, thick Atlantic blue. My sister out of the corner of my eye, a blur of peach skin and green eyes and hair the colour of peanut husks. Bees buzzing in the flowers nearby. She took my hand and pressed it into her belly. "I'm pregnant."

I propped myself up on my elbow. "Holy shit," I said.

"I know."

"I thought—"

"I changed my mind."

April and I had signed an oath. No marriage, no kids. She's already broken the first vow. But the second one was more serious. A child, a baby, why did she want one? So suddenly. What had changed? I looked at her flat belly. A little human would grow there. How could we raise the little human? We hadn't even taken care of ourselves. I returned to my back. We lay there, looking up at the sky, the ombre pattern of colour becoming more pronounced the longer we stared, a vivid, thick blue above us fading toward the trees to white. What kind of mother would she be?

"April."

"Yes?"

"I'm scared."

She laughed. "Oh, Julia." Her tone as though she were speaking to a child.

"What?"

"I'm scared, too." She stood up. "I have to show you something." She pulled me toward the house. Rod joined us from out of nowhere. He'd grown since I saw him last, no longer had the soft edges of a puppy. Now a sturdy, angular adult. He panted wildly and jumped up, his paws coming within an inch of my chest before artfully dodging away.

I rubbed his head, slapped his haunches. "Good boy."

In her pristine kitchen, April handed me a notebook. "Mom gave me this so I could help her with her garden. Ralph told me she's been writing things down ever since she was diagnosed with dementia." I ran my fingers along the cover of the book. Someone had written *Garden* in shaky script. "Read it." She was smiling. I opened to the first page. Mom's writing had changed. It was uncertain and light, big letters spaced far apart. Like a kid's.

"Remember: dahlias are slow to bloom."

"Remember: I put Julia's iris in front of April's rose bush and between the sharp-leaf spruce and the barberry."

"We have manure by the brook. Use it early."

"Pick out the eyes of the dahlias and split them."

"April's rose—open up!"

"Dahlias are the last one. Slow."

"The dahlias are very slow to start any flowers."

"This is a poem," I said.

"Right?" said April. "We'll publish her posthumously and become famous. Outsider poetry, and all that."

She dragged her own bicycle out of her shed and we made the trip up the South Mountain to Harmony together. We crept along lazily, through apple orchards and hallways of lilac trees, intoxicated and slowed by the fragrant juice of the flowers. At the South Mountain summit I looked down at the Annapolis Valley, spread out like a quilt, patched with farmland and lakes and rivers and red barns. *Like in a movie.* We trod west and then I saw my parents' house, set far back from the road, their long driveway paved since the last time I was home and the yard immaculately trimmed and tweezed. Mom's gardens flourished in the gold light of sunset. When she couldn't do the weeding and planting herself, April had helped her.

My sister and I pulled ourselves up to the top of the driveway, stopped at the edge and looked down toward the house. There was our mother, sitting on her favourite wicker rocking chair on the veranda, very straight and still in her bulky metal back brace. Her poor broken back. I saw the halo she'd mentioned, and the branches at her sides. The bullet around her waist. She looked trapped in a portable cage. April giggled. "Isn't she cute?" she whispered.

Mom noticed the cyclists who had paused in front of her house and she shielded her eyes against the setting sun, jutting her head forward as much as she could, trying to make out who we were. "Julia?" Mom shouted. I raised my arm and waved. "Julia!" she screamed, and started to laugh. She yelled my name, and then April's name, my name and then April's name again, over and over, and Ralph must have heard her because suddenly the front door flew open and he bounded onto the deck.

He spotted us. "Julia?" he called. April and I were laughing, unable, at that point, to respond to either of them.

"Go get her, Ralph!" Mom yelled.

Leaping down the steps two at a time, Ralph called my name once more, and ran up the driveway toward us. He ran up the driveway toward his daughters.

Acknowledgements

Without these people, I could not have written and/or published my first novel.

My family. All members near and far. More immediately: Mom, who taught me empathy and forgiveness. Laurie, who showed me where the high road is and how to aim for it. Tara, who displays every day the meaning of unconditional love. And whose belly laughter can make my belly laugh.

My second family. Gai, David, Lois and Parker. You've given me security, adventure, art and animal love.

My friends. To say there are too many to list makes me sound vapid or lucky or both. Luckily, I know I'm just lucky.

My early correspondent, Krissy Darch, whose letters I have saved in my inbox in a folder called Fuck Trauma, and whose questions inspired the research that led to *Pedal*.

My first listener, first reader, and first fashion consultant, Christine Ama. You know it's true: I wouldn't have written this book without you.

Poet and peer Lindsay Cuff, who graciously lent me her beautiful poem "Fission Theory," pieces of which are found in the final pages of this novel. Read her at tracesandtracks.blogspot.com.

My advocators. Editor John Gould for his attention and thoughtfulness; it was truly a gift. Vici, Andrea and Holly at Caitlin Press for their enthusiasm and belief in this novel. To my agent and advisor, John Pearce at Westwood Creative Artists, for taking a risk.

My teachers. Mary Schendlinger, who taught me about the noun and the verb, crucial lessons for every writer. Steven Galloway, who encouraged me to commit to writing at a very important time in my life. (In the early twenties, things can go one of two ways.) Deborah Campbell, who showed kindness and understanding at another pivotal moment. Ms. Graves, who trusted me with an enormous task and left an indelible impression, and Mr. Hanson, who urged me to learn the true meanings of words, for which I am extremely grateful. And bottomless thanks to Keith Maillard, my friend, thesis advisor, and respected author, who helped tape together the first draft of *Pedal* and send it off into the world.

My landlords. Michael and Duak, who show true generosity and kindness. Monica of Healing Aid Farm, truth seeker and community builder, thank you.

My partner and buddy, Taylor, who cooked and cleaned for me during the hard times. If there is a truer embodiment of love than the preparation of food and the maintenance of home, I cannot imagine it.

My allies. To the men and women who set aside adjectives like "shameful" and "embarrassing" and shared their stories with me—triggers be damned!—thank you. Storytelling is the good kind of power.